THE
ACADEMY
ALIGNMENT

DAVID DAVIS & ANDRA ST. IVANYI

Library of Congress Cataloging-in-Publication Data has been applied for.

Published in the United States by The Phoenix Organization, Inc.

ISBN (hardback) 978-1-4951-8608-0

ISBN (ebook) 978-1-4951-8609-7

Typeset in Adobe Canson Pro

Titles in DecoNeue Light originally designed by Jonatan Xavier

Illustrations & Design by Vashti Harrison

To our first fan Boo (the best uncle a guy would ask for),
my sister Victoria and her husband Karl
(my brother from another mother).
To my niece Etta Skye and nephew Connor,
who have been the light in my life.
To Sandra and Bee for reading the early drafts
and for the kindness and love they showed me.
To my best friend Adam for always being there
and lastly, to my writing partner, Andra:
thanks for taking this journey with me!
D.D.

To my husband Paul, for your patience and support …
and for all the years you spent
talking to the top of my head while I typed.
And to "David," who is every girl's dream writing partner.
A.S.I.

TABLE OF CONTENTS

THE
ACADEMY

ALIGNMENT

★

•

★

PROLOGUE

By dawn, the clouds were grey and thick, hanging unmoving above the forest. They had released most of their rain overnight, and the heavy downpour had made it impossible to hear the screams.

Huge blobs of water dripped off the wrought iron fence that surrounded the quiet campus. Its gates were closed, and the engraved crest on its front gate hung in silence, its two swords crossed and sparkling in the wet. Above them the words MAGNUS NOVUS ORBIS glowed. The campus was quiet, just as it had been an hour earlier, moments before the sky lightened. It was the kind of quiet that felt unnatural. No sound. No movement except that slow dripping.

Until someone exploded from the forest.

James Harken was running for his life from something he couldn't even see, arms pumping, lungs gasping for breath under his torn and bloodied shirt. He forced himself to keep going, eyes locked onto the school's crest with a fierce determination that made him look far older than seventeen. That crest meant something to him.

Safety.

He slipped in the wet grass. Scrambled to get up, pawing at the earth and then recoiling from it as if it burned his hands. He risked a glance behind him and fear sparked in his face. He whispered a quick prayer and kept running.

———〜———

Two hundred yards and a world away, inside the safety of the campus gates, stood a small stone chapel. It had been lovingly built forty years before the Constitution of the United States was signed, and all these hundreds of years later, students still filled the nave during the school year.

Dr. Browning, blonde and elegant, prayed quietly before an elaborate wooden altar, her fine features creased in distress. She could feel the dark figure slip into the pews behind her but she didn't turn. She didn't have to.

Professor Linden settled his bulk onto the wooden pew with a smirk.

"Think he's listening this time?" His voice echoed in the empty chapel.

Dr. Browning turned to him. "He's always listening," she said, her voice surprisingly gentle. "I just hope it's His will to act." With that they both looked up at the stained glass window behind the altar as if they could see James through it.

"Hope?" Professor Linden said. "Is that all you have left? That's so *sad*."

Browning eyed him steadily. "Rejoice in hope, be patient in tribulation, be constant in – "

"Oh *wake up*. It's so beneath you, this *clinging*. And to what? A cosmic bait and switch?"

She sighed. "Is that what you call faith these days?" Her shoulders rose slightly in a graceful shrug. It doesn't matter what he calls it. "We depend on it."

"*We* evolved past it," Linden says smugly. "And it won't save the boy."

They've been doing this for centuries, this back and forth.

———～———

James bolted for the fence, begging his legs to move faster, faster. His lungs were about to burst. The wind picked up, and another blast of rain pelted his face. A grey slime oozed from the ground behind him, filling his footprints as he pushed himself harder. The slime rose and slithered after him, making a low humming sound.

As he neared the fence, he thought he could make it. He thought he could summon every ounce of remaining adrenaline and leap over it. He got so close to the fence that he could see the sun shining on the other side of it, and the rosebushes so utterly still, unaffected by the wind or rain.

The shrieking intensified.

———～———

Professor Linden stared up at the stained glass. "Run, run, run if you must, James. The past is always faster." He leaned back in satisfaction, arms and legs splayed out in the pew. "Forget James!" he said. "Tomorrow we start all over again! A new semester of competition and amusement."

When that didn't elicit a response, the Professor tried again. "I've got him, Charlotte. It's inevitable." He snorted. It wasn't any fun, really, if he couldn't provoke something. *Anything.* "Think of the upside. Think of all he will be spared," he said.

———◦———

James threw himself at the fence and started to climb. The wind whipped his hair and clothes into a frenzy. He scrambled for his life to the top of the fence, grabbing it desperately, sensing but not seeing the grey slime curling and tightening around his legs. He couldn't kick it away. He couldn't pull himself free. The shrieking grew louder, an inhuman sound that made his head feel as if it were splitting from temple to temple. And then suddenly, only seconds from safety, James's hands were pulled violently from the iron fencing, the ligaments stretching and popping.

He screamed a terrible scream.

It didn't matter. He was pulled from the fence and dragged back to the forest.

Then the wind fell silent and the rain stopped. And all was still again.

———◦———

Inside the chapel, Dr. Browning went still. She nodded to herself. It was done. She willed herself to meet Professor Linden's smug expression. The sight of it was enough to inspire her.

"You're wrong," she told him, steel in her voice. "You don't have him yet."

CHAPTER ONE

DR. BROWNING

A thin mist clings to the ground. I can't help but scan The Academy as it sits, still and solid and elegant, atop this famed hillside, surrounded by forest. It's a beautiful school. And on this damp September morning, nothing is moving except a few barely visible tendrils of steam rising from the iron fencing.

I stop and stare first at the ribbons of steam, then at the dents where the metal melted under James's fingers. I pull my raincoat closed.

"I wasn't finished!" I whisper, leaning my head against the cold metal. A part of me still can't believe this happened, after everything I'd done to prevent it. But it happened. I can still see where James's hands gripped the fence before he was pulled from it with such stunning and unnecessary violence.

"Now what?" I ask aloud. I look around to make sure no one else is around. "How can we possibly move forward?" I collect myself. I will not be perceived as begging, or feckless. Or a failure. "I rejoice in an active mind making choices of its own. I do! But there must be balance!"

I straighten and set my jaw. I know he's watching, and I know he will try to twist my concerns into something warped and ugly.

But I have a larger problem before me now. Instead of souls prepared for the necessary hardships of being alive, I'm given lazy idiots. Yes! Shallow morons in a world that celebrates excess of every kind instead of urging personal sacrifice for something larger and more meaningful!

No more vague hints, no more pleading and hoping. It's time to stop marching around the city walls. It's time to declare my needs and fight.

"Thank you," I whisper, fiercely and with purpose, "thank you in advance for giving me a chance! For giving me *one* mind, a beacon to light the way!"

Silence. Nothing but silence. I smile to myself. Dab at my nose with a tissue. It's true: to an outside observer, nothing happened. But in a corner of my heart, I know something will. Soon.

Someone's coming. I tuck the tissue away.

Cole, wearing coveralls and a cap, comes to stand beside me. He peers at the fence; he'll have to fix it.

He has been fixing things at The Academy as long as things have needed fixing.

Cole seems to be in his mid-forties with short black hair and a forgettable manner, unless you look directly into his pale green eyes. He carries wire clippers in his leathery workman's hands, oblivious to the cold and physical discomfort in general.

"Doctor Browning," he says softly. He nods a polite hello as he sets his toolbox down.

He has to fix the fence. Soon The Academy will be swarming with students, and they can't see this. They can't possibly be allowed to guess what had happened here.

He has to fix the fence. It's the least he could do for James.

PROFESSOR LINDEN

So Cole is fixing the fence, slithering around as he has for centuries maintaining *the Balance,* as if that exists anymore. His idea of remaining neutral is a joke; he is forever rushing to Browning's side of the fence (an appropriate metaphor, if there ever was one). Never mind. It doesn't matter.

The truth is I don't particularly want the fence fixed. I wanted to look out my office window and see the bent iron posts, the scuffed grass, the lovely ribbon of color that marks, if only in my imagination, James's final, screaming path back into the woods.

I didn't necessarily want James to have to go in that way, but those were the consequences of his actions and ... well, so it goes. Bye-bye, James.

But what's more interesting to me is Charlotte down there in her perfectly tailored raincoat, struggling to maintain her optimism when there's clearly no reason to. I'd be the first to tell her, too. This whole thing with James has got her down, which I can't wait to remind her points to a sinful lack of faith for which she will have to repent one day. I'll make *sure* she does.

Another reason for my good spirits.

She thinks I can't hear her murmuring down there by the fence. I can. I have. I can always hear the lovely melody of a poor soul's wavering faith.

7

I light a cigar and step back from the lead-paned window. All in all, a good beginning for the new school year. I'm quite pleased.

I'm so pleased, in fact, I nearly forget someone's there. Someone I summoned. Time to tell him what to expect, time to get to *work*.

"The Academy's entire enrollment is only three hundred students," I tell him, because he's got a lot to learn. "Yet their parents control over forty percent of the world's wealth."

These are the details that I know will impress someone like him. And I'm right. His eyes light up at the thought of being so close to all that money and power. The avarice of today's youth gives me hope.

"Most of this year's students are returning," I continue, "but a few are new."

I pause to admire one of my favorite dioramas. Dozens of Roman soldiers stand frozen in battle, their weapons raised. Every helmet, every weapon, every military award on their miniature chests is historically authentic. Even the cruelty in their expressions is real. Maybe that's why this diorama, more than any other of the half dozen in my office, is the one I return to again and again.

"Only a handful of students are worth our attention," I say, taking a moment to collect my thoughts. How to best describe everything he'll need to know? I debate allowing him to find out some things for himself, but then remember: *I don't have the time.*

I push my hand into the diorama as if reaching into a pool of water. The entire diorama shimmers and then clears.

And I see Sophia Prescott standing in a pit of filthy water, her long brown hair piled high on her head, helping attach a pipe to a pump. I recognize it immediately: India. Two days ago. She's digging wells, dirty work, and as far as I'm concerned an utter waste of time. But to Sophia …

The villagers cheer as the pump gushes fresh water. Idiots.

Sophia smiles. She looks so happy, I taste the bile in my mouth. The images fade.

"Sophia likes to think of herself as a giver," I explain, "the kind of volunteer who is everywhere at once, toiling in the spotlight."

He's looking at me, curious, earnest, because of course all he sees is the diorama, nothing more. Still, I'm confident he has promise, at least for my intended purposes.

I don't tell him that what Sophia considers her greatest virtue is actually a strategic weakness. She's the kind who tries and tries, but can never do quite enough (because there is always poverty in the world, and evil), and this makes her vulnerable to manipulation. She seems to get some kind of high out of showing everyone what a good person she is, although it's a phase she'll soon outgrow. I've known her for years. If not for that car crash last year, she'd be in a very different place.

The diorama clears again and I focus. I know I have only a few moments to see what each student has been up to this summer. Now Sophia is cleaned up and riding in the back of a limo. I recognize the drive; she's cruising up the long road toward The Academy gates, right this very moment, wearing a silken orange sari and dangling gold Indian earrings. She thinks they look good, that they're a reflection of her new self. But the truth is they are nothing more than a way of advertising her generosity. She can't wait to be asked about them.

"Please! Just transfer twenty then," she is pleading into the phone. "For fuck's sake, you can't say no. I've already promised them."

She overpromises. It's one of her more reliable virtues. That, and her unshakeable confidence in her own righteousness. They will be useful one day.

"Of course I know what that's worth! I just spent five weeks digging wells there!" Her voice goes softer. "I can't. I spent my allowance on mosquito netting. But don't tell my dad!"

I do admire her capacity for deception. Her father's media company is worth $42 billion dollars. She fears (or knows?) he'll get upset about a little mosquito netting, which of course he could pay for with the change beneath his sofa cushions.

"Just transfer the money," Sophia is saying, losing her angelic tone. She pulls out the earrings in a fit of frustration and tosses them across the limo. "How would *I* know? You're a financial advisor, Gerald, *advise me!*"

I tell the young man standing stiffly in my office that Sophia will get what she wants. She usually does. Which makes her of special interest to me personally. We glance together out the window as the limo pulls up, tenth in the line of limos and Bentleys delivering children to The Academy this morning.

I take a few steps to another diorama and he follows. I'm sure he has questions but is too intimidated to ask. *Good.*

I move a miniature Egyptian slave out of a shaft of light.

"The alumni of this school are the world's CEOs," I tell him, trying not to sound too imperious. "International statesmen. Bank presidents and entertainment moguls. They shape our culture, our world. And so will their children." I move the slave in front of the great Pyramid of Giza. "However, we get to shape theirs first."

The boy can't possibly see the girl in front of the pyramid, the girl surrounded by makeup artists and stylists, but I can. And because she's a secret favorite of mine in a world where favorites are discouraged, and because the image is already fading, I try not to linger.

"Chloe Winters has everything a child of privilege could want," I say, my gaze devouring her pouting face. "Her beauty is an accident of nature; she has descended from Europe's royal families, and as dozens of portraits attest, they are a uniquely unattractive bunch. She is the daughter of Countess Alexandra of Flanders and Lord Richard Winters."

At seventeen, Chloe has a defiance in her eyes that I find incredibly appealing.

A hand dabs cover-up on a fresh bruise under Chloe's left eye. Oh Chloe, *what have you been up to?* Makeup artists apply foundation! powder! eye shadow! and soon, Chloe stares deeply at the camera -- now with a perfectly made up face and perfectly styled hair. Her long blonde mane blows in the wind and she appears as if she was born ready for this shot.

"Chloe lacks a tendency toward introspection. Which is without question a very good thing," I tell the young man, whose eyes flick to the side as he struggles to commit these details to memory. It's a pity he can't see the pyramid in the background as Chloe stands, arms outstretched, draped in bright silks that billow out behind her. She's glorious.

"But don't underestimate her," I warn. "She has untapped talents."

The image fades. I stifle a sigh. But then another image flashes by, quick as a wink, and I'm instantly cheered. There is Chloe in her trailer, her nose buried in a mound of cocaine with a gusto that makes me smile. I almost laugh at the thought of the frustrated stylists and the photographer pounding on her trailer door. Instead, I nod toward the window.

And there she is.

Chloe is huddled in the passenger seat of a vintage Ferrari now speeding along the campus perimeter and through the iron gates. It comes to a quick stop in the driveway. Richard Winters, her brother, drives and I can tell from here that he's annoyed. Eighteen, sharp-featured, aloof and a senior, he looks like a model for Abercrombie and Fitch. Personally, I have no use for him.

"Get it together," he tells her. "We're here."

But Chloe protests. "I'm sick." Richard rolls his eyes. "Seriously. I think I caught something in Egypt."

"No, you're hung over. And you're an embarrassment." There's no way he's falling for this again.

Chloe dry heaves into a silk Hermes scarf and then starts to cry. Richard looks away, disgusted. He doesn't know what's worse, the tears or the heaves. He pulls up behind the other shiny cars and parks in front of the stone arch that leads to The Academy campus.

She looks up at him tearfully. "Richarrrrd. Don't make me do this!"

"You'll be fine once you get in there and detox. Your class is probably registered already." He looks around at the students climbing from their limos. "I wonder if Sophia's here?"

Chloe stuffs the scarf into her $6,000 Birken bag. Of course Richard is looking for Sophia. He's such an ass.

"You know, she's not the angel everyone thinks she is!" Chloe snaps. "I can't *stand* Sophia."

Chloe is such a darling girl.

A Bentley pulls up next to Richard's Ferrari. The boy in the back seat locks eyes with Richard. It's classic. Like icebergs colliding.

"There's Volsky," Richard says, his voice dropping at the thought of another year spent anywhere near him.

"And Volsky can't stand *me*," Chloe whines again. Richard glares.

Chloe's right, of course. But wrong too. Nonetheless, I can't overwhelm this boy with too much information, so instead of elaborating, I move to another diorama. Stalingrad, 1942. My giant finger tips a Red Army soldier into the dust.

"Anton Volsky is the son of Vladimir Volsky," I explain. "Russian oil magnate and former member of the FSB. He and President Putin vacation together. His father is worth over $37 billion," I say, enjoying the flicker of amazement in the young man's eyes. I lower my voice a bit. "Which of course fluctuates a few million here and there depending on the price of oil."

I rest my hand on the floor of the diorama, and it clears quickly. There's Anton waking up in yet another beautiful bed, awash in silk sheets covered with a white fur comforter.

The bed didn't belong to him, and neither did the beautiful woman next to him.

Both belonged to another man who was, at that very moment, speeding toward his gleaming yacht, moored for the night in the Portofino harbor.

Anton dresses and steps out onto the deck, pausing for a moment to take in the bright Italian sunlight as if he didn't have a reason to hurry. He smiles as he hops into a smaller speedboat parked beside the yacht, its engines already running. And then he speeds away and I catch a glimpse of the other boat arriving at the other side of the yacht.

You have to applaud his appetite for risk.

But every risk has either a reward or a consequence. The sunlight blinded him, as it always will; Anton never saw the photographer in the distance snap his picture.

I hand a copy of Page Six to the young man. "I'm sure you are familiar with Anton's tabloid exploits." I shake my head, playing the part of the concerned uncle. "I've told him a hundred times to stay out of the light. It does him no favors."

I stare deeper into the scene before me. Anton's metallic blue Bentley, as if on cue, glides through The Academy gates. In the back seat Anton, tanned and smartly dressed, draws something on a pad in his lap. He stops. Frustrated, he tears the page off and continues.

The car comes to a halt as his driver takes his place behind the other luxury cars waiting to unload their passengers. Anton again considers his pad. Rips that page off and looks around.

"Why the hell have you stopped here?!" he bellows. "I don't wait in line. Pull up to the front!"

The Bentley abruptly pulls out of line, going the wrong way down the two lane road. Soon it reaches the front of the line, where a valet opens the door, addressing the young Mr. Volsky by name but avoiding eye contact, as instructed.

Anton marches past him without a glance. Letting his driver handle the angry stares of the people behind him in line! I peer at the inside of the Bentley. The back seat's floorboard is littered with Anton's rejected sketches. The image starts to fade and I squint. Is every single sketch a portrait of Sophia? The image is gone, too soon. Damn it. I needed another second or two.

I'm lost in thought when the young man speaks.

"Is this The Academy?" he asks. He is looking at my latest project and I'm pleased with his verbal nudge. It is time to get to the point of this meeting. I join him at the diorama that caught his attention; I admit it seems ordinary, hard to place, without historical details or any context at all to the untrained eye.

The truth is that this is the diorama I depend on most. And recently, this is the one that has made me the most uneasy.

It's the largest diorama, and mostly green. In its center is the campus, easily recognized. The miniature Gothic-inspired buildings face a web of rosebush-lined walkways, their little bay windows gleaming. The grass in the Quad is pristine. The lanterns glow.

Surrounding those buildings is a dense green forest, and I can't help but stare into it. In the middle of the forest is a mighty oak tree, larger and greyer than the other trees. If you look carefully, you'll see that its roots go so deep into the ground that they encircle the entire forest and every tree in it. Under its massive canopy are dozens of tiny Black Knights, lances raised.

I notice there's a figure on the ground, a figure so badly burned that nothing is left of its costume or features. It looks more like a charred twig. I remove it from the diorama, examining it briefly, although what I'd really like to do is savor the memory of it with a glass of Merlot.

"James Harken is to be replaced," I tell the boy, who nods as if he understands. I appreciate the gesture, but there is so much he doesn't know; the very idea exhausts me. Nonetheless, I can't afford even the shortest pause, and I refuse to linger in regret.

"James Harken *will* be replaced," I say, and I set a pristine White King beside the giant, grey oak. "But by an *unknown quantity.*"

What I don't tell him is that today is the day that will change everything.

CHAPTER TWO

PETER

I told her a million times I didn't want to go. Who the hell wants to leave their friends and everything they know to go to a school that's just daycare for rich kids?

She wouldn't even listen and shut me down before I could start.

"I don't care," she said. "You're going. It's non-negotiable."

My mom pulls out that "non-negotiable" phrase whenever she doesn't have a good reason for something but won't change her mind no matter what I say. Drives me crazy.

One of the cool things about having a single mom is that she usually listens to me. About most stuff, anyway. It's always been us against the rest of the world. She never pulls the "parent" card unless there is something she can't tell me and she normally tells me everything. We're pretty tight. Half the time I can change her mind but when she said "non-negotiable," I knew it was over.

I'd heard about The Academy my whole life, and the way people in town talked about it didn't help my mood. Everyone in Providence is connected to The Academy in some way. I knew a lot of kids whose parents worked on campus, either in the kitchen or on the security staff, but no matter who you were, your family was financially dependent on The Academy one way or another. Rumor had it The Academy privately funded everything from the Rec Center to our local park, but who knows? All that's for sure is that it kept most families afloat the way factories and farms do in other small towns.

Every once in a while, one of the parents would get drunk and whisper stories about their time working on top of the hill. I had a hard time believing what I heard about "The School of Kings" or its students. (We never saw the kids. Why would they ever want to spend time in Providence?) I always thought the stories they told were totally BS, because I couldn't believe people actually acted like that.

Even though The Academy was a thirty minute drive from town, it seemed like it was a world away.

So what the hell am I going to do there?

I was really pissed off for a few days. I didn't say much, didn't eat much. My mom thought I was punishing her. The truth is, I really *was* freaking out. My life was pretty good, as good as anybody's. I busted my ass all summer to get into shape because I was sure I'd make varsity in the fall, based on what the Coach said last year. I knew the teachers I wanted. I mean, all my friends went to Providence High; we *laughed* at the "yacht snots" up the hill. And with good reason. Half the kids at The Academy were regularly featured on the covers on the supermarket gossip rags that my mom glanced at but never bought. Who wants to deal with people like that?

I liked our little house and the crowded garage and the sad little garden no one ever took care of that just kept doing its best, spring after spring. I liked coming home after football practice and my mom yelling at me (and laughing at the same time) for eating all the raw veggies she just chopped up for stir fry.

Then, in early August, my mom sits me down and tells me I was awarded an "outreach scholarship" to The Academy! I was going to some *elite* boarding school.

"Give it back," I said. "Tell 'em to give it someone who wants it!"

"Peter," she said, crossing her arms. "You're going. Yes, it will be a big change, so prepare yourself mentally."

"Prepare how, exactly? Buy a Bugatti?"

She looked at me a moment and smiled as she shook her head, "You'll be fine. In fact, I'm betting you'll flourish."

"How can you be so sure?" I asked for the millionth time. "About *my* life!"

"I'm making the best decision for your future, Peter."

And I'm sure she really believes this. Nothing I said or did would change her mind.

After a few days of the silent treatment, my mom came into my room after dinner one night. She stood by the door but I didn't even turn around.

"I'm going to miss you, sweetheart," she said, and then added, quietly, "You can take your dirt bike with you." That was big for her, considering last year's accident. I knew she never wanted me near a motorcycle again. But here she was, trying to make it easier for me.

18

Trying to patch things up. Knowing I could have my bike with me at school did make me feel a little better.

At least it meant I could come back and visit her and my best friend Zach.

The next few weeks flew by, and now here we are in her ancient 1999 Volvo station wagon, towing my bike tied down to a small trailer in back. We have to take the hills slower because of that, and after a while, I notice all the limos passing us. A couple zoom by, then a whole line of them. I know exactly where they're all going and I start thinking that this drive, up this hill, is my last taste of freedom.

You'd think my mom would be happy, now that she's finally getting her way. She's not. Her eyes are moving all over the place. She touches the painted angel figurine that dangles from the rearview mirror. She seems nervous. And pissed off, as pissed off as I'm getting because she keeps trying to sell me on The Academy.

"I've told you why. A thousand times. It's an *opportunity.*"

"It's a day care for trust fund babies," I tell her. "I've told *you* a thousand times!"

"Don't tell me you researched them all already?"

Of course I have. "The internet's an amazing thing, mom."

She sighs. I'm being a tool, I know it. I just can't get myself to stop. My mom is a librarian and I grew up in libraries. She was the one who taught me to be prepared for anything, and that knowledge is power. So she can't be too surprised that I found out everything I could about the school weeks ago.

Which turned out to be a lot harder than you'd think it would be.

Because there isn't very much information on The Academy. They have a website but it only has the name, address and phone number. There's nothing else. No feedback from the parents, no random chat pages, no detailed descriptions of the campus or anything. Just their home page.

When you do a Google search for The Academy, the only hit it gets is the website, *nothing else*. How do you keep something off Google?

I turn away again and watch the greenery whiz by. "Whatever it is you're not telling me? I'm going to figure it out," I say. I don't want to piss her off more, but she's gotta see I'm not letting this go. "You know I will."

Her jaw tenses. She knows I'm serious. "I know, Petey. And then you'll understand."

I want to push her then, make her tell me, and yell, "*Just tell me the truth!*" But I don't. She's starting to look more upset than I am, and then I realize what she's looking at. We're here.

We drive past these huge iron gates that open onto a winding driveway. It takes us toward the biggest stone arch I've ever seen. And in front of it is a line of limos, each waiting its turn to unload. I can't believe it. Valets dressed up in uniforms moving luggage. Uniformed drivers giving them directions! Now I'm really starting to spin out.

Right there at the top of the stone archway is this huge crest, looming above everything. It practically glows in the morning sun, the words MAGNUS NOVUS ORBIS sparkling across a shield of arms. My mom and I just stare at it as we wait in the line of cars. I look past the archway to the campus, all these Gothic buildings with bay windows and enormous doors. I watch valets lifting leather luggage out of hundred thousand dollar cars.

My life's about to change. *A lot.*

Mom's still staring. She doesn't see the other kids getting out of the cars and heading through the arch, some of them glancing in curiosity at me and the Volvo.

"Seriously...?"

I yank the angel figurine off the mirror and jam it into my pocket. That snaps my mom out of it. She swallows as if she just grasped the reality of what she's doing. *Maybe,* I think, *maybe she'll take me home.*

DR. BROWNING

There's a moment at the beginning of each school year when I must acknowledge that I have prepared what I can prepare. I have done what I can do. Once that first car arrives, the school year has begun, as far as I'm concerned.

There's no more prep work to be done after that.

Of course today, I'm in constant argument with myself over everything, even over that. So here I am, the morning of move-in, toiling at my desk instead of outside greeting the arriving students.

I truly hope that's not an indication of how the school year will go. I say a quick prayer.

I look out the window and pause. Professor Linden is at his window, too, staring down at something that has caught his interest. What could that be, I wonder? And who's that next to him?

The thick drapes are tugged closed. I was sure I saw someone. Perhaps I'm mistaken. Who would possibly be in Professor Linden's office? School hasn't even started yet.

And what is he looking at? I get up from my desk to take a peek. It must be something of value, for him to gaze so intently.

At first I only see Richard sitting in his car arguing with his sister, again.

"Attending school isn't optional, you cow," he's telling her. Everyone knows that Chloe must graduate in order to access her first trust fund. If she doesn't, she won't get the money until she's twenty-five, and seven years without a trust is an eternity to these kids, especially one like Chloe.

Chloe balls up a silk Hermes scarf into a tiny, colored ball. She's crying.

"Take me home. *Please*," she's begging. "Or just into town somewhere and I'll call Russell."

Richard rolls his eyes. "Russell's in Paris, cleaning up after Mother. Good thing, too, or you'd have to explain that bruise."

Then he notices Peter's Volvo. "Who the hell is *that*?"

Chloe peers out the window, licking a finger to fix her eyeliner. She frowns at the car. "One of the staff's kids?"

"Why'd he park in the *front?*" Richard clicks the doors unlocked. "Grow up. Get yourself together and get out there, Chloe. *Now.*"

Richard hands his keys to a waiting valet and takes a ticket without looking at it. He moves to the school's archway, one eye on Peter and the Volvo. Chloe drifts after him, her makeup suddenly perfect, her hair in place.

Ah, the Volvo. That's what Linden's looking at. I am mesmerized, too.

Down below, Diana puts the car in park. She and Peter sit there a moment.

"I can't," he protests.

I know immediately who he is and why he's here. It's the new student. Our "outreach scholar." I scold myself again for not being out there to greet him, to be a welcoming face when he certainly needs one.

"Who *are* these people?" he asks.

And that's a very good question. Who are these people? I can't wait to meet him. I'll admit: I smile.

Inside the car, Diana sighs, "This is rough on me, too, you know." She grasps Peter's hands. I can tell he's trying not to groan.

"Not here!" he whispers, but he sees her expression and finally bows his head.

"Dear Heavenly Father," Diana begins. "We ask for your blessing on this very special day and pray for courage and guidance."

"Mom, *stop. Not so loud!*" Peter looks around and Diana's voice drops to a whisper.

"Show us your will so that we may follow it …"

"Mom." Peter sees Professor Linden glaring at him from the second story window. "*Come on!*"

He tries to withdraw his hands but Diana holds on tighter, "… that he can do anything through you, who gives him strength." She races to the end. "In your name we pray."

Peter tosses out a quick "Amen," grabs his new backpack and gives his mother a quick kiss on the cheek.

"Love you."

He jumps from the car before she can say it back, before he loses his resolve. I see him for the first time, and a peace settles over me. A strong, fearless young man. I think of Linden in the chapel, and I remember my own words by the fence this morning, and I remind myself I mustn't be smug. However, I wish I could tell my esteemed colleague, "*He is always listening,*" I would point out, "*and this time, it was His will to act.*"

Outside the archway, Peter moves to untie his motorcycle. A

well-dressed valet appears.

"We'll park it in the student lot for you, sir," the Valet says. "The students are meeting in the Assembly Hall, right that way." The Valet points and then is gone, along with the duffel bag.

Peter looks at the ticket in his hand. The Valet gave it to him so fast, he barely felt it. Printed on it is D-54. He has no idea what it means.

The three of us – the Professor, his mother and I – watch Peter move through the stone entryway. Diana hopes that he'll turn around one last time. He doesn't.

I see Linden turn in his window and say, "Now there's one we'll need to keep our eye on," his eyes focused on Peter's retreating back like a predator's on its prey.

I wonder briefly: to whom is he speaking? But the thought evaporates before I can examine it. I'm filled with a sense of gratitude I haven't felt in decades, and something else as well: hope.

Peter passes through the stone archway, where his footsteps echo unnaturally loudly. He digs the Angel Figurine from his pocket and moves to toss it into the trash. With his hand poised there, he looks up. His first look at the inner campus takes his breath away. He doesn't move.

Gothic buildings with towers. Expansive bay windows, majestic gargoyles and marble carvings everywhere. In the distance, a few last students disappear into a building. Peter is all alone.

I feel for him. I know he is intimidated. I know he is starting to realize that *things here are not what they seem.* It must be terribly frightening, even for someone like Peter.

I wish I could appear next to him and offer words of support.

24

He shoves the figurine back into his pocket and hurries to the Hall. He didn't need my words of encouragement after all.

I catch Linden's eye. I see the concern there. He looks quickly away.

I smile. I step back into the depths of my office, instantly forgetting whatever it was I was working on.

"Thank you," I whisper.

———— ～ ————

A few minutes later, the limos are gone. The once bustling parking lot in front of The Academy is as quiet as a grave. I scoop up my notes for my commencement speech and head for the Assembly Hall. That's when I notice that one car is left.

It's the Volvo, pulled off to one side as if it started for the gates and then forgot how to get there. I see Diana Foster inside, dabbing at her eyes, telling herself over and over that she made the right decision, and wondering how she will manage without Peter.

My heart breaks for her as she tosses the tissue away and puts the car into gear. She's about to pull away when she glances up; something near The Academy's crest has caught her eye.

She gasps in horror. "Peter!" she cries. She pounds on the horn. No sound. She fumbles for her seatbelt and finally unlatches it. She claws at the door. "PETER! *Come back!*" she cries as the door handle jams. She pounds at the window. Trapped.

I open the passenger door and sit down next to her.

Diana gasps. "Dr. Browning! Did you see that?"

She's so upset, she's not breathing. I put a gentle hand on her shoulder. "Diana."

"I can't, I can't just *leave* him here!"

We sit in the silence. I am overwhelmed by compassion for her, for her memories, not to mention what she just saw. Some things are impossible to forget.

"Breathe," I tell her.

Diana nods. Right. Okay. She breathes.

"I'm so glad you're here," I say. "I wasn't sure you'd come. Or if you got my messages."

"I *did*. It's just ..." A long beat.

"I'm looking forward to meeting him. He looks like a fine young man, your Peter."

Diana nods. "He is. But he's been asking questions. Questions I can't answer. And seeing things!" She steels herself against the tears, tears she has been fighting for weeks now. "And I keep telling him this is it. His one chance. Not many kids get an opportunity like this."

I take her hand. "You're right. And you have nothing to worry about. There is no safer place for Peter than *right here*. Inside these gates."

"He has no idea why he's even here. I couldn't tell him, could I? I mean, I barely ..."

"No. You've done the right thing, bringing him here. I promise." I smile. "It's an exciting beginning for everyone. Peter will flourish, I'll make sure of it."

Diana smiles gratefully.

"You must go home, Diana. And I must get to work before they find out how little I really do around here."

I know she wants me to keep talking, she's hoping I'll answer all the questions she has asked herself over the years. And she wants to be certain, too, that Peter will be happy here, that she is giving her son up to a better place, that she made the right decision and will have no regrets.

But there's only so much I can tell her.

I give her one more reassuring smile and head toward the Assembly Hall. I know she is probably peering out the window, tentative, scared. But whatever she thinks she saw is gone.

Diana sighs. She starts the car and pulls away, and when the tears come this time, she lets them fall.

PETER

I can hear the Assembly Hall before I see it, a low buzz of a hundred voices punctuated by that annoying high-pitched squeal girls make so often when they're excited. I'm planning to hang in the back, right? I'll scope things out from there and figure out what's next.

The second I get there, some usher grabs the ticket out of my hand and gestures for me to follow him.

"I'm just going to stand back here," I say but the guy is persistent. People are turning around so I figure to hell with it. I follow him.

He takes me up the center aisle toward the front of the hall – way too close to the front of the hall – and I realize my seat is right in the middle of where everyone is sitting. I've got to climb over a dozen legs to get there. Everybody is quiet and watching me until I finally get to D-54 and sit down.

Everybody's staring. I try telling myself I'm being paranoid, but no. Every time I look at someone, they quickly look away. Even the teachers on the dais with their black robes and colored collars are looking at me. A few people whisper. Is it my clothes? I run a hand through my hair. Nothing is sticking up. I break out my phone and pretend to answer a text when a blond woman walks to the wooden podium. She looks familiar and I try to remember where I've seen her before.

A hush falls over the room. Everyone straightens up. I hear a voice from the front say, "Good morning, Dr. Browning."

She smiles and for some weird reason, I feel a little better all of a sudden. Her eyes are kind and she looks like she wants to be there, which is more than I can say about the teachers at Providence High. They usually looked like they've been up half the night and were counting the days until summer vacation just like us. There is something different about her. I can't figure out what it is.

"Magnus Novus Orbis!" she says with a big smile. "A Great, New World! I'm here to welcome both returning and new students with the reminder that your presence at The Academy marks a new beginning, a fresh start for each and every one of you."

She pauses a moment and looks across the audience as if she is really trying to connect with it.

"The Academy is the only institute of its kind in the world. Your parents entrusted your educations to us, and we do not take this lightly. Why? Because we know that we are also entrusted with your *futures*."

Most of the students pretend to listen but there are a few who turn their attention back to me. Me, the new kid. And a townie, no less.

"You are all expected to rise to the top of your chosen fields. To excel. To *dominate*," Dr. Browning continues. "You have been given more than most ... so more is expected of you."

After a little more of this, I look around. Everyone is either looking right at me, or trying not to. Most the kids are on their phone, texting.

"And The Academy never falls short," Dr. Browning says, speaking more loudly. She's seeing the same shit I am. "Our standards are incredibly high. But so are the rewards."

Even the teachers are craning their necks to get a look at me.

Dr. Browning is getting irritated, I can tell. It's like I'm a goldfish in a bowl. I start thinking about my bike and the road back home, calculating the distance, how long it would take me.

Then, as if she could tell what I'm feeling, Dr. Browning looks at me. Her voice softens. "Know that the road ahead can be challenging," she says. "Know that you are *all* equipped to succeed. Thank you."

The students rise the second she's done. Their voices fill the room with an excited buzz and they group toward the exits. I'm the only one who doesn't move. Dr. Browning is busy shaking hands with the faculty. One of them, an older guy in a professor's robe, glares at me like I keyed his car. Kids rush by me without saying a word.

I pull out my phone and find Zach's name.

Get me OUTTA here!!!!!!

If anyone will recognize the misery in each of those exclamation marks, it's Zach. I press SEND.

CHAPTER THREE

PETER

After I send the text to Zach, I walk outside the Assembly Hall wondering where I'm supposed to go next. Several students walk by me but I might as well be invisible. No one says anything to me. Everyone seems to be in rush to go somewhere.

Finally a tall, blonde guy walks up. "Hey, I'm Richard. Peter, right?" I nod and he says, "Follow me." He sounds British but I don't get a chance to ask because he takes off like a shot. Since I don't know what else to do, I follow him.

That's when I finally get a chance to check out the campus. It looks old but weirdly unused too. The grass is perfectly mowed, like a golf course. There's not a single crack in the walkways. There's no trash anywhere, no students just hanging out. Pretty much the exact opposite of Providence High.

Most of the buildings look like they were built a hundred years ago. They all face the center of campus, which is made up of triangles of grass bordered by rose bushes with giant, waving white roses. Every single building is made of stone and with heavy wooden doors.

Richard hurries into a building with a brass plaque out front that has ROOSEVELT RESIDENTIAL HALL Built 1858 engraved on it. From the outside, it looks more like an ancient castle than student housing. He rushes up this huge wooden staircase with oil paintings lining its walls.

One of the paintings catches my eye as we go up the stairs, and when I pause to look at it, I'm practically pushed down the staircase by a valet carrying a large trunk. By the time he passes, Richard is gone.

I follow a bunch of valets carrying leather-bound trunks as they march up the stairs and disappear into several carpeted hallways. I finally spot Richard and haul ass down the hallway to catch up with him. I'm trying to stay out of everyone's way and grab a look at the dorm rooms but I keep getting bumped and shoved. A valet staggers by with a rolled up Persian rug.

Richard stops.

"This is you," he says, gesturing at a room. He rips off the name tag on the door frame and pushes open the solid oak door.

I almost fall over. I expected a dorm room but this looks like something out of one of my mom's magazines. *This* is where I'll be living?

I want to take pictures and text them to my mom and Zach. At least I know enough to wait until he's gone, but this place is amazing. High ceilings, recessed lighting, polished wooden floors. A giant window overlooking one of the rose gardens. A sink and mirror. I walk around while Richard sticks his head into the hallway to tell some kids to "stop screwing around." There's a mini-fridge, a microwave and an 80 inch flat screen TV built into the wall.

I try to act cool but *damn*.

"That yours?" He points to a huge bed surrounded by some kind of drapery. For a second I don't know what he's asking. Then I see it, placed carefully on a small velvet couch at the end of the bed: my Army duffel bag.

I nod. It looks so ghetto in this place.

"Who does all this stuff belong to?" I ask.

"You," he says, raising an eyebrow.

"There's been a mistake," I say, bidding a mental goodbye to the big screen TV. "They put my bag in the wrong room. Because none of this stuff is mine."

"It is if you're Peter Foster," he says. "It's *your room*."

Yeah right. Like I am going to fall for *that*.

"The cafeteria opens for dinner at seven," he goes on, sounding like a bored waiter forced to repeat the dinner special for the hundredth time. "Study hall is at eight every night but Saturday. Tutors are available but you have to sign up online. Lights out by midnight and – "

He stops when he sees me admiring a brand new, paper-thin computer on the desk. "I'm the senior proctor on this hall," he continues. I turn can't stop staring at the computer. "So to leave campus, you need my written permission. You listening?"

"Seriously, what do I do with all this stuff?"

"It's *yours* now." I can tell he is getting seriously irritated. *Whatever*. I lift up the feather-light computer, examining it from every angle. "This too? These aren't even out yet."

"They're prototypes. They'll be out in a year or so," Richard says, as if I were some backward child. "We get everything pre-market here."

"Like testers?"

Richard sighs. "No, like every student gets one, later runs a company and places an order for ten thousand. You can call it prototype testing, I call it marketing. Get it?"

"Yeah. But ..."

"Sorry if it's not your style. We weren't exactly expecting you."

"Who *were* you expecting?"

That stops Richard, just for a second. Then he rolls his eyes and tosses the balled up name-tag into a trash can, annoyed.

"Not you, that's for sure," he says so quietly I barely hear it.

"Look," I shoot back. "I'm not trying to be difficult, but this isn't my stuff."

"Right. Anything you don't want, just put outside the door. Cole will take it away." He hurries to the door.

"No, it's not that I –"

"Or else keep it. Or toss it in the bin!" He glares at me from the doorway. "Are we good then?"

I shrug. Okay, sure, asshole. Are they *all* going to be like this?

Richard yanks the door shut with a bang and the whole room goes silent. I'm relieved to be alone. I can't believe this place. I take pictures and try to text them to my mom and Zach. Each time I get an "Undeliverable" message. I figure I'll email them later.

I think of my mom. We never lived anywhere near this nice. There's wallpaper peeling in our upstairs bedroom and pipes that clang all winter. I wish she could see this.

I flick the remote and the TV bursts to life. First, The Academy crest flashes on the screen, and then a football game. Cheers fill the room and I wait until the score comes up. Cool. My mom would never let me have a TV in my bedroom.

Of course what she doesn't know, she doesn't know. *Maybe,* I think, *this won't be so bad.*

I click it off the TV and pick up the laptop. It probably cost five grand or more. I wonder about the guy who was supposed to be here and what made him change his mind. Maybe he decided to go to another school.

I pull the name-tag out of the trash and read it: James Harken. I drop it back in the trash and looked around again.

Thanks, James, I say under my breath. Whoever you are.

———— ❧ ————

Twenty minutes later I'm unpacked, and the only reason it took *that* long is because I had to setup my desktop. I built it myself and call it "The Beast" because, well, because that's what it is. It has the fastest processor on the market and enough memory to download an entire library. I admit, it may not look like much sitting next to that sleek, silver laptop, but thanks to what's under the hood, it will smoke most other computers.

The angel figurine, which for some weird reason I couldn't throw away, dangles in the window, refracting light. If anyone asks, I'll just say it was a gift from my mom.

Now that I've unpacked, I don't know what to do. It's so quiet. There are like sixty or so guys in the building and valets everywhere, but I can't hear a sound.

I consider wandering around a little, but the truth is I don't want to face anyone until I have to.

I put my helmet in the closet and do a double take.

The first time I opened the closet, I didn't notice anything. I hung up my dress shirt and the other button-downs I wear to church. It was just a closet (yeah, okay, a *huge* closet, like the size of my bathroom back home).

But this time, I put the helmet down on the floor inside the closet, and the door opened wider and caught the light. I'm stunned. *The entire inside of the closet is covered with names and symbols carved into the wood.* I stare. It looks like computer code as I start to look closer –

"Creepy, isn't it?"

I jump back a little.

In the middle of my room, sitting in a chair that I swear wasn't there ten seconds ago, is this guy. Brown, floppy hair. A big smile. Probably my age, or he could be a senior.

He wheels himself toward me and I realize: he's in a wheelchair.

"Charley Mercer," he says, shaking my hand in his Ironman grip. "Your suite mate." He points at a door in the far wall that must connect the two rooms.

"Peter Foster."

"I know."

I take a closer look. The guy is ripped. At least his upper body is. His legs seem much smaller.

He glances into my closet and sees my helmet. "You ride?" He rolls over and picks it up.

"Enduro," I tell him. "Modified it myself, but –"

"Holy shit, what happened?" He runs a finger over a huge gash on the helmet's side.

"Accident. Pretty bad."

"Looks like you shoulda been road kill."

I shrug. "Freaked my mom out." I'm not getting into details. Charley hands me the helmet and I put it back.

I have to ask. "So is every room like this?"

"Pretty much."

I nod, like it makes sense, like I was expecting this, like maybe I had a room like this back home. Without, you know, all those engravings on the closet door.

"What're these?" I ask.

"One of the best-kept secrets around here," he says with a laugh. I decide right then and there that I like this guy. He doesn't treat me like a massive pain in the ass, the way Richard did.

"Seniors write their names in their closets the night before graduation,"

"And what are these symbols next to the names?"

Charley shrugs. "No idea. You find out graduation day."

I look closer. "Wait a second, Thomas Edison, 1865. Thomas Edison slept in this room?"

Charley grins. "Charles Edison should be in there too. Most legacy students get the same room their fathers and grandfathers were in."

Wow. "How long has your family been going here?"

"Too long," he says, smiling.

I tap another name. "Warren Buffett?!"

"Yeah, well, he's my godfather. His father should be in there too, Howard Buffett. He was a Congressman during World War Two." He laughs at my reaction. "So you hang up your clothes with Amer-

36

ica's best and brightest. Congratu-dolences."

"What the hell am *I* doing here?"

"Figuring it out, I guess. Like the rest of us." He shrugs. Then he looks around the room. "Where's the rest of your stuff?"

Oh shit. "It's, uh, being shipped." That's the best I can do.

"Cool," Charley says, rolling back toward his room. "You need anything, just knock on the wall."

Suddenly pounding footsteps echo in the hall. Charley's eyes light up. "Feeding time! Come with me!"

———

You have got to be kidding me! is the first thing I think as we walk into the student dining room. Waiters in tuxedo shirts. White linen tablecloths. A salad bar with ice sculptures and fresh seafood. Real silverware and imported European bottled water on all the tables.

I'm surprised they don't have someone playing a harp in the background.

Charley leads me to a large table in the center of the dining room. "Don't let them freak you out," he says under his breath, wheeling himself up to what is obviously his spot at the table, since there's no chair there. I take the seat next to him and look at the other students at the table.

I don't know what I was expecting, but not this.

On the other side of Charley are two of the most beautiful girls I've ever seen. One is blonde, the other has darker hair, but they look like models. I try not to stare but it isn't easy.

They're having an argument about something but before I'm introduced, I recognize the guy next to them. That's Anton Volsky.

I'd know him anywhere because he seems to live on Page Six. He watches the two girls with a lazy half-smile, and for the briefest second, I think: *total player*.

They all nod a greeting at Charley but no one even looks at me. I study them all and can't believe they're my age.

Then the brunette waves at me, a little wave.

I start to say something but the blonde keeps ranting.

"Listen to me!" she says, in an English accent, obviously irritated to have lost her friend's attention for that split second. "I got a dozen calls after you abandoned me in Dubai!"

Charley winks at me. "Meet Chloe, on your left –"

So the blonde is Chloe. She doesn't even look at me but rails at the brunette. "Everyone wondered what happened to you!"

Charley continues as if Chloe wasn't even there. "Our Chloe is marginally attractive, morally adrift, and tragically unlovable."

The brunette dismisses Chloe with a perfectly manicured hand. "No one's interested in what happened in Dubai, Chlo–"

"–– *I'm* interested in what happened in Dubai," Anton says with a leer.

Suddenly Chloe turns to Charley as if she just remembered something. "You think I'm attractive? That is *so sweet!*"

She notices me, pauses, and then turns back to her friend without a word. Nice.

A girl carrying a tray veers toward the table. This girl is younger, a little nervous. Chloe holds up a hand and the girl stops. Sighs. And moves to another table.

What the hell was *that*? I'm starting to realize that there are a lot of rules here, rules I'd better learn before I make an ass of myself.

Chloe turns back to the brunette. "We *know* you, Sophia. Don't tell us you wouldn't do it again in a heartbeat."

Everyone turns toward Sophia.

"I regret doing it the first time," she's saying, obviously trying to shut down the conversation.

Charley says, "That's Sophia – " so only I can hear.

"Look we get it, we really do," Chloe says. "Charity work is trending right now. We just miss the *real* you. The one who used to be, you know, fun!"

Charley is so used to Chloe's interruptions, he keeps going as if he hasn't heard her. "— And Sophia is ... searching."

Chloe turns to me. "Sophia is our little well digger, getting all muddy in New Guinea—"

"India," Sophia corrects. "Can we stop?"

"—or *wherever* for people who will end up dying anyway." Chloe takes a sip of tea. "Off Sophia goes to help the sick and homeless so she can feel better about herself. And totally bailing on her real friends."

Whoa. Did she just *say* that? Because that's ...

"You're upset because I want to help people instead of going to another pointless party with you?" Sophia asks, and I'm liking her already. "Like I haven't watched enough spoiled boys drink themselves into oblivion."

"Those 'boys' were royalty," Chloe sniffs. "And we were guests of honor." She sighs. "We're just saying: the 'New You' isn't as much fun as the 'Old You'." She turns to the others. "Right?"

"Good! I hate to think of a near death experience going totally to waste," Sophia says. The table quiets. Chloe just looks at her blankly.

Sophia is obviously irritated.

"Haven't you ever wanted to do something good for other people?" Sophia asks.

Everyone stares at Chloe as she replaces her teacup in its fragile saucer. *"Why?"* she asks.

I can't believe it. *Who are these people?* I ask myself for the second time this morning.

Charley rolls back in his chair, laughing. He saw the look on my face. I'd better be careful. "It builds character," he says, and then adds, "but only if you have character to build on."

Anton leans in to Sophia. "So if it benefits you, too," he says, "how much moral credit do you really deserve?"

Sophia smiles sweetly at Anton but I can tell she doesn't like him. Or at least not right now. She says sweetly, "I was hoping a summer of unfettered drug use would do you in, Anton."

He chuckles. "Beginner's luck, I guess."

Sophia turns to me. "Hi and welcome. That's Anton Volsky, who has elevated being a dick to an art form. Ignore everything he says and you'll be a better person for it."

"Thank you," Anton says. He obviously considers that a compliment. What a douche.

I have Sophia's attention, only for a second. "I'm Peter Foster," I say quickly. There's a sudden silence at the table, everyone looks at me as if expecting me to go on. But what the hell can I say? That I have no idea what I'm even doing here?

Anton wipes his mouth with a linen napkin, looks at me and then nods at the girls. "Dubai. India. I yachted along the Italian coast. What did *you* do on your summer vacation, Peter Foster?"

Shit. My brain freezes. I'm not really ready yet for this kind of back and forth, but here it is. Already.

"Let me guess. A little fishing in your backyard pool?" he asks.

"—Ding, ding, ding! Dick Exhibit A," Sophia says, and the others chuckle.

I'm mentally pinching myself. *Wake up,* I say to myself, *get into the game! You can't let this douche bag humiliate you!*

Anton sees me hesitate. "I know! You had a family reunion at Disneyland and hooked up with your cousin." He licks his lips like a porn star. Chloe giggles.

At that second, I remember the last headline I saw with his name in it.

"At least I stayed off Page Six for screwing my best friend's mother," I say, *cold as ice.* The table goes silent and I have no idea what's coming back at me. But I can read their faces, and I know one thing.

No one expected this from a townie. Including me. I usually come up with a cool comeback thirty minutes after I need it.

"He shoots. He scores!" Charley says, and the girls are laughing. Relief floods my chest.

Sophia taps my arm and says, "You'll do just fine here, Peter Foster." She stands and pushes her chair in, taking a second to lean down and whisper in my ear. "Classes start in fourteen hours. Better get ready!"

I watch her leave. For a moment I feel really good, like I may have a chance at hacking this school. The moment is short.

Anton glares at me. "You'll never be ready," he says. He throws his napkin onto his plate and stalks off.

CHAPTER FOUR

PETER

I shut the door of my room and stand there, a little dazed. *What just happened?* I admit it: I'm a little freaked out. No amount of drunken stories from parents, stuff I read on the web or things I overheard people in town saying could have prepared me for people like Anton and Chloe.

Charley is nice enough. But he has hung with this crew his whole life, so how normal could he be? And where could I possibly fit in?

I fire up The Beast and get online to do a little research on Chloe and Sophia. After about ten minutes, I find their Instagram accounts, under fake names (of course). Chloe is all selfies and runway shots, and Sophia is nothing but charity events. I don't bother with Anton, because I don't really want to know or care.

I glance over at James Harken's laptop. It's a thing of beauty –

slim, gleaming silver and as light as a feather when I pick it up. It's technically mine, but I glance at the door to make sure I'm alone before I open it up.

The screen saver appears – an illustration of a cross with a weird three-pronged symbol sitting on top of it in the center of the page. "Issued to James Harken" blinks on the screen as it requests a PASSWORD. I type James's name.

ACCESS DENIED.

I try "The Academy" and then again in caps.

Both times: ACCESS DENIED.

That just makes me want to hack it more. I look at The Beast. I know I can do it, I've done it a thousand times. There is no firewall I can't crack given enough time. My mom would have never guessed that getting me a computer would lead to late night hacking at the library for fun. I never do anything once I'm in, I just love the challenge.

But it's late. I get the feeling this hack would take all night, and the idea of facing another day at The Academy after being up all night is more than I can handle right now. I close the laptop and marvel again at how light it is. I decide to start on it tomorrow before my first class.

———

BLEH BLEHBLEH

The sound pierces my consciousness like a jackhammer. I'm beat. I don't feel like I slept at all, but light is coming through the windows. I kept getting woken up in the middle of the night by some high-pitched music. Every time I turned on the light, it stopped! I couldn't figure out where it was coming from. It sounded like tiny bells and reminded me of those little music boxes they sell at the mall.

Finally, I was so tired, I decided to ignore whatever it was and sleep through it. Now I realize I slept through my alarm, too. Damn it.

I jump out of bed. I'm already twenty minutes behind schedule. First day, and I sleep through the alarm, which is a total first for me. Great start, Foster.

I wet my hair in the sink and throw on some clothes. I dig around for my class schedule, cursing the whole time.

First stop, Student Orientation with a special guest lecturer: the U.S. Ambassador to China. I race past the sign: apparently he's there to brief the students on his recent report to the President about U.S.-China trade relations and the shifting structure of import tariffs.

What am I doing here? I ask myself for the hundredth time.

Providence High once had the Lieutenant Governor come speak for its 100 year anniversary, but I don't even remember his name and he sure didn't talk about the shifting structure of anything. We called our first day of school Student Disorientation.

I'm one of the last to arrive and trip over everyone's legs to get to my seat.

"Making an entrance?"

Charley. Thank God. His wheelchair is parked at the end of a row and he makes some freshmen move over so I can sit next to him.

"Overslept," I say, wincing. "I shoulda stayed in bed."

I want to talk some more, ask him what the hell to expect here, but the hall quiets. *Fourteen minutes ago, I was dead asleep*, I think, willing myself to wake up. I rub my face a little. Maybe that will help.

"Get out your laptop, Foster," Charley whispers. I notice that all the other students have one. Damn! I should have brought James's. Just to blend in, because now I'm going to look like a total ass without it. All around the room are a hundred colored squares streaming a single webpage: the Ambassador's lecture notes.

I lean over to read what I can off Charley's screen when a swell of applause and some hooting makes me look up. I can't believe it. Bill Clinton just walked in and is smiling and waving from the stage! Bill Clinton! He's going to speak to us! I turn to Charley, a little bug eyed. Charley isn't looking at Bill Clinton, he's smiling at me. My reaction is very entertaining to him. I'm *amusing* him.

For once, I don't mind.

The former President talks for forty minutes, and I notice that a half hour in, the other students start to get a little bored. They act as if this happens every day. Maybe it does, in their world.

President Clinton finishes his speech and I'm clapping the loudest. I wish I could take a picture and send it to Zach, because there is no way he is going to believe it.

Charley rolls out with me as I head to my next class. "Clinton comes all the way to The Academy to give a thirty minute speech?" I ask him, incredulous.

"He can raise more money for The Clinton Foundation here, and faster, than he can at a hundred *other* fund raisers," he explains. It's clearly not that big a deal to him. "Plus alumni are expected to drop by and talk to the students every year or so. See you at dinner tonight."

And then rolls away with impressive speed.

The next few hours were pretty much standard high school hell, first day confusion and general disorientation. Everyone's catching up on summer reading and comparing class schedules. They always seem to be in a hurry to get somewhere.

I pause beside some rosebushes that line the walkway just in time to see the Secret Service escorting a jovial Bill Clinton to his waiting limo. I see Doctor Browning walking with him and giving him a hug goodbye.

I realize I'm about to be late to my next class. I don't even know what it is, everything on this stupid class schedule is abbreviated. And there's no way I'm asking anyone. I end up finding my numbered seat in Patton Hall without too much trouble, seconds before class starts.

The other students are all talking but then suddenly stop when the teacher arrives. He's a tall guy with a full head of hair, and he's wearing some kind of tweed jacket. He moves easily, like he's young, but he's not. I realize he's the same guy who gave me the dirty look at orientation. *Great.* When everyone gets quiet, the room sort of swells with respect, and I get the idea that this is a guy these students actually want to impress. I try to imagine why. He barely looks at them.

He says (to one in particular) that his name is Professor Linden, and launches into his lecture using some high-tech projection that glows on the wall behind him. We are studying "Medieval Military Order 1129 – 1291," according to the first card projected onto the screen. My schedule calls it MMO1 – yeah, I should have guessed, right?

All the students take notes on their laptops. Obviously the course work is streamed wirelessly to everyone but me. Swearing silently, I write everything by hand but that's way too slow, I know I won't be able to read half of it. I mean, it doesn't really matter because I've got a photographic memory and I'm not going to forget any of this anyway, but I don't want to sit here doing nothing. So I keep scribbling until my hand hurts.

Professor Linden paces. His voice is deep and he almost sounds like an actor reciting Shakespeare, the way he speaks.

"The Templar Knights originally depended on donations to survive," he says, "but by 1135, they found themselves beneficiaries of Christendom's wealth and good will." He pauses and smiles with half his face. "That came with all the accompanying corruption and loss of focus one might expect. Imagine: a warring, mobile state within a state, answerable only to the Pope, and with its own standing army! How *interesting*."

He looks around and settles his gaze on me. It's like he just noticed that he's not alone. He looks at me long and hard, and I can feel it. Like, in my bones.

"Often far from home and unwilling to trust conventional means of communication," he continues without missing a beat, "the Knights relied for centuries on a complex set of codes, symbols and glyphs that only they understood."

Behind him, the screen lights up with images of strange symbols, strings of digits, and odd symbols. I know I have seen them somewhere before, but where? Before I can place them, Professor Linden looks at the rest of the class.

"I'm sure you'll remember the winner of last year's Academic Prize, James Harken."

I glance up sharply. James Harken? That's –

The air goes out of the room. No one says a word.

"Don't any of you remember?" he huffs as if we've done something wrong. "For his paper on 'Mathematical Analysis of Cryptographic Algorithms found on The Academy Campus?'"

I can't take my eyes off the screen, where symbols flash by almost faster than I can process them, even when I sense everyone else in the room shifting uncomfortably.

"As a devotee of Freemasonry," Linden goes on, "James decoded Masonic symbols on our campus by using two of the most basic tools available to us all: a curious intellect and an unyielding work ethic."

The final image on the screen is The Academy crest.

"A student of immeasurable potential!" Linden booms proudly, "who was -"

A bell rings. Linden shakes his head, disappointed. The students file out and, feeling Professor Linden's eyes on me, I creep out with the crowd.

"You!" Linden gestures at me impatiently. "Where's your laptop?"

"It, uh, hasn't come yet. The one left for me is password protected and I haven't –"

"That's ridiculous. I'm sure Tech Services has provided you with all the necessary equipment."

"Yes. I mean, not yet, but –"

"This isn't an under-funded suburban high school, Mr...?" He waits.

"Peter. Uh, Foster," I say weakly.

"Nor is this some little Amish schoolhouse, Mr. *Foster*. We don't write by hand. Without a laptop, you will not gain access to my course website. You will not receive assignments. You will be unable to follow my lectures and submit your work ... and *you will fail.* Do you understand?"

I nodded.

"You have a laptop. Use it."

"Yes, sir."

All of a sudden, Linden's offers his hand.

"Welcome to The Academy."

———～———

I walk out of Linden's class and realize I have hit my limit with these people. I have to get away. Even for five minutes. I need to think, and process ... and breathe. I find a flight of stairs and follow them down to the basement, dark, and smelling of dust. I drag myself to a corner and drop to the floor.

I FaceTime Zach and get lucky with the reception.

"Hey, Foster child," he says, and I've never been so happy to hear my best friend's voice. Our mothers met when we were babies. We've been friends ever since. We know everything about each other. Zach is a little chubby and not really into sports, but he's an awesome musician (the highlight of the school's annual talent show) and I keep telling him he could do stand-up if he wanted to.

A half hour later, I'm still downloading my first day. I've told him everything, the good and the bad, and I feel lighter. Zach can always crack me up.

"Bill Clinton?" he asks, laughing. "My old friend. Did he recommend any particular brand of cigars?"

"I'm serious, Zach. They're all so…entitled." There's more to say, but too soon, I hear DONG! The final bell. I sigh. Above, hundreds of feet race through the corridors.

"What was that?" Zach asks.

I sigh. "I must be late for something. Catch you later."

"Hang in there, Foster," Zach says. He wiggles his fingers at me and the phone clicks off. I force myself to my feet and gather my books.

———— ∿ ————

That night, after an amazing dinner fourteen buffet tables long, I sat at my desk and finished up my homework. Or I should say, I finished the homework I could, since I still had no laptop. I called Tech Services twice and left messages, but no one has called me back.

I remembered what Professor Linden said and realized I couldn't show up tomorrow without a laptop, so it was time to break open the Red Bull and start the hack.

An hour later, study hall is over and I can hear the guys in the hall kicking something around and laughing. I barely pay attention. My desk is covered with wires; cables from my desktop snake into James's laptop. I type furiously as code scrolls across the big screen TV. I set it up as a mirror monitor for the desktop.

ACCESS DENIED.

Damn. I've seen that four hundred times tonight. I fight back waves of frustration.

The screen then refreshes to the same PASSWORD: _ _ _ _ _ _ _ against the cross and three-pronged symbol. I keep typing, but the same error message pops up.

Then I hear something. Whispering maybe? Whatever it is it's loud enough to break my concentration. What the hell…? I quickly open my door figuring I would catch someone planting a smoke bomb or something, but there's no one there. The corridor is totally empty. Wasn't it just full of guys a minute ago?

I look back at the computer. It's 11:41pm. No wonder. Wow. I sat there for four hours without moving! As I do the seventh inning stretch, I notice my closet door standing wide open. It was closed five seconds ago, wasn't it? Too much Red Bull.

I go to close it but stop when I see the names and the numbers engraved on the back of it. Oh my God. I peer closer. I can't believe what I'm seeing.

J. HARKEN '15, very recently carved. It has a bunch of numbers and characters carved around it, including the three-pronged symbol.

I back up. That wasn't there this morning. Who the hell came into my room?

I knock on Charley's door and push it open without waiting for an answer. Charley's doing pushups.

"What's up?" he asks, without breaking focus.

"You now anything about the guy who had my room last year?"

"Like what?" Charley bangs out another five pushups.

"I need his password for the laptop." Charley pauses. I shrug. "I should probably wipe his hard drive."

"What're you talking about? Your computer should be clean."

"Well, it's not. They were expecting this James Harken guy and prepped a new laptop for him. I guess they dumped his old hard drive onto – "

"You *guess*? You've *used* it?" Charley raises his voice, getting worked up all of a sudden.

"I can't use it," I say calmly, "not without his password! I've tried for two days to – "

"Call Tech Services!" Charley barks, pulling himself up into his wheelchair.

"I just need his password. I thought I could hack it by now," I say, realizing I shouldn't have said anything.

"Don't touch it, they'll take care of it!" Charley fixes me with an intense look. I imagine it's the kind a father gives his son when he's trying to keep him in line. "The last thing you want to do is screw that thing up. They don't even make replacement parts for it yet."

"Listen, I got my ass handed to me by Linden today," I explain. "If you don't know the password, no worries, I'll deal with it."

"Don't touch that laptop until Tech Services gets here. *I'll* call!" He pulls his phone from a pocket in the wheelchair.

"It's okay!" I say, backing out of the room. "I already called 'em!" I shut the door. *What's his problem?*

I hear the door click open. I guess I didn't pull it hard enough. Through the crack, I see Charley texting furiously, like his life depends on it. Then he grabs a pill bottle from somewhere under his chair and shakes out a few pills. Swallows them dry.

Squeezing the knob, I shut the door without a sound and make a mental note not to bother Charley with details again.

By 4:15am, I've almost given up for the night. I've hacked everything from my freshman year grades to the State Senate's budget, and I've never seen authentication obstacles like these. This is the kind of security I imagine NASA or the FBI has in place.

But something in me won't give up. I keep typing, and I keep getting the error message. In a moment of frustration, while I'm looking over at the closet, I get an idea. I've got to start thinking like James, not like a normal hacker. And then I remember what Professor Linden said about him and his obsession with codes and symbols.

I pull a lamp over to the closet so I can see better, and I write down the numbers carved into the closet door. ACCESS DENIED. I change the order and try again. ACCESS DENIED.

Then I get another idea and log on to The Academy's research database. It takes me minutes to find award-winning student essays and I scroll down to: "Mathematical Analysis of Cryptographic Algorithms found on The Academy Campus" by James Harken. That's it. I click on the link and I scroll down, slowing at the symbol illustrations. There's one of the cross and the three-pronged symbol. I print out the page and then put the three-pronged symbol printed on the page directly over the one on the door.

"Son of a bitch."

The four points of the cross correspond to engraved numbers on the closet door. I write them down starting at the top going clockwise on a notepad 42, 54, 72, 61 and then hurry over to the laptop.

I type them in and wait for ACCESS DENIED.

Instead, the computer goes black. Then it starts to boot up. I did it. I got in.

I do a little victory cheer and then the adrenaline starts to fade and suddenly I'm exhausted. I look at the clock. Three hours before classes start. At least I'll have a laptop tomorrow, I say to myself. *Time to get some sleep.*

I'm at the sink, brushing my teeth, so I don't even see the video window open on the laptop after it boots up. I just hear a voice.

"My name is James Harken. If you're watching this, I'm probably dead."

What was that? I turn and see the blurred image of a face on the laptop.

"And it wasn't an accident," James Harken is saying. "Someone had me killed to hide the truth about The Academy."

I spit my toothpaste in the sink. *What the hell?*

I go closer. The image focuses. It's a guy, my age, maybe 17. He's got sunken eyes with dark circles around them, and he's fidgeting. At first I think he's on some kind of meth binge but then I realize, no, he's really *scared*.

"You have two choices to make right now," he says, staring right into the camera. Right at me. "Either stop and delete everything on this computer ... or find out what's really happening."

The guy looks around, fighting panic. He readjusts the camera. Now I can see him in a room that looks a lot like this one, surrounded by piles of manila envelopes. He is scanning what looks like really old yellowed papers into his computer. His face fills the screen. He seals an envelope and tosses it onto the piles.

I must be seeing things. I'm exhausted. I can't – I mean, I am mentally unable – to take in any new information. The words "Tech Services" float through my brain and I'm about to click the video away when –

"Trust me when I say that you'll need this information to protect yourself," he says. Something in his voice stops me. "So decide. *Now.*"

I slowly pull my hand away.

"Okay. You're with me, then. First, I am *not crazy*." The guy scratches nervously at his face. He grabs a sheaf of loose-leaf papers and starts scanning a new batch. "I'm the first in my family to attend school here. Don't know about your parents, but no one told me shit about what this place is all about." He jams the just scanned papers into an envelope, his eyes darting about.

And that gets me. I sit back down, eyes glued to the screen.

"Even that crest! Magnus Novus Orbis!" he says grandly " 'Great New World!' I thought it was just for show, like everything else." He throws the envelope onto a pile. "Then some really weird stuff started happening and I thought I was losing it. That's when I looked into the history of this place and everything made sense." He remembers he didn't seal the envelope and quickly grabs it back. The guy's manic.

"Why do the richest and most powerful send their kids here? Think it's the education? Or for 'connections?'" he laughs bitterly. He gets closer. His eyes fill the screen, watery and scared. "I started to uncover what they're hiding."

I quickly reach over and turn down the volume. I'm getting a little creeped out and wish I'd just gone to bed.

"The more I find out, the less I want to know. Click on the links. You'll see what I mean."

Several link addresses scroll by the bottom of the screen.

James points to the pile of envelopes. "It's all in here. I wrote it all down, you just gotta find it before they do." A familiar sounding tinny melody plays faintly. He reaches out of frame and the melody cuts off.

"My time is up." He swallows and smiles, but it's a bitter, unhappy smile. "Remember: when things go really bad, you're only safe *on campus.*" He leans in until his eyes fill the screen. He's looking right at me. "Don't let 'em get you."

He tosses that final envelope away and the screen goes black.

The links remain, glowing.

What the hell?! Every nerve ending in my body is buzzing. There's no way I'm sleeping tonight. Don't let them get me? *Who?*

Holding my breath, I click on the first link.

CHAPTER FIVE

PETER

I watched the links. I couldn't believe what I saw. I knew the students here were planning to run the world one day, but I couldn't believe the shit they were into. Now I have video proof that would ruin all of their plans.

God only knows what they would do to me if they knew.

James Harken was writing a book. That much I figured out. And that book would expose them, so they must have killed him to keep him quiet. I remember how weird Charley got when I asked about James, and how uncomfortable (or scared?) the students in class acted when Professor Linden brought up Harken's name.

A bubble of panic rises in my chest. *I have to get out of here.* I press against the window latch. It snaps open, as loud as a gunshot.

The cold air hits me. I've got to think things through. I want to call Zach, call my Mom, but what the hell would I say? I could leave, I guess, but the sun is coming up. I saw the gates and the security cameras when I drove in; there's no way I can sneak out easily, much less in daylight.

Plus if I took off now, they'd know something was up.

I lean against the window. I'm stuck in this place for now. I sigh, and the window fogs a little. As I wipe it off, I see someone in a window across the way. I pause – who else is up at this hour? – and then whoever it is steps back and vanishes from my sight.

This is just getting too creepy.

I try to count the windows so I can see whose room that is, but I have to start over twice. I don't even know which building that is. God, I'm tired. Maybe it wasn't even a person. *Relax! Stop acting like a tweaker,* I tell myself. I glance over at James' laptop, which I slammed shut when I couldn't take anymore. I double check to make sure it's back at the password prompt and push it to the back of my desk.

Soon it will be time for class.

DR. BROWNING

I used to paint as a pleasant way of passing time. Now I find that no day feels well-lived until I've spent time before my easel. It's not what you might think: I am not bent on self-expression. I haven't the time nor the inclination. I'm told my work evokes a sense of lightness and peace, but that's not why I paint, either.

I paint because doing so enables me to do my job better.

I place a white polished stone on the easel. It shimmers as the light hits it and the colors in my painting come alive. At first I felt guilty looking in on my students this way. But with an adversary like Linden, one must grasp every advantage.

A polished stone. Something so simple!

But it works. Within moments, Richard takes shape beneath my brush. He knows what's on James's laptop, and thanks to Charley, he knows that it was left in Peter's room by accident (I assume, in my more charitable moments) or on purpose, in an effort to force poor Peter into an untenable dilemma (which is much more likely).

Richard struggles. He knows he can't really come to me. He knows I am not allowed to directly interfere with a student's choices. So he bursts from his room, yelling like a madman.

"This is a frigging *nightmare!*"

Peter, a little jumpy after a day of classes and no sleep, sticks his head out of his room. WTH??

Richard doesn't care *who's* watching. "Helloooo!" he rants. "Who the hell is responsible for temperature control around here! It's *moving air,* people, not brain surgery!"

Charley and others peek out into the hall warily, some still holding their tablets and books.

"My room is like a goddamn *sauna!*" Richard points at Peter. "Go find someone!" he bellows.

Peter pauses in confusion. He considers telling Richard to deal with it himself, but he's so exhausted he doesn't bother. He'll do it. He'll go.

It's a clumsy plan, but at least Richard is thinking.

Peter hurries down the hall toward the Security station. He doesn't see a very anxious Cole hurry up the opposite staircase toward Richard, careful not to make eye contact.

"I'm here, Mr. Winters," Cole says quietly, pulling his cap from his head. The rest of the students close their doors and go back to their studies.

"Congratu-frigging-lations!"

Cole hurries into Richard's room

Richard slams the door. "Do you know what my parents pay to send me to this place?" he shouts, louder than necessary.

Cole has clearly had enough of it, too. His expression hardens. He straightens his posture and looks Richard in the eye.

"I'm here," he says drily. "What is it?"

Richard loses his faux-outrage. He leans into his door to listen. Nods: they're alone.

"That new guy. Peter. He's in Jimmy's old room. He has his laptop!"

"We know," Cole says with a sigh. "A regrettable oversight." He speaks in a faint and hard-to-place accent. Few know that it's actually a careful blend of all the students who have ever attended The Academy.

"You know?" Richard asks. "What are you going to do about it? You realize Jimmy's computer was cloned for the first day of school. *Everything* is on that drive!"

"The laptop is no longer a concern," Cole says. "Your break from protocol, however, *is*. So you know what you will do now?"

Richard's eyes widen. *Me?*

"You will stay calm. You will keep your mouth shut. Am I understood?"

Richard gives a barely perceptible nod.

"*We* will handle this." Cole replaces his cap and walks to the door.

He lowers his voice. "And you might want to keep an eye on your sister."

Richard's shoulders sag. "There aren't enough hours in the day," he says, exhausted by the idea.

Cole nods. He understands. Gently, he says, "You may continue."

Richard takes a deep breath. "You got that?" he shouts. "It's a heater, man, not a nuclear reactor!"

Cole, hunched like an old man again, scurries out the door and down the corridor. He nearly bumps into Peter, who was told by Security that Cole was already there.

Cole pauses as he passes him. He whispers something into Peter's ear. I wish I knew what.

Peter stops. "What? Did you say something?" he asks, but Cole has already vanished down the stairway.

And now Peter is alone. The doors that line the hallway are all closed, and no one is making a sound. He looks around. He wonders where everyone has gone and why so suddenly? He has a remarkable intuition, this young man. The silence stretches.

The image begins to fade. Too soon! I scan the painting while there's something left to see. Peter quickens his pace. He is eager to get into the familiar safety of his room.

Moments later, the image is gone. But I saw what I needed to see.

PETER

From the hallway, I can hear this weird melody playing and it's clearly coming from inside my room. It's super high-pitched, and sort of mechanical sounding. Like miniature bells. *Why does it sound so familiar?* And then I remember: it kept waking me up.

I push the door open, figuring I'd finally follow the sound to its source, but I never get the chance.

I take two steps in – just long enough to notice that James's laptop, which I'd pushed back on my desk, is missing – and I'm about to shout for Charley when suddenly there's something in my mouth, gagging me.

I'm grabbed on both sides, really hard. Someone throws a hood over my head. Everything goes dark and I'm pushed to the floor. I try and fight off whoever it is, but there are too many arms pinning me down. My hands are wrenched behind my back and my wrists are zip tied together. Then I can feel myself being rolled up into something. I can't scream. I can't move.

And I can't hear much. Just urgent whispers, impossible to understand.

My stomach clenches in panic. I choke, sucking air. I make myself breathe through my nose. The laptop! This must be about the laptop! They'll kill me because of it! If I could just explain it! I swear I won't say anything! I try to scream.

I'm picked up and then I'm being carried. I try to follow the turns but it's impossible. I make myself go limp and it's a good thing, because soon I'm tossed down somewhere hard. I hear a trunk slam. Then silence until the car starts. What. The. Fuck?!

I can't move. I can't see anything. *Why is this happening?* I'm not embarrassed to say that a part of my brain is asking God to please take care of my mom. I'm all she has and I'm more worried about her and what she would go through if I just disappeared. Or worse. I did the same thing just before my motorcycle accident.

All of a sudden, I'm being carried again. After a couple of minutes,

I'm unrolled out of whatever they wrapped me up in and dumped onto a hard surface. The air is cool on my skin and I can feel the cold through my jeans. It feels like a stone floor.

All I'm able to see through the hood are vague shapes and little flickers of light. The zip ties binding my wrist are cut and I'm pushed into some type of chair. My arms are immediately tied to it. Footsteps echo and if I turn my head just right, I can hear the occasional murmur of whispered voices. But I can't make out what they're saying.

Then the hood is pulled away! I look around wildly, trying to get my bearings. I'm in some kind of basement or jail or something. The walls are rough stone with thick, rusted chains hanging off them. It's fucking medieval.

I'm sitting in a hard chair in front of a long wooden table. Six figures sit behind it in robes and hoods, their hands and faces obscured. Other hooded figures stand against the far walls, mostly in shadows. They are all absolutely still, but the place where their faces should be is directed at me. *They're all looking at me.* Torch light flickers on the wall.

I am only wearing jeans and a T-shirt and with all the adrenaline running through my body, I start to shiver. I take a deep breath and make myself relax. That's when I notice a large wooden guillotine! Right next to my chair!

Something gasps. Whimpers. It sounds like a baby. No one says a word. No one moves. I'm twisting my head around as best I can, but I can't see anything.

The leader behind the table finally speaks. The hood hides his mouth. "Peter Foster." It's a deep voice that fills the room. "You are accused of the most serious offense ever brought before this council."

I pull at my restraints, just to test them. They're too tight. I can't move.

"You have violated the most sacred right among us, that of *privacy*," the Leader continues. He nods, and someone I can't see unties the gag.

I swallow and stammer. "Who *are* you? What the hell are you – "

"— SILENCE!"

His voice echoes.

"You have thirty seconds to provide this council a defense!" the Leader barks. "Or you will be treated like the swine you are!"

He nods to someone standing behind me and before I can even turn, something screams bloody murder. I try to turn my body to see but the zip ties hold me down.

A pink thing is yanked out from under my chair. At first I think it's a baby because it's screaming in terror and twisting and squealing. Three Hooded Figures lift it onto the guillotine bench and hold it down.

SWISH! The blade falls. The screams stop. Blood splatters on my arm. I try to yank it back. "Jesus *Christ*!" Thick red blood pools across the filthy floor. I can see the pig head on the floor. The pig is still.

"Are you out of your mind?" I yell.

"You have fifteen seconds to answer my questions," the figure says calmly. A deathly stillness takes over the room. The loudest sound is me breathing, fast and shallow.

"Did you appropriate the laptop of another student?" the figure asks.

The laptop? This is about the *laptop*? I was right.

My mind races. How do I play this? Come clean? Pretend I

couldn't hack the thing? I scan the room for some clue, some expression. But I can't see a single face.

"I had no choice," I say, which is true. In a way.

From out of nowhere, the sharp end of a whip lashes the floor in front of me. I flinch. "What the hell!" Damn, that was close!

"Did you appropriate someone else's laptop? Yes or No!"

"Yes."

There's a pause. Then, slowly: "Did you enter into this laptop?"

In the far back, a tall hooded figure nods, very slightly. I blink, frozen. What the hell should I do? What if it's someone who hates me? Wants to trick me? It's a gamble. Maybe the biggest of my life. It's also the only help I've gotten. What do I have to lose?

I look away from the figure that nodded. "Yes."

"How?"

"I, uh, I entered the password and – "

"Who gave you this password?!" the Leader roars.

I recoil as if someone fired a gun next to me. I look up and the figure in the back nods again, barely.

"I--I figured it out," I stammer. "Off the codes inside my closet door."

A long pause. Some of the hooded heads turn away for a second, then back at me.

The Leader is calm again. "Did you view any personal material on that computer?" he asks.

I'm about to nod when the figure in the back of the room quickly shakes its head.

"Uh ... no."

After a moment, the Hooded Figures rise, all at once.

"The council has made its decision," the Leader declares.

"We do not tolerate liars."

I'm about to protest and deny everything when he suddenly points at me and bellows. "YOU LIE! AND WE SHALL TREAT YOU LIKE THE SWINE YOU ARE!!!"

The others converge on me like a swarm of demons. I can smell the smoky smell of their robes as they lean over me, tipping the chair back. I'm so scared, I can't breathe. The guillotine is perfectly positioned over my head.

I look up. A drop of blood wicks off the blade and falls, slow motion, onto my cheek. It's still warm. I lose it. I pull desperately at my bound wrists, so hard my elbows ache. I can't stop screaming, "No!"

"You must die!" the figure screams. Someone yanks the rope holding the guillotine blade.

It drops.

DR. BROWNING

He's asleep in front of the fireplace, the old sack of venom, in his favorite armchair. Asleep! A snifter of brandy and a half-smoked cigar are on the small table beside him.

I bend close enough to feel his rancid breath and imagine for the briefest instant what it would be like to hear the man's last breath. To watch and feel him fade from this earth forever.

Obviously he can sense the direction of my thoughts as a smile crosses his face. The globe on his desk starts to turn very, very slowly. His eyes pop open. "Hello, Charlotte."

"They've taken him," I say.

"Already?"

"As if you hadn't arranged it!"

"I did *not*."

Of course he denies it. He would deny the sun shining and be offended if I didn't believe him. I control my fury as best I can.

"Then you failed to prevent it!" I snap at him. "If something happens to him – "

"Dr. Browning!" Linden rises, indignant. He straightens his smoking jacket, flicking little bits of cigar ash off it. "I am not moved by your threats, if you haven't noticed. And while I enjoy seeing you all exercised, I'm equally concerned about the boy."

I glare. He points to his own blank expression. "That's concern."

"No, that's a sociopath's imitation of it." I tell him, "It's merely a guess at what *might* be an appropriate emotional response."

That stops him for a beat. He's so easy to knock off course, this one.

"I'm uninterested in *accidental converts,* you know," he says, huffing. "There's no sense of accomplishment in that."

I wait. He doesn't seem to be doing anything to help Peter and time is ticking away. I realize I'll have to provoke him further.

Such is the game we play.

"Your idea of accomplishment is simple treachery, Professor." There. I said it.

He stiffens. "I am the least deceitful person in this room," he says, and I stifle a groan. Not this again. "You, Dr. Browning, are a dog following the cruelest of imaginable masters. One who has obviously set you up to fail … again." He smirks. "Isn't that what you were lamenting at the gate a few short days ago?"

I admit I wasn't expecting that. I say nothing. We don't have time for this.

"Might not this sudden urgency be a measure of your languishing faith?" he asks.

Enough. "I want Peter back! Safe. And *you will make it happen,* Professor."

"Indeed I will," Linden says, buttoning up his jacket. "Because I wish it." He holds a playful finger up at me. "If it's not too late."

Oh how I detest him.

PETER

I'm screaming as the blade hurtles toward my neck. I think of my mom, of Zach, and the rest of my life ... all in a millisecond.

"NOO!!!"

Ka-THUNK. The blade stops half an inch from my neck.

Somewhere nearby, a voice booms in my ear.

"In the words of our immortal father, Sir Biggie of Brooklyn ..."

Rap music blasts from the walls. I shake my head to make sure I'm not hearing things. But no ... it really is Biggie's "Things Done Changed." WTF?

The whole group is singing along as Biggie raps about talking slick and keeping your mouth shut. The Leader is moving from side to side, his robes swaying.

I'm pulled up into a sitting position and I can't believe my eyes. The Figures all pull off their hoods. Anton, Charley (in his chair), Chloe and other familiar faces, all smiling. They high-five each other!

The zip ties are cut off and I stand up, a little shaky. It was a joke? This was all a fucking joke?! I wipe the blood and sweat off my face. The Leader, Richard, moves to me, all smiles, slaps me on the back. Behind him, the figure who helped me pulls off its hood and my jaw drops. Sophia. We lock eyes for a second, and then my view is blocked. When I look for her again, she's gone.

Anton pulls me up roughly. "On your feet, boy!"

Before I can say anything, or take a swing, Chloe's right there, her red lips the brightest thing in the room. She's smiling at me, too, as if I just won a race or something. "You did well, Pet-ah!"

Anton waves the whip. "Thought you were going to crap your pants!" he laughs.

Charley rolls up to me, "You're okay, right?"

"He's fine." Richard says quickly. His British accent is back.

"I just ... what ... why is ..." I can't even form a sentence.

"It's just a hazing thing, mate," Richard says.

"Congrats man, you're one of us!" Charley yells. "AND YE SHALL WANT NO MORE!" He's waving a beer stein in the air.

A big cheer goes up and everyone chants, "YE SHALL WANT NO MORE!!"

Everyone's laughing. Robes slide off, revealing colorful medieval costumes. Goblets appear in everyone's hands. I'm propelled by the group to a door that opens into a great room, with twenty foot ceilings and hay on the floor. The whole thing is decorated to look like a medieval castle: tapestries, tattered flags and shields on the stone walls, heavy wooden furniture with red velvet pillows everywhere.

The "bar" is a rough-hewn wooden ledge lit by a wooden chandelier. It's covered with wooden steins and brass goblets.

Chloe pushes a drink into my hands. "We're off campus!" she yells in my ear above the music. "So have a drink and relax!"

I take it all in. I'm finally calming down. This is something they do. This is how they party? It's incredible.

There's a couple in medieval costumes making out on a bench. Two guys in period costumes sword fight, and I mean, they are seriously trying to take each other out. A crowd around them shouts, laughing. I've never seen such rich costumes and decorations. It's like a Renaissance Fair for millionaires. Except with rap.

And suddenly I'm laughing, really laughing, high on adrenaline and relief. Richard lifts his goblet in a toast. "As we said at St. Jude's prep: 'Mazel Tov!'"

I bang my drink against theirs. "You guys are fucking crazy! Seriously. I thought I was freaking out with the laptop but this beats everything. I thought you guys had..."

I stop. What was I going to say? I almost give them all the ammunition they'd need to laugh at me for the next few years.

"What?" Richard asks suddenly more serious. "You did a lot of thinking about Jimmy Harken, right?" he prods.

I shrug. "For a second I thought maybe you had something to do with his disappearance."

The energy in the room concentrates. Everyone goes still.

"You did? All of us?" Chloe asks.

"Crazy, I know, I just – " I'm trying to back pedal.

"You think we, what, had him *killed* or something?" Chloe asks.

"No! God, no. I wasn't really thinking straight, I – "

"You wanna meet him?" asks Richard.

"James Harken? Absolutely," I say.

Richard throws an arm around my shoulders. I can't believe how nice he's being. "Right this way." He steers me toward a tall guy I can only see from behind, talking to some pretty girls by the bar. Richard leans into my ear. "I'm sure he wants to meet you, too," he says.

Before I can ask him what that's supposed to mean, the tall guy turns around. Athletic, put together. Has a face like an Ivy League lacrosse player. I put on my game face.

"Richie. What's up?" the tall guy asks.

"This is the guy I was telling you about," Richard says, nodding at me.

"So you got my room," he says. I'm confused. Whose room?

The tall guy grins at me. He holds out his hand. "James Harken," he says. "Nice to finally meet you."

My whole body freezes. I can't breathe. I look into his smiling face.

This is not James Harken.

CHAPTER SIX

PETER

Everything aches. My back. My head. My arms. Even my face, which I turn away from a very bright light. The sun. It's beating down on me through a huge window. I look around and finally realize I'm lying on the floor of the bathroom at the end of the hall.

I get to my feet and I swear my joints creak. It's like I'm a hundred years old. I splash some cold water on my face and do a quick check. I'm fully dressed but wearing only socks. How the hell did I end up *here* instead of in my room? And what happened to my shoes?

Then I remember last night.

Maybe the whole thing was a nightmare! Then I see the smear of blood on my arm. The pig. My wrists are raw from trying to pull them from the zip ties. *It really happened!* The last thing I remember was someone shoving a drink into my hand right before I was introduced to the fake James Harken.

Some asshole must have roofied me!

I hurry down the hall to my room. Just before I push the door open, I hear something coming from inside. That tinny music! *What the hell?* I open the door and the music stops. The room looks the same as it did last night. Nothing is out of place. The rug is straight. The bed is made.

And the laptop is back on my desk, just where I left it.

"Issued to Peter Foster" pops up as soon as I open it. It has the same illustration of the cross with the three-pronged symbol in the center. I type in my name, figuring it would be the temporary password, but ACCESS DENIED pops up. Not this again. I type in The Academy and get ACCESS DENIED a second time. Then I type in 42, 54, 72, and 61 – the same numbers I used to access James's computer. The laptop goes blank and then starts to boot up.

I rub my head. I need aspirin *right now*. Suddenly the adjoining door to my suite swings open. I jump. I'm still shaky.

Charley wheels himself in, "You okay?"

Are you kidding me? I want to ask, but Charley is my only real friend here. "Yeah," I finally say, struggling to keep my voice low key. "But where the hell are my shoes?" My mind is going a million miles an hour. "I don't even know how I got back here. What *happened*?"

He points. There are my shoes, by my bed. What?!

"What do you remember?" Charley asks.

Is he testing me? I glance at the blood on my arm. "I remember the pig, roasting and eating the pig," I say. He nods. I know I've got to go slow. "The guillotine. People in hoods. And James Harken."

He waits. I say nothing more, and finally he smiles. "Then you remember everything important. So relax!"

Are you kidding me? "But –"

"Because there are no Instagram photos of you in some not-so-flattering positions. You can thank me and Sophia later."

"Sophia?!"

Charley wheels himself back to the door.

"Wait!" I go after him. "Positions doing *what?*"

He looks back at me and smiles, "Breakfast ends in ten, dude." And he's out the door.

LINDEN

I stop in the doorway of Dr. Browning's office. She seems to be gazing at her latest attempt at abstract art, but she's actually listening in on the conversation between Charley and Peter. Nosy cow. I wish I could read the expression on her face but the light pouring in through the window hurts my eyes and I have to turn away.

I take another step inside, looking for some shadow to stand in, but there isn't any. How she gets any work done in here is beyond me. The tone is airy and warm, with light wood furniture and plants (*plants!*), making me wonder if she has ever entertained a serious, independent thought in her life.

I put on my sunglasses, which I always bring with me when I know I have to venture into her part of the building. At least *I* had the foresight to have my office built in the only section of the building that gets no direct sunlight.

Apparently she hears me. She doesn't even turn around. "He's a good kid," she says. "Or trying to be."

"You say that about them all. At first," I remind her. I try to focus but ... "Don't you have any blinds for these windows? I'm getting a headache."

She smiles at my obvious discomfort. "No, I don't." She nods to her plants. "Light provides nourishment."

Oh really? I want to list for her all the things sunlight can actually *reveal* and *destroy*. How it contributes to cancer, decay and ruin. I can feel my lips curling in anticipation but then – no. I can't let her distract me from the task at hand.

"I only came to talk about Cole," I tell her, applauding my own self-restraint. I sit down in one of her tiny chairs to let her know I don't intend to make this easy for her.

She finally turns, surprised. "Cole?"

"He has been more inept than usual this semester. Which is astonishing in light of *last year's* disaster." I bite off a cuticle and spit it out.

Dr. Browning cringes when I do this. *Good.* I sit back in the chair as if it's the most comfortable place I've ever been. As if I'll never leave. That should get her. Unfortunately, she doesn't seem to notice. She stares out the window instead, at the woods. "Aren't you going to thank me for getting your precious Peter back?" I ask.

"He isn't my precious anything," she replies without turning around. "Why would I thank you when you only *ever* act in your own interests?"

"Interest. Singular. I have but one." I grit my teeth. "And right now we're discussing Cole. He *must* be reminded of his function. We were promised a minimum of interference –"

"— I'll speak with him." Browning says. She's trying to shut *me* down! "Soon. Or *I* will."

She says nothing. I know where her head is. She can't tell, but I'm laughing at her.

"Stop staring out the window," I tell her with a wave of my hand. "He's *never* coming back."

CHLOE

It's time to hit my spot! I snatch my ciggies from the nightstand.

There's a small alcove behind the girls' residence hall. Centuries ago, the ladies' maids used to gather here to wait, so it has a little stone bench, perfect to grab an early morning smoke. At least walking up and down the stairs is good cardio. My hair is still wet, so I've got to be quick. Luckily, there are no surveillance cameras on campus or I would have to wear more than a bathrobe. You never know *what* will end up on TMZ or Page Six.

My cigarette is almost lit when a hand grabs me from behind. Every kidnapping scenario my father ever tried to scare me with flashes through my mind. I'm shoved against the wall. My elbow is ready to do some serious damage to someone's Adam's apple when I realize who's holding me. I recognize the cologne.

Anton. I know what he wants. I turn around. His face is really close to mine and there's something in it this morning besides hunger. Anger. I like that.

I hesitate a second, only to make him think I'm debating it. I'm not, really. What else is there to do on a Tuesday morning at The Academy? I take my time untying the knot on my silk bathrobe. I know what drives him crazy.

He doesn't wait. He can't wait. He spins me back around to face the wall and lifts up the robe, taking me from behind. Anton is never boring. At least he has *that* going for him.

He whispers into my ear. "I was wondering..."

I smile and grind against him as he moves slowly up and down.

"What made you think leaking that photo to Page Six was a good idea?" he hisses.

I freeze for just an instant and my eyes pop open. *Does he know it was me or is he guessing?* He starts to move a little faster and I relax. He can't be *too* upset, right? Besides, my mind is on other things now.

"Maybe you thought you were helping?" He whirls me around so we're face to face. He goes at it even harder now. We lock eyes. "You know," he continues, "you thought you'd make Sophia jealous so she'd come back to me." Anton's eyes are bright with anger now, and that just sends me. I'm so close ... and then he stops.

"Well?"

I stop grinding. "Hooking up is one thing, Anton. But it's way too early to *talk*. Unless you brought coffee?" I start to pull back. That does it. He buries himself inside me. We close our eyes and shudder together.

Boys and their toys. Take something away from them and they want it even more. Now I really do need a cigarette. I push him away and straighten my robe. I make a flitting gesture with my hand: go away.

"She didn't, though, did she?" he asks, zipping up. "Come back to me." I notice that some hair has fallen across his forehead, giving him a bit of a tousled look. *I did that,* I think.

I light my cigarette, which I managed not to drop this whole time. I exhale a smooth puff of smoke at him. He doesn't break his gaze. "I can't make her love you," I say, which is only partly true. The fact is *I can make Sophia do anything.*

"If me with other women doesn't make her jealous," he says, suddenly becoming Mr. Strategy, "we gotta try the opposite."

"You with other men?" I ask. I even amuse myself sometimes.

Unfortunately, he doesn't take the bait. I forgot that talk of Sophia robs him of all his humor and three-quarters of his brain. "No. Convince her I'm the only one who could ever make her happy."

I roll my eyes. It's ridiculous, really. Why does *everyone* have a thing for Sophia? She's about as interesting as a pair of smelly tennis shoes. I've had enough. I'm bored. "Why don't you just *tell* her?" I ask. "Not the truth, of course, that you wouldn't know real emotion if it bit you on the ass. Tell her ... here's a thought ... that you love her."

He seems to consider it for a millisecond, but Anton lacks the confidence for any emotional honesty and has no interest in any relationship that doesn't involve domination and manipulation. (I, on the other hand, have a great deal of respect for emotional honesty. I avoid it at all costs.)

He shakes his head. Obviously he is done thinking for the day. "Figure it out, Chloe," he orders, as if I were his servant. The *nerve.* "Today. And neutralize that townie, Peter Whatever. The one sniffing around her."

I mouth the word "neutralize?" Does he even know how idiotic he sounds? I almost laugh but I can't. I'm playing a role, something my mother taught me to do to perfection.

"*Distract* him," Anton says slowly, as if I were a child.

"Oh for God's sake, I'm not –"

"-- *You owe me,*" he says.

I bristle. I'm not his little puppy, taking orders. I imagine putting my cigarette out on his $4000 jacket. Instead, I toss the cigarette away. "Page Six wasn't my idea."

"I don't care. Do this for me, or everyone will know how you got that black eye." And he walks off. *The arrogant bastard.*

I want to go after him and rip his face to ribbons but I remind myself of the bigger picture. It's true: he has been a great ally in the past. Maybe, *maybe,* if he can help me get the old, fun Sophia back, it's worth lending a hand here. I'll have to think about it. And I better get to the bathroom.

I look at my phone and realize I'm already running late.

Five minutes later, I'm refreshed. No time to think about my wardrobe, so I put on the emergency "anytime" outfit my stylist put together. She finally came up with a numbered system that even the drycleaners at The Academy can't screw up.

Fifteen minutes until class and ten minutes worth of makeup! Where *does* the time go? And why can't they start classes at a decent hour?

Twelve minutes later, looking like a right Ready Freddy (as my mother used to say), I hurry to class. I might just make it, I'm thinking, when I round a corner and bump straight into Cole. He's holding a large white flower with a giant bug crawling on it. I give him a wide berth.

"Excuse me, Lady Winters," he says, the only person on this side of the pond to use my title. He fits the blossom and the beetle into a small box.

"Aren't you supposed to kill those?" I ask, pointing at the horrid little thing.

"I'm just transporting them!" he answers brightly, and looks about ready to explain. He doesn't realize I was merely being polite. I wasn't hoping for a tutorial from the gardener, thank you. See? *This* is what happens when you talk to the help.

———⊱———

After classes, I spend a few minutes engaging in a Twitter war with this über bitch my agency just signed. "The new face of Ford," they called her. *I think not!* She can't know that the profile I'm using is totally fake, and the press won't know the rumors I'm starting about her meth habit are, too. She'll soon be just another victim of Page Six.

Pondering that puts me in a brighter mood as I watch Sophia try on dresses before dinner. We have our own suites, of course, but we share this dressing room between them. It has tall windows, cedar lined walk in closets (of course) and a wall of beveled mirrors. It's okay, I guess.

I notice the gold earrings she's fitting carefully into her pierced ears. "Ooo pretty. From India?"

Sophia smiles as she nods, "A memento from this summer." She leans into the mirror to apply lip liner. She got so lucky in the lip department and doesn't even know it.

But there's my opening. Time to move. "About what I said the other day at breakfast. Some people don't understand why you're doing all that charity work. But I get it," I tell her as she tests the outfit with a pair of Jimmy Choos.

"I don't do it for attention, Chlo."

"Of course not! That Peter kid just doesn't know you like I do." I see her eyes flick up at me in the mirror.

"He was drunk anyway," I add with a dismissive wave. I examine my nails. They *are* flawless.

Sophia stops. Full turn. "Wait, what did he say about me?"

Well, there you have it. *Dance, my little puppet!* I hesitate, as if it's difficult to explain. "Anton was telling him about your work in India. What did Peter call it?" I pretend to think a moment. "'Pretentious posturing.' Something like that. It's like he thinks it's all an act."

"He said that? After I –" She stops herself.

"After what? What did you do?" I'm instantly alert, wondering what I missed.

"Nothing. I can't believe he would say something like that." She returns to her eye lining, clearly hurt.

"You're worried what a drunk townie thinks?" I ask incredulously. It's time to play the best friend. (I'm very good at this.) "Every girl on campus wants to be you, Sophia! You're gorgeous. You've got the mighty Volsky crawling for the crumbs of your attention. Please. Forget little Peter Whatever."

"Don't talk to me about Anton," Sophia says with an annoying little pout that would probably melt the heart of every male on campus.

"Sophia, give the guy a break. He made a mistake," I say, as if compassion came easy to me. "And really," I sigh. "You of all people should know what *that's* like."

CHAPTER SEVEN

PETER

Zach sounds just as freaked out as I was.

"What'ya mean, it wasn't him? Then who the hell was it?" he asks. I've been calling him all day and he finally picked up.

"I have no clue!" I say. "But it wasn't *James Harken.* What the hell did they do with him?" I really want to know what the hell are they gonna do with *me*, but I can't say that.

"Dude, calm down. Gimme a second to think."

"They must know I know something!" I say, keeping my voice low because I'm hurrying to library to do some research and I don't want anyone overhearing a word.

"Just shut up a second and listen. No one caught you watching the videos. And no one knows you made a copy of the hard drive, right?" Zach asks.

"I guess. But –"

"You guess, right. No one knows shit. *They* think *you* think that party guy was the real James, who might actually *be* the real James for all we know. Don't interrupt!" he says, somehow knowing I was going to. "For now, just play it cool. Okay? We'll figure this out."

This is why he's my best friend. I agree. I'll play it cool. We say goodbye.

Hell, maybe Zach's right. Maybe that *was* the real James Harken and the guy on the laptop was someone's idea of a prank? Still, those links … I can't shake the feeling that there's more going on here. And something Laptop James said sticks with me: the only way I can protect myself is to find out what's really going on. Because seriously, if they aren't worried about what I know, why go to the trouble of introducing me to the fake James?

I head up the steps to the library and stop. There is something strange about the building's exterior. It's been bugging me all week. I step back and check out the one side of the building. Even from a short distance away, I can see that each stone fits perfectly together in a kind of weird pattern. The building is so old that the stones have faded with age, so you really have to look for it, but the lighter and darker stones have been used to form a pattern. That's when I see it.

My mind flashes at all the different places I've seen it before. On James's computer, on the screen during Professor Linden's lecture, in James's essay, on the closet door and on my computer now. It's a three-pronged symbol four stories high, so subtly built into the front of the library I would have never noticed it if it weren't for Professor Linden's lecture. Holy shit.

Then I remember why I was hurrying to the library in the first place. At the front desk, I make myself relax and ask for last year's yearbook. I figure there's got to be a photo of James Harken in there, right? That should settle it.

A librarian disappears for a few seconds and then comes back with a yearbook. It has last year's date embossed on its cover, which is obviously very expensive leather. I don't take it for a second, so the librarian nudges it closer. She's a chubby black woman who seems to know everything about everything, just like every librarian I've ever met.

She gives me a once over through her giant black-rimmed glasses. "This is last year's," she says. "Special edition books, compiled essays and articles on the history of The Academy can be found over there –"

"–in reference." I say. Then I explain, hoping it might earn me a little goodwill. "My mom's a librarian. I spent a lot of time in libraries as a kid."

A beat. Nothing. No common ground here. Her eyes take in my rumpled clothes and pause on my flip-flops. "Um, ma'am ...?" I say quickly before she can react to them.

"Mrs. McCarthy," she says quickly, an eyebrow up. *Like I should have known.*

"Mrs. McCarthy, you must remember James Harken."

She just stares at me from behind her large glasses.

What did this guy do? I wonder. Everyone reacts the same way. Silence. "I figure he must have spent a lot of time here, researching the school," I add. Maybe that will get her to at least admit the dude existed.

"He did," she says carefully. "And I understand he won't be returning." I wait, hoping there's more. There isn't. "If there's nothing else," she says a bit louder, "I'll leave you to your work." She gives my flip-flops one more look and gets busy with her computer.

It's as if people are scared to talk about him. I take the yearbook to a carrel where no one can see and open to its back pages. I scan the index. "Harken, James .... p. 7, 28, 35, 61." Finally, I'll get some answers!

The first photo is of a group of students running track. One guy who could be James has his face hidden behind another runner. I realize I have no idea how tall Laptop James is; I only ever saw him sitting down. And every second guy in this school has the same haircut.

The next photo is a bunch of guys laughing. Some, including someone who *could* be James, aren't facing the camera. Damn it. I go to the next one, and there I can see what could be the back of James's head again. He's holding what looks like a futuristic iPad and pointing to the three-pronged symbol.

I make a quick sketch of it.

Frustrated, I turn to page 61. These are the headshots. It's got to be here. But *I can't believe it.* The page is missing! I check twice. It goes from 59 to 62. Opening the book wider, I see where someone carefully cut out the page. *Are you kidding me?* I slam the book shut.

That's when I notice Sophia speed-walking out of the library.

It's not just that she helped me the other night. There's just something different about her. Sure, she's wearing an outfit that costs more than my mom's car, I can tell that from here. But she doesn't look like she's trying so hard, like some of the other girls. Like Chloe. Sophia's dress is simple but really accentuates the positive. And there are a lot of positives.

I dump the yearbook back on the front desk and hurry to catch up with her. She seems to sense it and speeds up. I call her name. She moves faster. *Jesus.*

Finally I sprint across the quad, right up to her.

"Whoa. Running boy."

"Yeah. Varsity … this year," I say. She looks at me blankly. Doesn't she know what varsity is?

"Lucky you," she says in a dismissive tone that totally confuses me. Wasn't she the one who saved my ass last night? What's with the *attitude?*

"I talked to Charley," I say, hurrying to get to the point, "and he said – "

"Charley? Which Charley? The totally delusional liar Charley?"

"Uh … no?" *Why she is so pissed?* "My roommate Charley. Wheel-chair..?" I mime him pushing the wheelchair. "He admitted taking some crazy pictures with your phone last night, and– "

"So? Unless you're here to apologize, I have nothing to say to you." She stands there, waiting for me to …

"Apologize for what?!" I ask. *Is everyone at this school bi-fuck-ing-polar?* "I didn't – !"

"Your *non*-apology is *not* accepted." With that she stalks off.

"If you'd let me finish a sentence, you'd realize I'm *thanking* you for helping me out last night." That stops her.

"I didn't help you and I have no idea what you're talking about," she says, stomping back to me, her voice really low. "Now please just go away."

Okay, that's it, I officially hate this school and everyone in it.

"Fine," I say. "Just tell me what this is." I hold up the paper with the three-pronged symbol on it.

Sophia sighs and squints at it. Then she brightens. "I know! Those are the ski trails at Telluride, right? This part's the lodge, and –"

"Never mind." I tuck the picture back in my pocket, wondering why I even bothered. "I'm an ass. I assumed you'd be different from the other Trust Fund Babies. Don't know why."

"Like you know anything about me!"

I lower my voice so only she can hear me. "I know you helped me last night." That lands. I can see it in her face. "So just tell me," I continue before takes off again. "What happened to James Harken? Because we both know that guy at the party wasn't him!"

She looks around quickly and makes sure we're alone.

"Was James a friend of yours?" I press, quietly.

"No! I barely knew him! Third years don't really talk to lower-classmen." She's practically whispering. "Listen, you got past initiation. Now be smart. Keep your mouth shut, *especially about me*, and your head down."

Before I can ask any more questions, she storms off magnificently across the quad.

LINDEN

I marvel often at the vagaries of human nature and people's constant quest for power in all its forms. This seeking of power must be more gratifying than wielding it, I assume, because I've noticed that no one is ever able to set his own limits. No matter how much power a person accrues, he always wants more.

The idea makes me smile as I turn to Anton's father, who sits by the small fireplace in my office.

Vladimir Volsky is a man of enormous physical strength; he clearly has not left his Soviet gangster life too far behind, even as evidence of it is now covered by an air of mastered elegance. He reeks of money, and I like the smell: it's money he has taken, not earned. Russians, regardless of the era, strive to dominate every environment, always. They do this, they have done this, by warring and stealing and extorting and enslaving. I admire them tremendously.

"Your son is excelling academically and socially," I assure Mr. Volsky with my most indulgent smile. He waves away my words with a meaty, manicured hand.

"I am not interested in his schoolwork. Or his playmates," he says in a heavy, guttural accent. Music to my ears.

"No. Of course not." I do not take umbrage at his brusqueness. I know him too well. I am a patient man, and I must let the plan unfold. Best if it comes from him.

"He allowed himself to look like fool this summer," Volsky continues with an expression of distaste. "Before I give him more responsibility, I must be sure he is ready."

I wonder briefly if he is holding me responsible for Anton's extra curricular activities. (I applaud them, mind you, but it would be unseemly to take credit for the young man's exercise of free will.) "Anton might surprise you if you – "

"Anton never surprises. He only disappoints. But that doesn't concern you. I am here to ask your opinion about something else. I need to know …" Volsky leans forward, his eyes ice cold. "Can he control the actions of others to his own advantage?"

That is a very good question. It's one I've pondered myself of late.

I walk over to my Stalingrad diorama, pretending to be deep in thought. "Anton has made tremendous strides in his time here at The Academy."

I look down at the diorama and what I see there transpires in an instant.

Sophia on a cushioned windowsill, surrounded by three girls. Their hair is styled just like hers. She is holding court; they chatter and laugh happily.

Anton approaches. The girls back off like well-trained staff. "Hey," he says, but without his usual swagger. "I thought you should know that Peter kid is talking. About you."

Sophia sighs. "I heard. It's no big deal."

Anton's eyes narrow. "Really? You don't care that he's going on about you and him *hooking up last night?*"

Oh, bravo, Anton. The look of shock on her face quickly turns to rage but she covers it.

"I figured you wouldn't want that out there. I can deal with it for you –"

"-- No!" she barks. Clearly she has seen Anton "deal with" things in the past. She calms herself down. "Thanks. But no. I'll handle it."

Anton nods, but it obviously pains him to do so. She sees it, too. She stands up to leave and takes pity on the boy.

"Anton, just because things didn't work out between us, doesn't mean I stopped caring about you." He gives her a pathetic little smile as she goes. I can't help but feel a flicker of anger. I turn my back for *one single second* and all my hard work to get Anton on the correct path erodes in the blink of an eye.

Emotions are self-indulgent in general, but this peculiar notion of human "love" is particularly baffling. It serves no purpose but to warp reality, which in turn inhibits the true nature of man and rewards him with a sense of fraudulent, short-term pleasure. It turns noble prospects like Anton into moronic, babbling idiots! It is, plainly put, a scourge.

But with every setback there is a small victory. Turning the corner and inching into a shaded alcove, I see the anger in Sophia's face. She is stewing about what Anton just said. *Hooking up*?

People are so predictable, especially once you get a firm grasp on their weaknesses. Vanity, for example. Sophia wants to be considered generous, but she doesn't exhibit it when called upon by circumstances. She could confront Peter and demand the truth. She could merely shrug it off. She could forgive him wordlessly, as I'm sure Dr. Browning would suggest.

But people don't do that. It's not in their nature. Certainly Sophia won't, thanks to her vanity. That's what makes her so delightfully predictable. There she is, scrolling through the photos on her phone. She finds it: an image of Peter, eyes closed, with an apple in his mouth. He has obviously passed out. Next to him is a pig's head with a bottle of vodka in the side of its mouth (I have to laugh. It *is* clever).

Sophia pushes some buttons. She just posted the photo to The Tunnel, and in an instant ensured that everyone will have a good laugh at Peter's expense.

A short distance away, Anton hears his phone blip. He sees her post and smiles. Then it begins to play a tune: screaming horns and then a choir. The opening bars to the national anthem of the Russian Federation.

"*Papa?*" he whispers into the phone.

Alignment

The image fades and I see only my diorama again. No matter. I will see him soon enough.

———⟐———

Minutes later, Anton is there in my office, striding past two huge Russian bodyguards standing inside the door. They nod at him. Vladimir signals at them to go. Then he embraces his son, but without warmth.

"Papa. *Chto eta–*"

"Everything is fine. Speak English."

Anton stops, chastened.

"I can not stay," Vladimir says. "Did you see the stock numbers?"

Anton nods. "And I remember your promise," he tells his father. "I want to be a bigger part –"

"— It's not enough to want," Vladimir says, his voice rising. "You must earn it, like I did."

"I *know* that," Anton replies as Volsky narrows his eyes at this little exhibit of attitude.

"Maybe so, maybe not," Volsky says. "*I* came today, not lawyers. They insist your behavior this summer proves you are too young to run a company. Even a small one."

"I relish the chance to prove them wrong!" Anton snaps back.

"Your reputation is your greatest weapon," Vladimir continues, "your most valuable possession. Perception is *everything*!"

Anton looks down, embarrassed. I so enjoy the way Volsky treats Anton as his life's greatest disappointment. Which he may very well be.

Now Volsky paces, his eyes never leaving his son. "These men you will do business with, they will seek out your every weakness. And they will exploit it. Like your feelings for this girl."

"Buried. I swear it!"

"Good. You must be ruthless in protecting your image." Volsky rests a massive hand on Anton's shoulder and starts to apply a vise like pressure as he talks. "The foolishness must stop. The women. The drugs. The public photographs."

"It is done. Finished."

How much longer can Anton keep his voice even and mask the pain? I wonder.

Vladimir takes a long look at his son, a look without confidence or warmth. He seems to be studying his character, unconvinced of its worth. "Maybe so. Maybe not," he says again, finally releasing the boy's shoulder.

He pats Anton on the arm and walks out.

Anton stares at the door for a beat. He rubs his shoulder, lost in thought. I clear my throat and he suddenly remembers I'm there.

"We were going to move on Foster," he says with regret.

I shrug. What can I say? I'm not allowed to push.

"I mean, I *want* to. But not now. I can't be a part of anything now."

"The choice is yours."

It doesn't matter. It's merely a delay, this newfound resolve of Anton's. It won't last long. I'll just wait it out. If there's one thing I know how to do, it's wait.

I'm always rewarded in the end.

CHAPTER EIGHT

CHLOE

Sometimes you just have to put on a floor-sweeping frock and dance, preferably by an infinity pool and holding a glass of Chardonnay, while all the well-dressed men watch and the women pretend not to. That's the mood I'm in. I'm hungry for glamour. Or danger. Or both.

But I'm nowhere near an infinity pool, or a Valentino Haute Couture show, or any of the other things I truly love. I'm stuck here at The Academy (again) and no one cares. Not even my brother Richard, who should recognize how wobbly I get shut away here, and who is too much of a bootlicker to do anything about it.

I shouldn't even be here. The words make a loop through my brain, repeating again and again. The weight of it is nearly too much to bear. I want to choke someone.

I realize it's too soon in the semester to feel this desperate. That blackness doesn't usually hit me until February. But none of my usual distractions seem to be working. *Distractions.* That's when I remember what Anton said. He wants me to *distract* Peter, who seems to be afraid to look too long at Sophia, as if she were the sun.

I start to get angry, but just for a second. Who the hell is he to talk to me like that, essentially *commanding* me to become Peter Foster's pitiful *distraction!*

He's pathetic, Anton. His single-mindedness might make him successful in business one day, but it also ensures that he's the most boring person on the planet. I'm not kidding. He has no sense of humor, no passions other than inflicting his will on others, and absolutely no flair for fashion. He's not that interesting a lover, either, even when he's exerting some effort. But it's too much trouble to say no, and our little secret might come in handy one day, so I just go with it.

I have little interest in distracting Peter Foster. I know nothing about him, mostly because that's exactly what I want to know about him: nothing. I can't be expected to fill my head with useless information, where it will take up room and crowd out the things that are really important, like the newest fabrics coming out of Milan and the floral-slash-impressionistic inspiration for Vera Wang's Spring Collection. Fashion is everything to me. And Peter Foster is less than nothing.

I lean into the mirror and examine my face, a painter examining her canvas. *Flawless.* I do a quick mental inventory of my wardrobe, my frame of mind, my time constraints. I think of Peter Foster again, in those scruffy jeans. He certainly has a body on him, and I wouldn't mind peeling back a few denim layers and taking a closer look at it, if I could get some type of guarantee he wouldn't actually *talk* to me.

The image of Peter's muscled chest causes a shift in my mood. I imagine him checking me out, top to bottom, slowly. And liking what he sees.

At that moment the fog lifts. It occurs to me that I've hit upon a winning solution, a way to give Anton what he wants and still beat back these back-to-school blues, at least for a week or two.

Peter Foster. He'll be *my* distraction.

I immediately know which outfit I'll have on (the sheer pastel green Tory Burch), which sunglasses I'll peer over, which strappy heels I'll wear. I know every step of this dance. I'll touch his arm so lightly he won't be sure it happened at all, and I'll back away with a lingering smile, holding his eye with a promise. I'll get him flat on his back in record time, and *I'll* be the girl who blows his mind. Not Sophia. Not an underclassman on a dare, not the frumpy slags from his provincial high school. *Me.*

The first step is the easiest. Just be in his line of sight when he's off-balance. It takes me about five seconds to get a copy of his class schedule and since I don't have the patience to wait until whatever daily detail knocks Peter off track, I do the honors myself.

There he is, walking across the quad. Right on schedule, time to get to *work.* I walk toward him so our meeting seems accidental.

"Looks like you had fun last night," I say, looking down at my phone. He's a little confused and lacks the sophistication to hide it. His eyes linger on my cleavage; I expected nothing less. I hold up my phone and he takes a good, long look at himself, passed out next to the pig's head. His expression is priceless. *Super funny.*

He reaches for the phone but I pull it away. "Relax!" I manage between giggles. "Sophia posted it on The Tunnel. Only students have access to it."

"*Sophia* posted that?" Peter asks, as if he'd never imagined she could do such a thing. Such is her saintly image, which makes it extra fun to tarnish. I push my sunglasses onto my nose with a smile, and walk off before he can ask any other stupid questions. I'm sure he'll come after me.

And of course, he does. *They always do.*

But before he can demand a second look, his phone chimes, and he looks at it. I turn back to him and see the surprise on his face has turned to something else. Dread.

"Really," I tell him. "No need to get all wound up. It's just a *photo*. And not the worst I've ever seen."

He shakes his head. That's not it. He holds up his phone so I can see the message. He has been summoned to Dr. Browning's office immediately.

DR. BROWNING

As I walk into my office, Peter is standing before my desk, waiting. I'm pleased. He's a well-mannered young man, my Peter. He doesn't sit until invited to do so. I see him scan the flowers pots by my window, each containing an exquisite, rare flower – although he can't be expected to know that. He takes in the enormous painting on the other wall, the painting I moved off my easel just this morning. It's an abstract painting of a highly detailed maze.

"I didn't mean to make you wait," I say with a smile. He must be quite intimidated. "I'd just like to have a quick chat, introduce myself." We shake hands.

"You just want to *talk*?" he asks.

"Well, yes," I say. "I assure you, you don't want to hear me sing."

We laugh and he relaxes and nods at the painting. "You paint that?"

"It's a work in progress, really. A silly hobby. Keeps me from chewing my nails."

"I remember you," he says. "You came to the house a few times to see my mom."

"Last spring. I had to persuade her to let you come to The Academy. Our first Outreach student." I gesture to the chair. He sits, and I do, too. "Everything going okay?"

He can tell it's a sincere question. He shifts. "It's a little weird. I mean, different. From what I'm used to."

"Weird makes sense." I nod. It does. But Peter and I have more in common than he knows. "When I first got here, in my twenties, it was a bit of a shock," I tell him. "Where I grew up, we had chores, not servants. In fact, *I* was given extra chores for asking too many questions!" I can tell that strikes a chord. "Once I even asked my mother why we have to kneel in church. She said, 'because God likes it!'"

"Sounds like my mom," he says with a smile.

"I thought it was a lousy reason, to be honest. Took me years to understand there really isn't a better one."

We sit in the silence together a beat, smiling. His face changes as he struggles with something.

"Why me?" he finally asks. "I mean, *here*. Why was *I* chosen for this program? It makes no sense."

"Why *not* you?"

I know it's not the answer he was looking for. I know it doesn't satisfy him.

"You want to know why you're special," I continue, willing to go as far as I'm allowed and no further. "I can only assure you that you are. But special in what way, exactly, is something you'll have to figure out for yourself ... just like everyone else."

After half an hour talking with Peter, I watch him head back across campus toward his room. I wonder if he absorbed everything I said. I don't want him to feel limited by his background.

"*Look at your classmates, for example,*" I told him. "*They're on the very same journey. They appear to be lucky beneficiaries of incredible privilege and wealth. And they are. But that's not all they are.*"

Peter cuts through the parking lot. To him, it must look like an exotic car convention. He pauses over a Ferrari Dino, a Bugatti, and a vintage 1928 Jaguar.

"*Despite their wealth, in some ways the students here are broken and hungry. They've lived lives of neglect you can't imagine.*"

He runs a hand over an immaculately restored 1962 Ford AC Cobra. There isn't a speck of dust on it. He looks over at the corner of lot, where his motorcycle is parked. It looks small, alone and caked in mud.

"*How does one measure privilege and wealth, anyway?*"

I hold the pale stone in my hand, feeling its weight and smoothness, and gaze into the painting. Now I can see Peter back in his room, lost in thought, cleaning his dress shoes with a rag. He reacts to a thump from the hallway and discovers a valet pulling freshly cleaned (mostly handmade, leather, Italian) shoes from a trolley and leaving them at each room's door.

"Just leave 'em here outside your door Monday through Friday night before 8pm," the valet explains. He sees Peter hesitate. He suspects why. "It's free."

"My job is to prove to each student that you have a unique obligation to yourselves and the world."

I don't think anyone, other than his mother, has ever said a word to him about what he might owe the world. He stares at his shoes (not handmade, and not Italian) I bet he is wondering if he just heard the world's greatest pep talk, or an incredibly elegant load of bull –

Suddenly, Charley barges into his room and invites him to a Call of Duty tournament on the third floor. "Can't," Peter says. "Test Monday." He holds up his history book.

I follow Charley upstairs. He and the other students will play Call of Duty and laugh uproariously, mostly because of the cocaine they snort at a rate few can afford. Only Anton, for some reason I have yet to discover, is not partaking. His lack of participation is very suspicious.

Despite his impressive mental discipline, Peter may not yet have the strength to resist certain elements at the school.

In his room, Peter completes a set of 100 pushups and drops to rest on his bedroom floor.

Two floors up, almost directly above Peter's head, a young man and a freshman girl have sex, rippling and slipping in a sea of dark silk sheets. The bathroom door opens and another girl quietly gets into bed with them. They barely pause.

"But before you can change the world, each of you must first learn to

master yourselves. And that is infinitely more difficult."

The painting starts to lose focus. I see Anton walk past the bowl of cocaine, nearly empty but not quite. He eyes the party's damage with regret – the empty glasses, the full ashtrays, a few scraps of forgotten clothing.

Peter climbs into his bed and turns off the light. I can't see him anymore, but I can feel his uneasiness. I know he keeps asking himself why he was chosen to come to The Academy. What is expected of him? Does he have the qualities he'll need to succeed?

Yes! I want to tell him. You will be tested, but yes, you do!

I wish I could be more specific. I can't. I am not allowed to tell him what he needs to know. All I can do is provoke him to think more deeply about his future, and I hope I did. I hope my question resonates as he falls asleep.

"What direction will you take, Peter?"

PETER

It's Saturday morning and the place is deserted. I mean, there's no one here. Nothing stirs but the birds. The air is cool, the sun is just coming up. It's like a giant bomb went off and vaporized everyone but me.

Oh wait. There's a maid in the lounge, dusting. I can usually hear the hum of the student dining hall chatter when I'm halfway down the steps but not today. Today, the tables are empty. Only two Asian girls sit at a corner table, talking to each other quietly in Korean. Waitresses in uniforms polish silver at the other end of the room, hiding their yawns.

I chug a glass of fresh squeezed orange juice and decide to go for a run. I haven't worked out all week and I really feel it. Plus, I need to get out of my head. I can't stop thinking about that picture Chloe showed me. I looked like a jackass.

I shouldn't be surprised that they found it so funny. I mean, we don't know each other so they're going to make a big deal out of it, right? Still, I can't believe Sophia would post that photo *anywhere*, I don't care if only other Academy students can see it.

Why would she do that? I know she's pissed about something, but what the hell? First she saves my ass and then the next day, she posts that picture to embarrass me. Either she is totally bi-polar or I'm missing something.

And that's another thing. My whole first week at school, Chloe pretended I didn't exist and that was fine by me. Then all of a sudden this light goes on, and she's not only looking right at me, she's smiling and talking to me, and standing way too close to be an accident. I have no clue if she was hitting on me because I have no experience with girls like her. She's probably just messing with me.

I make it to the running trail. Like everything else at The Academy, it's incredible. It winds behind the main buildings and goes around the entire campus.

I stretch out my hamstring, which has started to pull a little.

My mind drifts back to the things Dr. Browning said yesterday. At first I was like, yeah, I saw that on an inspirational poster in the Counselor's office at Providence High. But all of the stuff she said was meant for someone just like me, someone who comes from nothing. I don't think she was just blowing smoke. I know it's crazy but I got the feeling she really meant what she said, and now I can't stop thinking about it. She thinks I have potential. And she expects me to fulfill it.

She made me realize that's one thing that sets apart the students at Providence High from the students here. Not just the money but the expectations the school holds out for the students. She thinks that if they can change the world, I can, too.

I stretch, feeling as if I'm the only one on campus.

"That looks painful." Professors Linden's voice pulls me back to reality.

He's in his usual jacket and tie. On a Saturday. Doesn't he own anything else? He's just looking at me, from my running shoes up, expecting me to say something. For a second I wonder if I'm doing something I'm not supposed to.

"I'm, uh, going for a run."

"Smart. Could save your life one day," he says, with a sort of snap in his voice. He seems like a totally different guy today. Almost happy.

"Where is everyone?" I have to ask. "This place is dead."

"You didn't see the King's Parade this morning?" I have no idea what he's talking about. "That's what we call the shiny limos out front, all lined up to take students to the City. I'm surprised they didn't invite you along."

He waits for a reaction. I look away. I actually did get an invitation from Charley but it was sort of last minute, and he was just being nice. I told him I had to study, that I had stuff to do. The truth is I heard him talking with another guy about what they were planning for the weekend. There's no way I could pay my way. I figured I would just stay on campus and work out.

"I'm moderating the Chess Club Challenge in the library...?" Professor Linden continues, nodding toward the library.

Sitting in the library on a day like this, with Linden in his tweeds, would definitely be my version of hell. "I'm not really a chess player."

Linden smiles at that. "Neither am I," he says. "I'm a 'dabbler.' And *I'd* rather be in the City, too."

Something about him makes me feel like I could ask him anything. So I do. "What do they do there? In the city?"

"Well, they spend their allowances," he says. "Most of which exceed my monthly paycheck." He's smiling, not whining. Like it's a big joke to him. "They search for bigger thrills and higher highs," he goes on, sounding amused. "They're unsupervised teens who have never known a limit they couldn't exceed with impunity. What else would they be doing?"

I look at him then and he smiles at me, as if he knows what it's like going to school with these people. Is it possible? Maybe we're more alike than I thought. I don't think he tells the other students what he really thinks of them.

He walks off toward the library without another word, just waving one hand in the air as he goes.

———— ～ ————

I've always loved to run. Now I'm pretty close to done. My feet are hot and I'm soaked in sweat. I figure I ran about five miles total, including the sprints. It felt great to push myself. I stop near the back gate to stretch and catch my breath. After that, I figure I'll walk another mile or so to cool down.

I'm stretching my quads when I notice something at the base of the wrought-iron fence. It's easy to spot because it's out of place, and nothing on this campus is *ever* out of place. I move a little closer and see half-wilted flowers, a teddy bear, a white candle. It takes me a second but I realize it's a memorial of some kind. I've seen them by the freeway, put there by friends at the site of a bad accident.

A heart-shaped note reads *"James RIP"*. It takes me a beat to make the connection: James Harken! So he didn't go to another school. He *died*. Holy shit. No wonder they left all his stuff in the room.

I pick up a white rose. The handwritten note attached to it reads:

"Your work will live on. Always YOUR S."

I put it back. There are too many unanswered questions to think about, and my head is already full with Chloe, Sophia, Anton, Professor Linden and everything Dr. Browning said. Not to mention the whole laptop thing. I grab the fence to stretch my quad …

And suddenly everything goes weirdly dark, cloudy, and I'm running as fast as I can, dodging branches. I'm being chased by something.

I'm so scared, my throat is pinched and my lungs are on fire. I run. A tree branch suddenly bends and twists to grab at my shirt and I leap back to get out of its grasp –

Suddenly my vision clears and I'm right where I was! I'm on the running trail, next to the memorial. My whole body is shaking, and I'm still out of breath. The sun feels extra bright. The hand that held on to the fence stings, like a rope burn. I stare at it. *What the hell was that?*

I regain my balance and look around. I'm alone. I must be seeing things. "Get a grip," I mutter to myself. "It's all in your head."

I put both hands on the fence. Maybe it was some type of endorphin overl –

– Someone is screaming in my ear! I'm here at the fence, but on the other side of it, my whole body aching with the effort to climb up it. Every muscle is straining out of pure animal panic. I look down just long enough to see some grey slimy thing wrap around my leg. *Fuck!* I pull myself up and over the fence, but it pulls me back.

I realize it's me, screaming! I can't stop. It pulls me off the fence –

-- and I land on the ground with a thump. Suddenly: silence. My heart is pounding. I get quickly to my feet, a little jumpy, freaking out. I'm back on the campus side of the fence. Everything is perfectly normal. There's nothing slimy anywhere.

What is happening to me?

Then the adrenaline drains away. My muscles are suddenly heavy. There is no way in hell I am touching that fence again. I back away.

I take one last look at the memorial and jog slowly back toward my room. I get it now. I understand why those notes and flowers are there by the campus's back fence.

That's where James Harken was killed.

CHAPTER NINE

PETER

There's no feeling like going fast.

I downshift my bike into third as I come up on a sharp right hander. It hugs the road as I push through the turn. I've always been able to escape on my Enduro. When I'm riding, there's no room to think about anything else; whether it's a winding road or forest trail, the ride takes all my concentration. I love getting in that zone.

I left The Academy about fifteen minutes ago. I finally come out of the twisting canyon turns and hit the piney country road that leads to Providence. I open up the throttle. The engine starts to scream and ...

CRASH! A fluorescent bowling ball demolishes a set of fluorescent bowling pins. A group of guys who work at the Walmart start cheering two lanes down.

Alignment

I'm bowling with Zach. The night out is a gift from my mom and Dr. Browning, who must have figured I needed a few hours of normal. Zach is nearly done lacing up his bowling shoes but I haven't even started yet. I haven't shut up since I got here.

"... and then it just vanished?"

I nod. "But it was *so real*. I could smell the rot coming off the trees."

Zach grins. "Mighta been a flashback from whatever they put in your drink."

CRASH! Another strike nearby, another loud cheer. Zach and I have been coming here our entire lives. It's the local hangout, with air hockey and pool tables in back. It's half full of people and I know most of them. I wave at the mom of a kid I played T-ball with when I was five. She waves back and it gets me thinking: I used to feel at home here. Now it feels so different. Why is that?

"You really think these visions, or whatever they are, have something to do with this James Harken guy?" Zach asks. "And why leave flowers by the back gate in the first place? It's not like he died there."

"Unless ... he died there," I say with a shrug.

"Well," Zach says with a straight face. "That would *suck*. I mean, dying at school."

I shake my head and look around as people high five and joke around. I think about how much has happened to me since I left Providence. Did I ever really have that much fun here? I pull the portable hard drive from my backpack.

I know it isn't safe to keep at The Academy. I didn't know what else to do with it after they took James's laptop. I hand it to Zach and he slips it into his backpack.

"This is so 'Homeland,'" he says, grinning. "I'm *on* it."

"Jesus, Zach. Just put it somewhere. And if you have to, you know, *if something happens*. Give it to my Mom."

He nods at my feet. "Lace up, you lazy bitch. Time to have some fun." He sees me hesitate. "What's wrong?"

I look at the shoes. I never thought of it before but…"They're kind of gross," I tell him. "I mean, how many people have worn them *this week?*"

Zach gives me a look. "We've been coming here every Tuesday since third grade," he says and then asks, "and *today* you decide the shoes are gross? Drink the Kool-aid much?"

He's right. What the hell is wrong with me? Where did that even come from? I lace up the shoes and thank God I have Zach to keep me from turning into one of *them*.

"I'd say it's nice to see you back in town," he says and then smiles. "But my mom told me never to lie."

I pick up a ball and line up my shot. "She lies every time she says she loves you." Just because he was right doesn't mean I am going to let him get *too* cocky. I let the ball go, aiming perfectly, and immediately walk back to the scoring table. I don't even have to look back to know it's a strike. Then I hear the ball crush the pins. We high five.

"Now *that's* something they can't do at The Academy," I say. "They probably don't even know what bowling is."

"What I can't figure out," Zach says, looking at me a little more seriously, "is why you're even *there*."

———～———

He's absolutely right, I think on my ride back to campus. I haven't hit the curves yet and am enjoying five miles of smooth, straight country highway before I have to really concentrate. The engine's steady drone is hypnotic as the trees on the side of the road fly by. *And if I he's thinking that, everyone on campus must be, too. Why me?*

Later that night in the dining room, I overhear everyone catching up on the weekend. It doesn't sound real. Half of them went to New York and the rest flew all over the country to a party or event. They talk about it the way I would talk about going to the movies. No big deal.

I see Charley, Sophia, Anton and Chloe talking more than eating, as usual. The only available seat is next to Chloe and I take a chance and sit in it. She barely registers me (thank God).

"You guys have to shut up," she tells the others, who are cracking up at one of Anton's jokes. "My head is killing me."

"Chloe, Chloe, Chloe," Charley says. "How many times do we have to tell you that Coke and vodka are not part of the five major food groups!?"

"I've been telling her that since sixth grade," Anton says, and everyone laughs. Even Chloe cracks a smile.

Charley turns to Anton. "Hey, I didn't hear any wild stories about your weekend. What's up?"

But Anton just shrugs. "My partying days are behind me, I'm afraid. I've got bigger plans."

"Oh, spare me," Chloe shoots back. "A straight and narrow Anton Volsky? There is no such thing."

"No, that's good, Anton," Sophia says.

"How is it you guys all know each other?" I ask. Anton glares at me. He wanted to keep talking with Sophia. *Too bad.*

Sophia sort of ignores me but Chloe perks up. "Sophia and I met at Verbier," she explains. "Skiing. Fourth grade." She nods to Anton. "And Anton's parents used to vacation with mine in the mid-90s, before we were born."

"A few years later, we'd have taken bubble baths together," Anton grins at Chloe wickedly but Chloe just glares at him over her sunglasses, "And Charley ..."

"-- I've never seen any of you blue collar trolls in my life," Charley says with a grin.

Sophia sighs. "We only let him hang with us because every April we run away to his parents' beach house in Praia do Sancho."

Everyone smiles at the memory but Sophia turns serious and says, "But this year you guys can't trash the plane! My dad was pissed."

They laugh. I have no idea what they're talking about, something Sancho, but I don't let on. I'll look them up later.

Suddenly, Chloe grabs my arm and smiles at me. "Praia do Sancho is the most awesome beach in Brazil." She takes off her sunglasses and smiles. "Come with us this year. You'll love it." She lowers her voice a little, looks directly into my eyes and whispers. "No tan lines allowed."

She lets go of my arm and returns to the conversation. Huh? She *wants* me there? And was that a reference to them all going around topless? I glance over at Sophia and Anton catches this.

"What a great idea!" Anton says, fake as hell. "We don't even have to pay for the charter or crew, just gas for the jet. What was it last year? Something like twenty grand a piece?" He looks at me. "Chump change, right, Peter?"

Everyone shifts uncomfortably, but they wait for my reply. *What a tool!*

"Sure," I say, trying to keep my voice normal so no one can tell how pissed off I'm getting. "Or we could fly commercial and give that hundred grand to Sophia's village," I say. "For clean water. Maybe save some lives." I look around the table. "Tough decision, huh?"

The whole group tries not to laugh and I can tell they think Anton is as big an ass as I do. His jaw clenches. "Like the decision to let someone like you in The Academy?"

"If you got a problem with where I am ..." I say, standing up and getting ready to end this, "... you can always try and move me."

Anton rises from his seat and I'm staring him down, thinking *Game on!* but Charley quickly wheels himself between us.

"Guys! You're on campus," he says. "And everyone's staring. *Everyone.*" He nods to Linden and Dr. Browning's table. They're watching us.

"This place used to have standards," Anton says in a voice just loud enough for our table to hear.

"Then why'd they let you in?" I ask.

Anton just stands there for a beat and then relaxes into a kind of self-satisfied smile. "Sounds like someone's ready for a bigger audience," he says. He takes out his phone and presses a couple of buttons, and then he walks away.

LINDEN

I can't be blamed for moments of doubt. And there are many such moments when I consider Anton's value to the cause. It's not that I doubt his potential as a fine addition to our family one day, but the characteristic I most appreciate about him, the ease with which he can be manipulated, is often the one that causes me the most frustration.

I saw him challenge Peter in the student dining hall. I don't know nor care what the confrontation was about, but it could have derailed my plans for them both. I imagine it was provoked by a triviality, or jealousy; I know how quickly Anton's judgment is impaired by his obsession with that damned girl. But he restrained himself, possibly thanks to my countless lectures on the critical importance of when, where and *how* to engage one's enemies.

And that restraint gave him the opportunity to post the picture of Peter to Page Six, where I'm sure it caused Browning no small amount of distress. Not only was her precious Peter passed out in the photo, but the subsequent scandal was the first of its kind in nearly a decade. The Academy made the headlines! Not for very long, of course, but long enough to force her to field calls from parents (there are a few who care) and alumni (concerned about the school's image, even though they raised hell here themselves), not to mention the hours on the phone required to clean up the mess after I had the offending photo taken down.

There is no longer a record of it anywhere on the Internet. Nor will there be any future stories directly involving The Academy on Page Six or in any other tabloid. It took three well-placed calls to ensure this won't happen again. I can only guess how many people were fired for running the story in the first place.

The main administrative building is still bustling with activity this morning. No doubt half of the activity is related to completely "sanitizing" the news, and the other half following up to ensure those who were interested in the story are discouraged from pursuing it. Journalists can be such an irritation if not properly directed.

A frizzy-haired teacher named Miss Rizzolo, representing the Board in disciplinary issues this semester, sits outside Dr. Browning's office. Several chairs away, pale with embarrassment, sits Peter. I give them a look and enter without knocking.

My amusement at the sight of them is immediately tempered by the fact that it is too damned bright in Browning's office. It seems like I have been here more this semester than I have in the past two years. I turn away from the light and get right to the point.

"You know Rizzolo will push for expulsion," I tell Dr. Browning, "or suspension at the very least. And you can't very well argue Foster doesn't deserve it."

Dr. Browning is accustomed to my dispensing with the niceties that open most civil conversations. I have little interest in civil conversations, to be honest, and she gave up concealing her contempt for me decades ago. In these small ways, we have forged a tenuous truce (for now). She stops her pacing. I'm dismayed to see that she's not as stressed as I'd hoped.

"So help him," she says with a shrug. "You have as much to lose as I do."

"And what will you do for me?" I ask.

"I already promised to talk to Cole," she says, which is almost insulting given that she agreed to do that before any of this happened. "Besides," she continues, irritated. "I don't need help. I just need --*we both need* -- a clean escape."

There's a knock at the door and before I can respond, a stricken Peter is ushered in, accompanied by Miss Rizzolo. "You did say your office at 10 am sharp?" she asks.

Dr. Browning nods at Rizzolo and takes a seat at her desk. "Peter," she says coolly. "I assume you know why you're here."

"I don't know how that photo got posted on Page Six!" he says.

"You're not being blamed for that. But it's clearly a picture of you, and you do appear intoxicated."

I adopt a very paternal and concerned tone. "That behavior violates the posted rules of The Academy, I'm afraid. We can't have that."

Browning nods. "You must understand how disappointed we are. Personal responsibility and consequences are keystones of character development, and –"

"-- I don't know who took that picture! Or when," Peter blurts out.

"That's because you were, as they say in the finest circles, *blotto*. Thanks to my limitless connections, however, the photo has already been removed," I say to save him from implicating himself further.

The look on Peter's face is just what I hoped for. Relief and gratitude. He believes he owes me now, which of course, he does.

Browning sees this, too. "Please wait outside," she orders. Peter glances around, pained, wanting to say more. He thinks the better of it and leaves.

The second the door shuts, Miss Rizzolo's nasal voice fills the office. "Suspension would send a valuable message, especially this early in the school year," she whines, lacking any understanding of the larger agenda before us.

Dr. Browning digests that and nods. She turns to me with a questioning look. I decide to have a little fun.

"I couldn't agree more," I say brightly. I'm not going to make it *that* easy for Browning. Miss Rizzolo tries to hide a pleased smile.

Time to increase the stakes. "This is a clear infraction of school rules," I say, turning toward Miss Rizzolo to emphasize my support of her position. "A literal interpretation would require expulsion, to be perfectly frank."

Dr. Browning's eyes widen. Even Rizzolo looks surprised.

"Really?" Dr. Browning asks. She's trapped and has no choice but to say, "Then I'm to recommend expulsion to the Board? Have him removed immediately from student housing?" She checks her watch. "His mother can be here within the hour."

A strained silence stretches as the weight of the decision hangs in the room.

Neither of them looks very happy about it, but there's nothing they can do now. I savor Browning's discomfort a moment longer. But everything must come to an end, and Peter is much too important to let go.

"This will send a clear message to every student on campus," I continue. "I mean, *really*. Giving someone like him false hope is quite cruel."

"False hope?" Miss Rizzolo asks. Of course she fastens on to that phrase. I knew she would.

And then Dr. Browning catches on to the game. She probably remembers the last time we played a version of it, years ago. She turns to me, arms crossed. "You were right," she says. "I'll admit it." She heaves a sigh that might just be overdoing it a touch and turns to Rizzolo. "Just yesterday, Professor Linden was telling me how surprised he was that someone of Peter's background lasted this long."

Miss Rizzolo gives me a dark look. "His *background?*" People like her fascinate me, really.

I give Dr. Browning a pointed look. "That was a private conversation," I say, lowering my voice. "But since it's just us, I'm glad you brought it up. Saves us from going through the motions."

Miss Rizzolo is frowning so hard I fear her hair barrettes will come springing off her head.

Dr. Browning jumps in. "I think Professor Linden is referring to the near impossible challenges Peter would face at The Academy."

"Of course I am. There's nothing wrong with telling the truth, and the truth is that someone of Peter's limited means will never make it at a school like this."

Miss Rizzolo frowns. She can't stand me, and now I have become her ally but for a reason she finds abhorrent. It's a delectable dilemma, but I have no doubt she'll side with Peter, whom she just tried to suspend, rather than with me.

"He's a very respectful boy!" she says, backpedaling. "He turns his work in on time, he's very smart, he's engaged in the classroom and—"

"But we've already wasted so much time on him!" I interject. Impatient. I've got a cigar waiting back in my office. "Is it really in our best interests to deprive *all the other students* of our attention for the advantage of *one*?"

"Our best interests?" Rizzolo repeats, slightly dazed.

I heave a sigh worthy of the stage. "Our energies should be expended on behalf of those who show real potential. Like ... Anton Volsky." I say. I see Miss Rizzolo's eyes widen and I smile. Not only is *low income* Peter getting kicked out but Volsky will benefit from it.

"As opposed to a charity case," I continue, "who won't ever be capable of functioning in this world. I'll bet his mother even clips coupons! I mean, realistically, the odds are —"

"Charity case!" Rizollo is literally pale with anger. She spins to Dr. Browning, her eyes flashing. "Dr. Browning, I would like to withdraw my complaint and ask for lenience for Peter!"

"You would?"

"It's his first infraction," she offers weakly. Behind Rizzolo's back, I raise my eyebrows to Browning. *That was too easy.*

"I see," Browning replies, as much to me as to the shaking Rizollo. She closes the file on her desk. "Very well," she says with a nod, as if the decision were a difficult one. "I will let this one go on your recommendation, and note it as such. I'll remind Peter that his probationary period has ended. He gets no more chances."

Miss Rizollo nods gratefully. "Thank you." She gives me a contemptuous look and marches out the door, pulling it shut loudly behind her.

I have to say I am rather pleased with myself and must look it because Browning narrows her eyes at me, a rare smile playing on her lips.

"Clipping coupons?" she asks, incredulous.

I nod at the door Rizollo just shut. "Every Wednesday. In the break room." I smile. "Like clockwork."

When they say the devil is in the details, they're right.

CHAPTER TEN

PETER

Tree branches bend and crack in the wind. I'm surrounded by black and grey, running as fast as I can. Why? *Why am I so scared?* A low-pitched humming rises from the earth. It terrifies me. And it's getting closer.

I run to a clearing and stop: a huge oak rises up above the other trees. Suddenly a branch shoots out from its center and wraps around my arm like a vine, yanking me toward it, *dragging* me across the forest floor. Within seconds, I'm right up against it, pushing away, screaming. I can feel the bark moving under my hands. It looks like it's melting.

The center of the tree trunk changes shape when suddenly a hand *breaks through it* and grabs a fistful of my hair. I scream and fight but the hand pulls me back to within inches of the tree, where a *face*, its mouth open in a scream, pushes outward through the trunk.

I recognize him instantly. It's James Harken.

"Get me *out*!!" he screams. Grey sap oozes from his mouth like he's a part of the tree. I pull at his arm as hard as I can and get him halfway out, but he's covered in a sticky sap and I can't hold on. I pull harder but then another set of arms, black and charred, close around his neck. He's yanked back into the tree. The trunk closes and forms a scar: that three-pronged symbol.

"No!!"

———— ❧ ————

I wake up screaming.

The sheets on my bed are soaked with sweat and I look over at the clock. It's 3:28am. I feel like I just ran a marathon. My whole body aches and I'm hyperventilating. Totally spent, I make myself breathe. That's when I hear that tinny melody again. This time, I don't care. I just lie there, exhausted but too scared to fall asleep. I listen to the music until it stops.

DR. BROWNING

The garden around the chapel is lovely, filled with blossoms so big they're even visible at night. I pause beside a white one as a green beetle – a beetle of unusual size, I might add – tiptoes around a petal and disappears inside it.

The blossom contracts in one ferocious move. It shrivels into nothing, crushing the beetle, and dropping out of sight.

The symbolism is not lost on me.

I find Cole napping in the chapel. He knows I disapprove, so I make no effort to quiet my footfalls as I enter the nave. He has spent a good deal of time here since he lost his precious anuscript. I sit down next to him and his eyes pop open. He struggles to sit up and mutters a curse under his breath.

"My thoughts exactly," I say gently. "This whole business is moving much faster than I expected." After a beat, he pats down his hair. He's pretending he wasn't just napping, so I will, too.

"Nothing you can't handle, I'm sure," he says casually.

I keep my gaze straight ahead. "I continue to search for your Manuscript. I intend to be the one who returns it to you."

"I appreciate your efforts," he says, "*and* your intentions. But you didn't interrupt me for that."

"I assured Professor Linden I'd ask you to back off," I begin, maybe a bit too pointedly. "But now I've decided not to. There's no turning Peter back now, not after what he has seen." I hope I don't sound too discouraged.

"No," Cole says simply.

"I've told you before, Mr. Cole. You are our keystone, the keystone that locks us all together." I make an arch with my hands and touch my fingertips together.

He frowns at the implication so I quickly add, "And keeps us in place, right? Without you, we'd ... collapse."

"Dr. Browning, if you're not asking me to 'back off,' ...?"

"Peter will need help I can't give," I say, and finally look directly at him. "I know it's an impossible request. Last year, you made it quite clear—"

"-- It's a new school year, Dr. Browning. Anything can happen." Cole takes out his antique pocket watch, glances at it. "But there will be a price to pay," he says, almost in a whisper.

I nod. I know this. "There is always a price to pay."

We sit for a moment. Then Cole clasps his hands together and nods as if something important has been decided.

PETER

I have to get some sleep, I keep thinking. The Red Bull doesn't even work anymore. I can barely stay awake through Miss Rizzolo's lecture. Plus I can't stop thinking about last night's nightmare. I draw in my notebook just to keep my eyes open; the page is filled with sketches of that three-pronged symbol. I see it everywhere now, even when I close my eyes.

Between classes, I see Sophia talking with some girls. I remember what Chloe told me about Sophia posting that picture on The Tunnel. I charge up to her. The girls bolt.

"You almost got me kicked out!"

"Karma's a bitch," she says like she has nothing to do with it. *What the hell is wrong with these people?*

"Are you kidding me?!" I yell. "I was kidnapped, some tool roofies me, and then my picture ends upon Page Six! There I am, in front of Dr. Browning, taking the blame for something I didn't do. And all you can say is, 'Karma's a bitch?'"

"My friends told me what you said about me," she says self righteously, as if I got what I deserved. "And if you let anything – *anything* – slide by you in this place, you might as well paint a target on your forehead."

"I didn't say anything about you!"

She stops for a second as if she never thought of that. Then she dismisses the idea. "Whatever. I only posted the photo on The Tunnel. I have no idea who hates you enough to post it on Page Six."

Suddenly I do. "*Anton.*"

"Anton? Then you should count your blessings. It could have been *a lot* worse." She notices my drawing of the three-pronged symbol sticking out of my history book. "Planning a ski trip?" she asks sweetly.

I look over toward the woods. "It's on a tree out there."

Her smile vanishes. "What?! Even *you* can't be that stupid. Those woods are off limits!"

"*Off limits?*"

"You'll get expelled!" she snaps back, obviously irritated that she has to spell it out for me.

"Expelled. For going into the woods?"

"A couple years ago, a student got killed by a bear out there!"

"Sophia. There are three bears in New York …and they're all in zoos."

"You almost got kicked out once," she says, shaking her head. "And now you're going to get yourself killed. *For what?*"

I want to tell her. I want to tell someone so they can assure me I'm not crazy. Somewhere deep down I feel like I can trust her, I don't know why. Then that photo on Chloe's phone flashes across my brain. What kind of an idiot would trust her, knowing she posted that?

"You wouldn't understand," I finally say.

Sophia rolls her eyes. "Then go. I didn't think you were going to make it here anyway."

I watch her leave, and I suddenly feel very alone. Then I look past her, at the woods. That's where that giant oak tree is. I can feel it in my bones. And that's where I'll get some answers.

———～———

I hurry back to my room after classes and change into my running clothes. I don't see how I have a choice anymore. Either this is all in my head or I've stumbled onto something incredible. I can't do nothing. The video, the visions, the dreams, whatever this is … it's not going to stop until I figure it out and *make* it stop.

I jog across campus. No one is at the track when I get there. After my third lap, I get near the back gate and notice the padlock. Was that there last time? I don't remember. I look up at the sharp spikes on top of the wrought iron gate: no way am I climbing over it.

I decide I might as well finish the laps. Maybe a run will clear my head and I can finally get some sleep tonight. But the next time I run past the gate, I stop. *What the hell?* The gate is now slightly open. No padlock.

I look around to make sure no one is watching. The gate is like a waiting invitation. I take a deep breath and step through it, tensed up, expecting something bad to happen. But nothing does. The place is still. Quiet. I wait. Nothing. I relax a little, and turn toward the forest. Instead of the usual rush of excitement I get for breaking the rules, I get this terrible heaviness in my gut. I tell myself it's just nerves.

I walk toward the forest, remembering that the last time I felt like this was just before the motorcycle accident. For the first time I realize how big the forest and how closely the trees are spaced. *How am I going to find this thing?*

As the tree line gets closer, the feeling gets worse. Finally, I turn back. Something isn't right. I should at least have a compass so I don't get lost. I'm ten feet from the gate, almost back on campus, when I hear a voice.

"Help!"

I stop. Is that a girl? Or an animal in the woods? It could just be the wind … right?

I take another step. I hear it again: "Please help meeee!"

It's coming from the forest! I scan the tree line. Someone is in trouble. Who is she? *Where* is she??

"Hello …?! Can you hear me?" I yell but the wind carries my voice away.

"Help me!" the girl's voice cries out desperately.

I start to run toward the forest as fast as I can. A few feet from the tree line, I look around. There's no one there. I can't see but a few feet into the woods, they're so thick and –

"Help! Please!"

Screw it. I run. I'm just about to take the first step into the woods when everything goes black.

CHLOE

The things I do for Queen and Country.

There's Peter, in the wet grass by the running track, out cold. I take the opportunity to get a closer look at him, and even in that low-rent athletic wear, he still looks *good*. He's breathing, always a good sign, but he is obviously unconscious.

I shake him at the bicep, which feels warm and very taut. *Not bad at all.* "You okay?" I ask, putting on my best concerned look.

He startles awake.

"Oh my God!" I shriek. "Were you *sleeping?*"

"No!" Peter jumps to his feet, probably a little faster than he should have. He wobbles a little and rubs the back of his head. "Someone hit me." It's true. There's a smear of blood on his hand.

"If you're very nice to me," I say. "I won't tell anyone you were off campus without permission." And then I can't help but ask, "*How on earth did you get back here?*"

"I have no idea." He actually looks a little confused.

I take in his shorts and shoes, caked with grey mud. "Doing what, I don't even *want* to know."

I spot some students and staff starting to walk toward the track. "Quick! Come with me." I lead him around the corner into the Chapel garden. I used to come here a lot to catch a smoke last year. It's a small garden, old and worn out. I point out the faucet to him, and he rinses off his shoes.

"I actually have a lot of practice at this," I say. "Covering up for my friends after blackouts."

"I didn't black out! Some son of a bitch *knocked* me out!"

"Last year," I go on, not really paying attention, "Sophia blacked out at the Met Ball. So embarrassing. She had a *crazy* year, even by Sophia's standards. I mean, she insists she's clean but... *come on.* Sophia has zero willpower, we all know *that.*"

He looks at me as if he doesn't understand the English language. "Aren't you friends with her?"

Maybe he's gay, which would explain why he is concentrating on those damn shoes instead of on, say, *me.* Then I remember how he watched Sophia leave the dining hall. There's no way he's gay.

"Good thing Sophia spends all her allowance on that silly Indian village." I lean closer as I let him in on the secret. "Otherwise *that* plus anything else she can get her hands on would go ..." I gesture, "... right up her nose."

Peter is processing that, I can tell. And I'm enjoying myself. "She seems perfect, I know. And then when they find out the truth, guys always want to *rescue* her. Makes me sick." He frowns.

"What?" I ask with a little defensive pout.

Peter rubs his head again. This time his fingers come back really bloody. "I'm gonna beat the shit out of Anton, *that's* what."

"Have you heard a word I've said?"

"I don't care if I get kicked out, that guy is going down."

"Slow down there, boy. That's *not* how it's done. You *will* get expelled, you'll be a pariah the rest of your life ... and *he'll* get a great story to tell for the next three years."

"So I'm supposed to walk around here with a target on my forehead?"

I sigh. *He's cute, but not clever.* Still, I have to admit his anger and willingness to use violence excites me. But there's a time and a place for everything, I learned that in third grade. He has to learn how this works, how to identify weaknesses and use them against people to get what you want. It's not nuclear physics.

"Use your imagination," I tell him. "Think strategically. Anton's image is everything to him. What could possibly be more fun than tearing that down?"

I can see the gears turning, so I toss him a mischievous smile and add, "With a little anonymous help from me?"

Back in Peter's room, a bright white square glows in the middle of his monitor. Slowly an image bleeds in and there it is: a hand drawn sketch of Sophia. Nude, her chin tilted up, her mouth partly open. I wouldn't tell Anton this unless he had a knife to my throat, but it's actually pretty good. Tasteful even. It doesn't really show that much of her naughty bits, but there's that birthmark near a very intimate place. That's how the girls will know it's authentic. And once the girls know …

The image enlarges briefly, flashing the monogram at the top of the page.

ANTON VLADIMIR VOLSKY

Moscow ~ Paris ~ New York

I squelch a giggle. Anton has been working so hard on getting Sophia back. When she sees this, she'll freak out and *never* hook up with him again. That's the price you pay for ordering me around, *Anton.*

Peter eyes the nude sketch longer than I consider necessary. *Enough already.* He is clearly having second thoughts about posting it, but let's get real. If anyone deserves it, it's Anton.

"Go *on*, you know you want to," I say in my sultry voice. That should get him to man up.

Even then, he hesitates. Everyone wants to be the good guy. Why is that? It's soooo boring.

The "Tips for the Tunnel" banner is already on the screen. I lean over the keyboard and press my chest against his shoulders as I type: "Hey Anton! It's never ever Ever EVER gonna happen!"

My "accidental" boob brush makes Peter blush. I didn't think guys did that anymore. He just stares straight ahead. Still, he doesn't push the damn button to post the picture. One more nudge should do it.

"How's your head?" I whisper into his ear. "Still bleeding?"

His eyes narrow at the memory and that's all it takes. He presses ENTER. The JPG sketch uploads, hanging there in the ether a beat.

We wait. Peter nervously rubs his hands on his legs.

Then the comments section explodes.

"LOL seriously Volsky is an ass"

"Too funny"

"never happen with me either"

"right on!"

They keep coming, comment after comment, mocking Volsky just the way I planned. I squeal with delight. Good times!

Peter pushes away from his desk, staring at the computer. He's not laughing. He's not even smiling. I was hoping for at least a satisfied glow or a grateful hug but here I am, risking my reputation by being in the Townie's room after midnight, and he has gone all Gloomy Gus on me.

Before I can snap at him, the comments ticker zooms up to fifty in less than a minute. So who cares? What's done is done, and I won't let him ruin my good time.

"Welcome to the big leagues," I say trying to cheer him up. After all, what are *friends* for?

CHAPTER ELEVEN

LINDEN

WHERE IS HE??!

I plow through the darkened school corridors with only one thing on my mind. We were promised, *promised*, "a minimum of interference!" And now this!

I hurl open one door, then another. Cole hears me coming and has half risen from his chair. Too late. I throw him against a wall. I hold him there by his throat. "You *cheat*!"

"Be careful, Professor," he warns in a strangled voice infuriatingly devoid of fear.

"You *interfered!*"

He tries to swallow. Hell if I'll let him.

"What happened," he asks softly, "the last time anger overwhelmed your better judgment?"

Hate bubbles up from my bowels. But he has a point. I can't afford another misunderstanding because of this creature's incompetence. It cost me dearly last time. I let him go with a shove.

"After everything I've done for you..." I snarl.

"Emotions can be frustrating, Professor," he says, so calmly I want to tear his head off. "I see you're not quite getting the hang of them yet."

"*I'm* not the one who allowed that Manuscript to get out there!"

"That has nothing to do with Peter."

Not *yet*, you useless piece of garbage. "So you haven't found it yet?" I ask.

"I'm too busy cleaning up after *you*," he shoots back.

"I *saw* that boy entering the forest! Of his own free will!" I move to within an inch of his face and hiss. "What deal did you make with her?"

Cole pulls a handkerchief from his pocket and dabs at his neck and forehead. "I don't make deals."

"I don't care how many centuries you've polluted this place, you are not going to stand in the way of –"

Cole raises his hand to interrupt me. "I heard you. Calling the boy."

Damn it. He heard me. *How?* Did he see me in my office? I fight the urge to smile; it *was* one of my better performances. Peter was so determined to be the hero and save the girl. Utterly predictable. But how did Cole hear me? He doesn't have the grey stone – he *can't.* James does.

Cole can tell where my thoughts have gone. "That was a clear infraction, Professor. You over-stepped, just as I was warned you would."

Oh he was *warned*, was he? I go to grab him by the throat again but think the better of it. "Listen to me, you pathetic fool. This isn't just about *me*. Browning's no saint. She manipulates. She cheats.

You can't see it, can you? She's exploiting you."

Cole folds his handkerchief as if he has all the time in the world, then looks up at me with exasperating calm.

"*We are all exploiting each other*," he says quietly.

———————◇———————

I hurry back to my office. I must recalibrate. I've lost valuable time already.

A gifted military commander is one who can make decisions based on information that shifts and changes by the minute. That's how I see this, as a military undertaking, and I intend to triumph. I'll have to force my opponent into unconditional surrender. To do this, I must assimilate new information, make strong decisions and push ahead. My focus must be on Peter, not on the injustice of Cole's bias.

I move a tiny oak tree inside a display case. Then I place a Union soldier at the base of it, musket up. I do all this, I think of all this, while Anton paces in my office and unloads his latest litany of complaints. The boy tries my patience.

"I was so close!" he whines. "Sophia is totally past the Paris thing. She even *told* me. And ComEx was practically mine."

I flick some dust off the display case and wonder if it was a mistake, spending so much time and energy on Anton. He is scheming to get Sophia back, I can tell and it's time to get him back on track.

"You really think your father – or *hers* -- would allow you two to be together again?"

"Their feud has nothing to do with us!"

I have a considerable amount invested in this boy. He is the sole heir to one of the biggest empires in Eastern Europe and will make decisions that will control the price of oil. Occasionally, he shows great promise. Yet there are days like today when I worry if he will ever be able to wield such power successfully.

"Don't be naïve. If you want ComEx, or any part of your father's business, you'll have to end your obsession with ... that girl."

"But I really – " Anton blurts. And then stops. He shakes his head, dismissing the thought. He wouldn't tell me that he really "loves" her, would he? Could he possibly be that stupid?

"What. You really what?" I goad him, to punish him and to train him. He can't let things like that slip. He doesn't answer. Can it be? Can he actually be considering sacrificing a lifetime of enormous power over global events for ... a *girl?*

He finally stages a recovery. "I really... wish my father would change his mind. I can run ComEx, I know I can!"

"Then stand up like a man instead of begging like a boy," I say without even looking at him. "Earn it. Prove you're willing to make the sacrifices necessary to get what you want."

He is silent, fuming at me. Let him fume. "Forget Foster for now!" I tell him. "Forget the girl and her self-indulgent charity. Focus only on ComEx. Owning it will make you one of the wealthiest and most powerful businessmen under twenty five."

"I will!"

I put my hand on his shoulders, such a simple gesture, one that engenders a kind of intimacy. I'm sure he'd like his father to do this, too, but with affection and concern, instead of dominating through brute strength. "Anton. Is that company truly your top priority? Before anything else?"

"Yes." He didn't even hesitate. *Good boy.*

"Then I will do everything in my power to make sure it is yours," I tell him, pretending that I didn't set the ball in motion hours ago.

PETER

I'm at my desk after dinner, looking at a whole bunch of three-pronged symbols and trying to figure out what the hell they have to do with James. I hear a series of thumps in the hallway and suddenly remember: it's almost eight.

I grab my dress shoes and drop them outside my door. They've got a coating of grey mud from the forest on the bottom and for a second I think I should wipe them off. It's kind of funny, seeing all the piles of shoes outside all the doors in the hall, waiting to be collected by the shoe shine guy. Some look pretty dirty, which makes me feel better. I'm about to shut my door when I'm stopped cold.

Another pair of shoes in the hall has the same grey mud on them. Wait, wha??

I walk to the door – I gotta get a closer look – and pick one up. Before I can inspect it, the door is flung open. Richard stands there, yanks the shoe out of my hand and tosses it next to the others.

"You can thank me later," he says, shooting a glance up and down the hallway. "Stay out of the goddamned forest, Foster! You have no idea what's out there."

He slams the door shut.

It was Richard, not Anton! I walk back to my room in a daze and click onto The Tunnel. I touch my head and I don't know what makes me feel worse, the bump on my skull or the 874 comments on that stupid post. Anton is a jackass, but now that I know he didn't knock me out, I feel even guiltier about posting the sketch. The comments were brutal. Even Alumni got into the act.

What the hell do I do now? Take my chances with Anton?

I am wondering what that would look like when I hear the tinny melody, muffled but unmistakable. Grateful for something else to think about, I go looking for its source. I open drawers on my night-stand. I pull up the mattress. The sound is coming from underneath the bed frame.

I slide underneath the bed, and there it is. A black lacquered box is wedged between the box spring and the wall, and the music is definitely coming from it. I pull it out as gently as I can.

I sit down on the bed and open it up. The melody cuts out. Inside is a gold watch on this velvet pillow. It must be solid gold, I figure, because it's so heavy. It's got thin Roman numerals around the edges and a black crocodile watch strap that doesn't have a mark on it.

I open up the laptop and find a photo of the exact same watch on eBay – I can't believe the asking price. $385,000.00! For the last three weeks, I've been sleeping on top of a watch worth three times more than our house in Providence. Unbelievable! I flip the watch over. The tiny inscription on the back reads:

Always Your S

It has a space between the R and the S, just like the note by the gate. I stare at it. What the hell do I do with it? I consider hiding it in the dresser but that's the first place anyone would look. I slip it back under my mattress but keep looking at the case. It looks almost as expensive as the watch.

I lay down on the bed and turn it over, looking for hidden com-partments. The inside of the box's lid has that same the three-pronged symbol on it. That thing is *everywhere* and I still have no clue what it means.

I trace the symbol with my finger and suddenly –

-- it explodes in a flash of blinding white light! I drop it and shield my head but it makes no difference. I blink my eyes hard several times and when the light starts to clear, I'm standing near a cliff's edge. I shake my head trying to wake up. I see a couple: Sophia and *James Harken!* They're on a blanket, enjoying a picnic. Beyond them is an expanse that glitters. My eyes focus: the ocean. Sophia looks different. Her hair is shorter and she looks so happy. She hands James the black lacquer box and says "Happy Anniversary." He smiles and opens it. The watch catches the sunlight, blinding me.

I press my hands into my eyes. Darkness. Finally bits of white start to fill in the darkness and I realize where I am.

Back in the forest. And there's that giant grey oak tree again. My stomach goes heavy with dread. The three-pronged symbol is carved into the tree's massive trunk.

And then the melody starts playing. It sounds like it is coming from inside the tree. I try not to freak out. *I don't want to be here. I just want to be back in my room.*

But I reach out to touch the tree, half curious and half scared to death. The second my finger brushes against the trunk, everything goes quiet and dark, it's as if I were suddenly locked inside a coffin. I can't lift my feet. I can't raise my arms to push the blackness back.

Roots from the forest floor wrap around my feet, then my legs. I open my mouth to scream as thin, wet roots poke into my ears and mouth. I whip my head back and forth, screaming, but they're going down my throat now, suffocating me –

And suddenly I am sucked downward and delivered SPLAT! back onto my bed. I'm heaving, breathing really hard, staring at my desk, my TV, my carpet, all undisturbed. Silence. But I'm covered in layer of sweat, and my shoes have grey slimy mud all over them. I gag and cough up bits of grey sap.

What the hell is happening to me?

I open the black lacquer box in a fury. The symbol is gone, there's nothing inside it but that little velvet pillow. I hurl the box across the room and scream.

CHLOE

I can't wait to see Anton's face. The thought kept me from falling asleep last night and I guess I wasn't the only one buzzing with sweet anticipation. No one at school can talk about anything else this morning. (Even Our Table isn't immune to speculating how our Russian Tsar wanna be will handle this latest setback while I employ my most convincing wide-eyed, innocent look.)

Charley tells us that a guy from Roosevelt Hall overheard Anton on the phone with his father last night, begging for forgiveness. Begging! Oh I can't stop smiling at the idea! Poor Anton is so desperate to run that company. And he's desperate to get Sophia back. We all know he can't have both.

Knowing Anton won't be able to trace anything back to me (I've been careful to construct a detailed, unshakeable alibi, should I need one), I have a hard time concealing my utter joy. This is going to be a fucking *brilliant* day.

That's when I look at my most recent distraction and try to imagine what is going through his little Townie head. He seems subdued. Then it hits me: he feels guilt! The most useless of emotions! (Any decent therapist will tell you that.) His expression of self-loathing would be comical, but I deserve someone to celebrate with, and who else is there? He is seriously crushing my happy vibe this morning. I glare back at him. He looks even more miserable. *Crikey.*

The only one missing from breakfast is Anton, but he's the topic of every table's conversation. Charley keeps looking at his phone and updating us. "Eight hundred and ninety eight comments in eight hours. Not bad."

"Kept you up all night laughing, did it?" I ask Charley, taking pride in an accomplishment no one knows is mine.

"Wish I could stick around for Round Two," Charley says. "But I'm flying back to PA tonight. Big Carnegie Gala."

"So bail!" I tell him. "Things are finally getting interesting around here." I wouldn't miss this for New York, Milan and Paris Fashion Weeks all rolled into one.

"My dad is getting an award. Again. Must honor the Canned Food King!" Charley says.

"And the keeper of the Trust."

"That, too."

Out of the corner of my eye, I see Peter lean over to Sophia.

"I have to tell you something. *Now.*" he whispers to her. He's not going to spill to *her* of all people, is he? He better keep his mouth shut about me!

"Maybe you could just *post* it," she snarls back at him.

"We need to talk. *Alone,*" he says, and I try to kick him under the table. I miss but don't get a second chance because suddenly the dining room goes utterly still. Everyone looks up: Anton's here.

He pauses, taking in the silent humiliation. Most of the students look at him and giggle. A few high-five. Anton straightens and makes the long walk across the dining hall. He turns to a group of girls at a table, "Got a problem?" They look quickly away. He finally makes it to our table.

"Ah, Anton! Top of the morning to you!" Charley greets him cheerfully. "We were marveling at our student body's many hidden talents. Weren't we?"

Peter shoots him a dark look. "Shut up, Charley."

But Charley doesn't shut up, and I want to hug him. "I play violin like a cripple," he says theatrically. "Chloe can say the alphabet backwards, starting with "zed." You can sketch like a man in love. And Peter here…" Charley smiles at Peter, his confidence waning a bit. "Peter, what can you do, exactly?"

Peter glares. The muscles in his jaws tense, just like in the movies, and it's a real effort to not to laugh out loud.

Anton says nothing (*nothing*, Anton?) and looks at Sophia. This is it, the moment I've been waiting for. What will Sophia do? Slap him? Cause a delicious scene in the dining hall? I can barely breathe.

But Sophia, or whoever this uptight schoolgirl is who so resembles Sophia, just nods demurely at the seat next to her.

"The salmon crepes are delicious," she says quietly, sipping her tea like a right princess, avoiding Anton's gaze.

He slowly sits down next to her and motions for a waiter to bring him coffee.

Maybe, I think with a hopeful jolt, she's just toying with him, extending his suffering until he's comfortable and unsuspecting, and then she'll kick him when he's down! I wait, eager, playing that scene out in my mind. But nothing happens. Sophia just continues to take dainty little bites of her breakfast biscuit. It's too soon for the joke to end here! I want to shout. Certainly we can squeeze more mileage from it!

But no one says a word. They're following Sophia's lead, being as gracious and forgiving as kittens! I can't believe it. Will I *ever* get the old Sophia back?

Anton catches my eye and *what is that I see? Gratitude?!*

My brilliant day just turned to smoldering shit.

In a last ditch effort to save the moment, I turn to Peter. "I bet Peter can do all kinds of amazing things," I coo, as if being in the same room with him were more than my fragile femininity could bear. "Do tell us, Peter."

Anton turns to Peter, his eyes the color of ice. "Yes, Peter. Tell us what you're good for."

No one moves.

PETER

I'm pacing in the laundry room, waiting for Sophia. I suggested it because I never see anyone in here. After fifteen minutes, I've already rehearsed what I'm going to say.

She finally shows up. She starts to say something but stops and looks around. "Wow. I had no idea this was even here."

Seriously? "Where do you do your laundry?"

Sophia looks at me like I am learning impaired. "I send it out like everybody else. Now, what the hell is so important?!"

Of course you do, I want to say, but I can't afford to piss her off. I set down the black lacquer box. Sophia looks at it, says nothing.

"I thought today was my lucky day. Guess who found a little bling under his bed?" No reaction. I take the watch from the box. "Turns out this sucker's worth three hundred eighty grand on eBay."

She just stares at the watch.

"What am I saying? Like you shop on eBay." I point to the inscription on the back of the watch. "At first I thought this said 'Always yours,' like the note on that rose left by the gate. But it has the same space between the R and the S. That's when I realized that what it really says is *'Always your S.'*

I pause. She gives me nothing. "'S' for Sophia."

I hand her the watch. "So why'd you lie to me?"

She examines it and hands it back. "Cute. But it isn't mine."

I roll my eyes. *Why is everything so difficult with these people?*

"I know you gave it to James." She just looks at me. *Fine.* I keep going. "On a cliff near the beach."

Her eyes widen a little, and start to tear up. She looks at me for a moment as if making a decision. "Who told you?"

"No one. I *saw* it!"

Her eyes narrow. She clearly doesn't believe me. "Seriously. Tell me. How did you know? I didn't even tell Chloe!"

Of course I can't tell her. Like I'm going to get into the details of my own insanity.

"Peter."

I know she isn't going to tell me the truth if I don't share this with her. *To hell with it.* I have to tell *someone.* I have to make sure I'm not losing my mind.

I tell her everything.

She just sits there, taking it all in as if it's just normal conversation. I finish with "... then I was back in my room, with this *grey slimy mud* all over my shoes." I pause. "That's it."

After a moment, she gathers her books. "I gotta go."

You gotta *go?* That's all she has to say after all I just told her? *Hell no.*

"Your note said, 'Your work will live on,'" I say, refocusing. "What work, Sophia?"

Sophia swallows. "James and I were friends, okay? So what? That doesn't mean I have any idea what you are talking about."

"I haven't slept in three frigging days," I tell her. I know my voice is rising but I can't help it. "I can't eat. I can't think of anything else. So tell me what I need to know, or I'll find someone who will."

Sophia freezes for a second. I can practically hear the debate raging in her head. Finally her shoulders sag a little. "We met in rehab last year, James and me." She brightens a little. "Malibu of all places. You ever been?

"To *rehab?*"

"To Malibu!"

"Uh, *no* and *no.*"

"After my meltdown at the Met, my parents sent me there to 'recover'. It was James who really got me on my feet again."

"So what happened to him?"

She stalls. Looks away like she's thinking of a lie, or some way to get me off topic. I press on. "I need your help, Sophia. I need to find that tree and get him out of it..." I run my hand through my hair and add, "... *and out of my head.*"

Sophia, pale, leans against a washer. "All I know is he was researching the history of The Academy. It started as an Independent Study with Professor Linden but then James got ..." She breaks off, searching for the word. "... like, obsessed. Writing constantly in this *journal*. He was so protective of that thing, he never even let me read it."

"His journal? Where is it?"

"I figured *you* had it." She looks around anxiously and I can tell I've got seconds left before she bolts. She looks down at her hands and says, "It's got that weird symbol on it, the one you were asking me about in the quad."

"There has to be more. Come on, Sophia. Help me. I know you know more than you're telling me."

"*Help* you?" she asks, her temper rising. "So you can keep grinding on this, no matter what I say, with *no clue* about the danger you're putting other people in?" I try to interrupt but can't stop her. "Like there won't be a price to pay if I get involved?!"

Huh? Price to pay? My confusion pisses her off even more.

"Don't you get it?" she shrieks. "They find out I'm helping *you* and I'll disappear! Or turn up dead! *Or be stuck in a wheelchair for the rest of my life!*"

She stalks out of the laundry room. I'm so stunned I can't stop her. That's when it hits me.

Charley.

CHAPTER TWELVE

PETER

I race up the stairs of Roosevelt Hall in thirty seconds flat. I'm done with these games.

I bang on his door. "Charley, come on! Open up!" Nothing. The door is locked. I race into my room and try to push open that door, but it's locked too. I pound harder, "No more bullshit!"

Then I remember his trip home for the weekend. I race back down the stairs as fast as I can.

When I reach the top of the hill on the far side of campus, I can see a helicopter waiting on a neatly outlined helipad, blades spinning. And there's Charley, his leather overnight bag on his lap, pushing his wheelchair toward the helicopter as the pilot comes out to greet him.

I hop over the small fence surrounding the helipad and yell out, "Charley!"

He can't hear me but the pilot sees me coming and frowns. Charley follows his gaze. "Nice of you to see me off, Foster!"

"I gotta talk to you. About ..." I catch my breath and point to his legs. "... what really happened."

"You know what they say," he says brightly. "It's not the sex that gets you but the chasing after it!" He hands the bag to the pilot, who gives me a dark look and disappears into the helicopter.

I don't laugh, I don't smile. I don't give Charley anything. I want answers *now*.

His smile fades. "You aren't going to let this go, are you? Sophia was right." He gets my surprise. Sophia? "There are no secrets at The Academy, Foster. Lesson number one."

"I gotta know, Charley." I hesitate because once it's out there, I can't un-ask the question. I haven't made up an explanation in case I'm all wrong. And what if he tells me I'm out of my fucking mind? I suck it up and ask. "Is James stuck in a tree in the middle of that forest?"

"The Tree of Souls, to be exact." He says it casually, like we're discussing the weather.

That just sits there a second. *So I'm not crazy. This is really happening.* It takes me a second to recover, and when I do, Charley has already rolled his chair up to the helicopter door.

"Where is the Tree and how do I get him out?" I shout above the whirring blades.

"You don't!"

"Please, man," I beg, no longer willing to hide my desperation. "I'm a wreck. I gotta know the truth. I can't live this way."

Charley waves his hand over his lap. "Better than living this way,

Foster. Think about it." He rolls up to a mechanical arm that hooks onto the wheelchair and lifts him and the chair into the chopper.

"Sorry!" he shouts down to me. "I'm not going to make the same mistake again!"

I've got seconds. By the time Charley gets back, it will be too late. I'll be dead from exhaustion … or something else. "He was your friend! *You owe him!*"

Charley hits a button and the mechanical arm pauses. He stares down at me, and I can tell he's getting pissed. "James was just like you. Kept chewing at it! And the deeper he went, the more paranoid he got! He wouldn't tell me anything in the end. He kept all the information he discovered on his hard drive. Kept saying it was for my *safety*." He looks down at his legs with regret. "Didn't matter much in the end, did it?"

The pilot catches Charley's eye and points urgently to his watch. Charley nods and turns back to me. "If you want to get him out of that Tree, then you'll have to do it alone, because I sure as hell am not risking my life again."

"Just tell me – "

"For God's sake, Foster!" He looks at me a moment and sees the determination and relents. "I don't know where the Tree is, but you need the last two stones to get him out. I think James has the third one. He was looking for it when he disappeared."

"*Stones*??!" Am I hearing this right? Stones? As in … rocks?

Charley flips the switch and the mechanical arm lifts him into the chopper.

"Where are they?" I shout and lean inside the chopper.

The pilot waves at me to get back.

"Charley! *Where are those stones?!*"

"Browning and Linden's offices!" he shouts. And then he says something else I can't hear. I put my hand to my ear – *what?* "They've each got one!" he shouts louder. "Everything has to be in balance, Foster. Lesson number two!"

I start to back away as the chopper engine revs up. I stagger backward, pushed down by the blast of air from the rotors. Charley closes his door and the chopper rises into the cloudy afternoon sky. I watch it go, dazed.

Seconds later, I'm alone on the hill overlooking The Academy. It's perfectly still and quiet. I can see the Chapel, the quad. The rows of roses, all the incredible buildings with their turrets and bay windows.

Behind them, dark clouds start to roll in.

I force myself to breathe normally. But each time I exhale, I whisper the same thing over and over.

I'm not crazy. *This is really happening.*

CHLOE

Sophia admires herself from every angle. She's wearing a pretty enough gown, with tucks at the waist and jeweled straps. Still, I've seen it a hundred different places. It's so *safe*. I know she expects me to say something. So I don't.

What I really want to do is throw something at her. *Just pick one, you indecisive cow!*

Friendship has required me to be subjected to the most boring fashion choices of the season for over an hour and forty-five minutes. *What happened to her?* I wonder as she tries on another conservative gown. The old Sophia was all about bold choices, pushing the envelope, making a statement. She was exciting and interesting. Now she follows the trends instead of setting them, and everything she does is without an ounce of creativity or confidence.

It makes no sense, really! We had everything. We were the "it" girls, on the list for every club that mattered. I mean, it wasn't a party until we got there! But what happens? One little car accident and she becomes this born again *whatever* with no sense of fun or *joie de vivre*.

"Angel Sanchez," she says, interrupting my thoughts. "What do you think?"

"I think it's irrelevant. There are no Vogue photographers at the U.N." I probably should have been kinder, but ... I forget these things, and I don't have the patience for them anyway. "Really, Soph. It's not Milan. It's the U.N! They won't even know who Angel Sanchez is."

Sophia holds up yet another lavender gown. "You think Malala will be there?"

"I doubt it," I say, as if missing Malala were a huge disappointment. But let's be honest. Who will even remember the girl's name in a year? This whole charity thing is getting old. It's a passing fad and everyone knows it. Remember when celebrities adopted babies from third world countries? Like *that*. Who does *that* anymore?

I've had enough. Every friendship has its limits and I've reached mine. I'll rave over whatever horrifying, boring frock she pulls out next, even if it's a bloody bathing suit, just so we can be done.

"Anton wants to fly me to New York for my speech," she says, and I

147

perk up. Wait a second. Have I gone about this all wrong? Anton has always been her greatest weakness. If they get back together, it's only a matter of time till he breaks her heart again. Once that happens, I'll definitely have better chance at getting the old Sophia back.

"That's ... sweet," I say. "You'll take him up on it, won't you?" We both know how nice the ComEx private jet is: the plush rugs, the expensive champagne, the leather seats. (Not to mention the private bed in back.) And we both know what it will mean if she accepts the offer. There is no *halfway* when it comes to Anton.

She sighs. "You think we can just start up again, Anton and me? After everything that happened?"

"Of course you can! You saw those sketches. He adores you. You belong together."

Sophia looks back at the mirror. Doubt fills her face. "I don't know."

"Imagine what access to the Volk Oil fortune could do for your little Indian ... people," I say. She gives me a weird look. "What?"

She shakes her head quickly, that little "oh it's nothing" gesture, but I know it's *not* nothing. She only does that when she has a secret she's dying to tell. Luckily, she's easy to crack. You just have to remind her who she really is ...

"Just think of Anton as moral support. After all, no one would blame you for being nervous. You'll be surrounded by all those accomplished people at the United Nations." Sophia brightens for a second but still won't *spill*. "Being with all those people who have, like, really changed the world for the better!" I continue pretending to be awed. "It must be intimidating for you."

"They aren't the only ones who changed things for the better!"

Sophia squeaks. And then out it comes, a gushing torrent that nearly knocks me over. "I have a $30 million check for Village Works!" *She what? How?* "From my Dad. I'm announcing it Saturday!"

I really should write an owner's manual for Sophia one day. She is so easy to manipulate. Still, I'm gobsmacked. Her father doesn't trust her with *anything* (for good reason) and now he's waving a check for the thirty mill in her face??! There has to be more to this.

"Major win for you," I squeeze out.

"Well I *earned* it," she says.

"You earned it? How? Are you selling orphans now?"

She smiles and tells me everything. "We were digging wells, remember?" she says, her voice just above a whisper. "I sent soil samples back to the States! Turns out the area is loaded with Californuim."

I arch an eyebrow, so she explains. "Californium is used in nuclear reactors. It costs about $27 million *a gram*." She practically levitates with happiness. "My village is sitting on the largest supply of it *in the entire world*. And guess who gets the mining rights? In return for a sizable donation, of course."

"That's great, Sophia," I say, forcing a smile.

"But you can't tell anyone!" she says, quickly.

"Of course not!" I say in my most reassuring voice, as in *how dare you suggest I might*. "All your hard work is finally paying off. That's just ... *great*."

Sophia leaps off the bed with renewed energy and disappears into the shoe closet. I need a few minutes to think this through, but I have to make sure there isn't more I should know.

"What did Peter want to talk to you about so badly at breakfast?" I ask.

She emerges with a pair of $650 Manolo Blahniks (but they're last season's). "He just ... needed homework for Global Finance class." She waves the shoes around next to her dress. "Approved?"

"Approved." I say without really looking because *seriously, who cares?* "I guess the new kid's still laboring under the delusion that he's going to make it here."

"Well, he figured out all by himself that that wasn't James at the party," Sophia says, scooping up the dresses and hauling them back to our walk-in closet.

"So he's not a total idiot."

"And kind of cute," Sophia shoots back.

There she goes. Anytime I show interest in a guy, Sophia is there two seconds later doing her "rescue me" thing. I stretch out on her bed and notice that a drawer by the bed is partway open.

"Don't you think?" Sophia asks from the closet. Don't I think Foster is kind of cute? *Like I would tell you if I did.*

"In a total slumming downtown way. With a makeover. Maybe." I open the drawer and peer in. There's a photograph there. I stare at it. My hands start shaking and I can't breathe. I really, *really* can't breathe.

Inside the closet, Sophia drones on and on but I can't make out the words. My stomach clenches. I pull the photograph into the light and stare: there Sophia sits with James, their arms around each other. They're on a beach, tanned and smiling. They look so happy. I feel like I have an iron bar lodged in my throat.

I stuff the photograph back into the drawer, barely able to see through my tears. Sophia's voice floats from the closet. "I don't know if I should go classic or trendy. I have, like, seven interviews!" I shut the drawer closed and tip my head back until the tears drain away. "Should I give Chelsea Clinton a call?" Sophia asks, oblivious. "She would know."

James. That dumb bitch took James from me.

"I'll be speaking at the UN about my charity!" Sophia drones on. "*My charity.* Wow. I love saying that. Six months ago, I wouldn't have thought it was possible for me. Not ever."

I walk out without saying a word. I can't listen to that voice a second longer. It isn't until I've locked the door on my suite and totally shut her voice out that I start to breathe again. The next thing I know, I'm in the bathroom, I don't even know how I got there. I'm crying now, for James and for myself. The blackness is taking over now. *I have to stop it.*

I open the medicine cabinet. I pour some lovely little pills into my hand, and I feel a weird rush of affection for them; they will stop the pain. I never take more than two, but this is different, this is so much bigger, so I take four. I deserve it. I crawl into bed and hide my face, and I let the sobs come.

The pills start to kick in five minutes later. I imagine myself lying on a raft on some ocean. My parents and friends cry and call to me from shore, "Chloe! *Chloe, come back!*" but I pretend I can't hear. I thank the doctors and scientists and whoever else created these amazing ways to make my rage and my pain so small and far away I barely recognize them.

DR BROWNING

I wait for the coffee maker to do its magic. My early morning coffee ritual in the faculty lounge is one of my favorite parts of the day. I breathe deeply, savoring the moment: the aroma, the rising steam, the increasing warmth of the cup. Most importantly, I enjoy the serenity of an empty lounge.

One must revel in the simple pleasures of being human.

The moment is ruined when Linden comes waltzing in. He immediately opens and closes the cupboards, almost rhythmically, as if enjoying the clattering noise.

I keep my expression perfectly neutral. But after he slams shut the ninth cupboard, I can't take it anymore. "Oh, for heaven's sake."

He gives me an apologetic look that's about as sincere as a circus clown's. "Sorry. Looking for the honey."

Of course. The honey. Before I can snap back, Cole hurries in, quickly shutting the French doors. Linden and I watch, amused, and he quickly closes the door to the tiled patio, too. He moves quickly, with real purpose.

I offer my cup. "Coffee, Mr. Cole?"

He stands there stiffly, as if preparing a formal speech. He clears his throat. "No. Thank you. I have an announcement to make."

"In the faculty *kitchen*?" Linden says, purposely throwing Cole off his game.

"It won't take but a moment," Cole says, struggling to stay on point.

"My office is twenty feet away," Linden continues, undaunted.

"I'm here to remind you both," Cole says, "that the lines have been redrawn despite your recent ... misadventures."

The temperature in the room cools. Linden and I are instantly on guard.

"Redrawn *how*?" Linden asks before I can.

"Redrawn as in ..." Cole clearly hadn't considered that we might have questions. He lets out a frustrated sigh. "As in, *your accounts are reset.* You are neither credited nor blamed for past indiscretions." He pauses as if he were expecting a protest. None comes. "You can consider yourselves beginning anew."

"I *knew* he would try something!" I say, pointing at Linden.

Linden pretends to take offense. "Me?!" He looks ready to explode in self-righteous anger.

Cole raises a hand to stop him and looks pointedly at *me*. Imagine!

"Just so you understand," Cole says. "Nothing goes unnoticed, Dr. Browning. *Nothing.* From now on, you are to work within the accepted boundaries. No future transgressions will be permitted." He holds us both with a stern look. "*Do you understand?*"

PETER

I remember this place from my run around the campus track. I saw it from a distance and couldn't figure out what it was until I saw the horses. Now I'm up close, and it's even bigger than I thought. It's a full size equestrian complex with several arenas and expensive looking stalls. Like everything else at this school, it doesn't look like it gets a lot of use. It's practically deserted.

I walk into the main building and head toward the only tack room with a light still on. That's where I find Sophia, dressed in riding clothes and shiny brown riding boots. She's unbuckling the leather straps of a bridle and I wait for her to notice me.

I look around at all the saddles and riding hats hanging there and finally ask, "Is this, like, your PE credit?"

She looks up, surprised. Then she goes back to the bridle. "No, this is where I board one of my horses. They only let me bring *one horse*. How cruel is that?" she asks.

"To you or the horse?" I ask.

She rolls her eyes and turns to face me. She's still a little sweaty from her ride. And I'll admit she looks hot in the outfit, even when she's glaring at me. "What do you want now?"

I hold out the Breguet watch. Sophia takes it. "Thanks."

I really hope I did the right thing, giving that back.

She drops down onto a bench and looks at me with a little smile. "Would you?"

I don't know what she's asking me until she raises her right leg and gestures to her boot.

I want to tell her what she can do with the boots. But I came all the way here for answers. I pull at her foot.

"I have a question," I say, with a grunt. The freaking boot isn't coming off.

"So that's why you gave me back the watch? Nice." She twirls a finger at me to turn around. I'm getting a little pissed, but she's got this playful little smile on her face, so I roll with it. I turn around and her boot appears between my knees. It moves upward and snuggles into my crotch, gently.

"Pull," she says, practically in a whisper.

I fit my hand under the heel of her foot and the boot slips off. Then the second boot slowly makes its way up into my crotch. I glance back at Sophia and she's just watching me, like she's testing me. There's something vaguely sexual about the whole thing, and it's not the worst feeling in the world.

I slide the boot off, a little slower this time.

"Okay then. Tell me about that tree?" I finally ask.

"I told you. I'm not getting involved."

"But you have some idea of where it is, right?"

"I can't help you." She thinks a second. "Or I *won't* help. Not sure which."

"Why not?"

She slips on a pair of embroidered slippers. "James was a beautiful part of my past. But the past is ... past."

"Deep, Sophia. Seriously. But this –"

"-- I can't, Peter," she says with something that sounds like regret. "I have to think about my future."

"No one will know you told me. I promise."

"They will know someone told you." She hands me back the watch. "Keep it. Helping you isn't worth the risk. And I don't owe you anything."

"Why is everything always so calculated with you people? I owe you, you owe *me*," I say. She looks like she's getting seriously pissed. I don't care. "Sometimes people just help each other because they can."

"Like I need a lecture from you!" Sophia's eyes narrow. "Get this through your head, Peter: everything here is a trap. Or a lie. Or both. And every choice you make is one you can't ever undo. *Nothing will destroy you here faster than trying to help someone else.* So if you see a chance to help someone, *walk away!*"

Sophia slowly walks to the tack room door and pauses. "See how easy it is?" she asks. And then she's gone.

CHAPTER THIRTEEN

DR. BROWNING

Tiny dust particles dance on the sunlight streaming into my office. I dab more paint on the canvas. I regret I am not a skilled enough painter to capture these lovely, peaceful moments; contentment is so rare. Still, I find satisfaction where I can.

It rarely lasts long. There is always something to be done. I'm grateful for the burden placed on me; I take my responsibilities seriously. But I would appreciate a little more time to enjoy the moment before being called to action again.

I peer into the painting, willing it to come alive, and it does. I see Sophia.

I'm not pleased. I consider letting it go (years ago, I may have) but I've learned that nipping certain things in the bud ensures a great deal less heartache later on.

I remove my painter's smock and hurry to the dorm's main kitchen. I stop at the sight of Sophia in a starched white apron. She's chopping carrots on a shiny industrial-sized counter. *It's worse than I feared.* I hoped she'd only need a minor bit of course correction.

Several photographers snap pictures and call out directions. Sophia beams, clearly in love with the cameras. An assistant positions lighting umbrellas, redirecting light onto trays of vegetables.

I let the door bang shut and they all turn. I glare at the photographers, irritated that they snuck on campus while I was admiring dust particles and sunbeams. I can't afford to lose focus for even a moment.

Sophia freezes as if caught doing something she shouldn't. "Teen Vogue is doing this Future Global Leaders thing!" she quickly explains, obviously hoping I'll be so pleased for her that I'll overlook breaking the school rules.

"I didn't authorize any photographers on campus. And you *know* our policy, Sophia."

She looks down guiltily and mumbles, "It's for a story on Village Works. They wanted 'action shots.' I didn't think you'd mind."

She knows how much I support her efforts with Village Works. I even approved its classification as an Independent Study so she can get academic credit for it. But she also knows that no photographers or press are to be allowed on The Academy grounds without written authorization, especially given the PR nightmare we faced with Peter and that photo.

But I am more concerned about Sophia's growing need for attention. Has she forgotten why she started Village Works in the first place?

"Sophia, good work should be its own reward. You don't need to shout about it from the rooftops. And if you have to sneak around to do something, that means you shouldn't be doing it." I am as gentle with her as I know how to be. "That's why you told the gate guards you had my permission instead of seeking it. You knew what my answer would be."

I have to remember to have a talk with those guards.

"But all this attention will be so good for Village Works ..." Sophia says, but weakly, seeing my expression. I do not compromise when it comes to integrity, not ever.

"All that matters is the good you do, not *what you get* for the good you do."

I can feel a growing heaviness in my chest. There is only so much I can say. Unchecked vanity has the power to lead us all down a very dangerous path. Even so, I can't push Sophia much more. She has to be responsible for her own decisions, and I can't step much closer to the line without going over it.

Thankfully she relents and agrees to send the photographers packing. I return to my office. But instead of feeling good about a job well done, I am uneasy. I'm not entirely sure my words had the intended effect, and what are a few wise words next to the lights and cameras of Teen Vogue? It's not that I don't trust Sophia. Well, yes it is. I would very much like to trust her but her seeking the spotlight so brazenly worries me.

I sit back down in front of my painting and sigh. It hurts to watch it. But I can't look away.

In the kitchen, Sophia smiles nervously at the impatient photographers. "Sorry. Ummm, listen ... you guys have to go."

No one moves. They're confused. Leave? So soon?

Sophia sighs quietly. It's a tough moment, when the "want to" and the "should" collide. I'm not without compassion (I was young once too). Then she says, so quietly I barely hear it, "I wish I were back in India. Life is so much simpler there."

A flash goes off. Then another. Sophia slowly brightens. She looks at the row of photographers before her as if she has never seen anything quite so mesmerizing.

"You can use that quote," she says, "if you want to." She starts chopping again, or pretending to.

When the whirr of the cameras starts up, I know that this particular battle, this time, has been lost. I can no longer interfere. She made her choice. I hope she'll be able to stop before she goes much further down that path. I already begin to make a backup plan in case she can't.

I decide to keep a watch on her throughout the day.

————— ᵔ —————

After the photo shoot, Anton and Sophia picnic under a tree on the west side of campus. Sophia watches the clouds, troubled.

Anton, wanting to be the only thing she sees, leans into her line of sight. "We're set!" he says. "I arranged it with my pilot. We leave Friday after last period."

"Don't take this the wrong way," Sophia says quietly, "but I think we should take it slow."

"Of course!" he says, as if he thought of it. "Me too. Slow. Careful. That way, you can see how much I've changed."

Sophia smiles at him a bit uncertainly as he clinks his ice tea with hers. After a moment, unable to meet her eyes, he goes on, "About those sketches ..."

"Just forget it, okay? Add them to the long list of 'just-forget-its' from last year."

"Agreed." He gives her a sideways look. "Whatever happened last year is done. I've let it go." He notes the expression on her face and suspects she isn't so convinced. Then something in the distance catches his eye: an opportunity. Peter. On a bench across the quad, working on his laptop.

"I *have* changed, you know," Anton says. "I'll prove it." Without waiting for her encouragement, he gets up.

Peter, engrossed in a webpage of computer codes, looks up and sees Anton coming. He quickly shuts the laptop and braces for the worst.

"Listen," Peter says. "I only put that sketch up because some asshole sucker-punched me from behind. I was sure it was you."

"It wasn't," Anton replies in a tone that is neither threatening nor friendly.

"I screwed up," Peter says. "Honest mistake. If I could fix it, I would."

"You cost me millions of dollars. You can't *make that up*." He lets Peter twist on that for a moment. "But *this*. Admitting your mistake. Good strategy. Well played."

"It's not a strategy, you pompous ass. It's an apology."

Anton looks at Sophia, who shields her eyes from the sun and watches them with some concern. She's clearly trying to read their body language.

Anton turns back to Peter. "You say you want to make it right. But you can't. You'll have to suffer, knowing that."

Peter shifts uncomfortably as if he's wondering the same thing I am: *where is this going?*

"However, I refuse to live with the anger," Anton said.

"No shit. How Ghandi of you."

"This is *my* strategy," Anton says a little louder, and Peter stiffens as if expecting a punch. But Anton just extends his right hand.

Peter looks as surprised as I am. Slowly, uncertainly, he shakes Anton's hand. And there's Sophia, watching them from a distance, probably wondering what to make of all of this.

Anton swaggers back over to Sophia and drops down beside her. "If *that* doesn't prove I'm changed man, I don't know what will."

Sophia smiles to herself, plucking a flower from a nearby bush. Anton waits, obviously expecting more. Finally he has to nudge her. "You okay? Because you've been, like, somewhere else today."

Sophia shrugs. "Yeah, I guess. Dr. Browning wasn't very happy about the photo shoot I just did for Village Works. She thinks every act of charity should go totally unnoticed. I tried to tell her I was trying to raise awareness but she thinks I do it for attention."

"She's clueless," Anton assures her.

"Sometimes. But she has helped me a lot with the whole charity thing."

He shakes his head. "I wanted to help, too, you know. But I guess its too late now."

"Why is it too late?" Sophia asks.

"Because of the big money dump from your dad."

Sophia inhales sharply. "No one knows about that yet!" She looks around, irritated, and lowers her voice. "You can't tell anyone, Anton. Especially your father."

"Promise."

She stares at Anton and I know she wants to believe him. To be able to trust him again.

"I have to go practice my speech," she says, pecking him on the cheek and hurrying away.

―――――~―――――

Hours later I get confirmation of my worst fears in the form of an email from Sophia's father.

I don't have to look for her. I know she's in the stables practicing her speech. The polished wooden doors glow and a light shines from inside. I hear her voice as I approach.

"...which is why it's imperative for us to come together and help these villagers."

It breaks my heart to see her work so hard and then have this happen. I step into the light and she searches my face, no doubt fearful I'm there to scold her for continuing the photo shoot when she promised to end it.

"I have some bad news."

It takes several minutes to tell her what I know, and to give her a printed copy of the email. She looks at it, but doesn't really read it. She seems dazed.

"I don't understand."

"Village Works. Your father pulled his funding. I'm so sorry," I repeat, running a hand over her arm.

"But ... what about the mining contracts?" she asks.

I shake my head. "Apparently another company, a rival he knows well, outbid him. He blames you. I'm sorry. I don't understand it all myself."

"Dr. Browning, Village Works is *everything* to me!" She's about to cry.

"I know."

"For the first time, my dad said he was proud of me! I proved that I could do something meaningful in the real world!" she says, her voice cracking. I pull her into a hug. That's all she wants, this broken girl, to do something meaningful outside the enormous sphere of her family's influence!

"And you will. Someday."

I let her cry for a while and then I wipe her tears away. "It's nearly midnight. Why don't you finish up here and go to bed? We'll sort it out in the morning."

I hoped she would let my words be her comfort until morning, but before I'm even out the door, she is fumbling for her phone.

LINDEN

Every day is a battle in a war that never ends. Every victory is a step closer to, every defeat a step further from, attaining total victory. I have studied all of military history and one thing remains constant: while the foot soldiers celebrate victory of each little battle, the generals know they cannot afford to. Their entire focus must be on the larger goal: winning the war.

As I secure my stone under the miniature oak in my diorama, I see the fruits of my latest work unfold.

"Daddy? It's me." It's the voice of a young woman, choking back tears. Sophia is in the stables. "This is, like, my third message. And I left two more with Mrs. O'Connor, but ..." There's a delightful desperation in her voice. Almost melodic. "Please call me back. Please? I just want to know *why!?*"

She turns off the light in the tack room and heads back to the dorms. It occurs to me she doesn't have the full picture. There's something she should see.

A few seconds later, the sprinklers go on.

There's Sophia, head down, hurrying to her room. But thanks to my quick thinking, she'll now have to choose to go through them and get soaked, or go around. As I anticipated, she opts for the longer route back to her dorm via a pathway that will take her right by the male students' lounge. I know Anton and his cohorts are celebrating there; I have already received two notices warning about the noise.

The huge bay window is ablaze with light. Young men shout. Sophia pauses. Her eyes focus and search for someone, and she hears a voice on the TV. Her expression goes from curiosity to suspicion. She slips inside Roosevelt Hall and hurries to the lounge where Anton and his crew watch late night TV. She hovers by the door, unseen.

The guys hush each other as the business news comes on. "In a last-minute press release from the business desk," a voice intones, "Volk Oil has just announced that its subsidiary, ComEx, will now be managed by the youngest CEO ever, Anton Volsky."

A whoop goes up in the lounge.

"The younger Volksy's first move is a confident one: the purchase of mining contracts in southern India. This bold maneuver preempts the prior bid made by US-based Prescott Technologies ..."

In the hallway, Sophia's expression turns to one of disbelief and horror.

In the lounge, Anton's cell phone rings. He steps toward the door to answer it but that's a little close and I can't risk him seeing Sophia. So the volume on the TV suddenly drops (with one click of a button, *oh how I love technology*), so he stops before he gets to the threshold and never sees Sophia on the other side of it.

"Hello, Father," he says boldly. "It's on the news. Just now." He puts the call on speaker for his friends to hear.

"You have what you want," says his father's emotionless, heavily accented voice. "ComEx is yours."

"Yes. Thank you."

"Finally you think like a man. Hopefully this continues. We will see. Good night, son." Anton smiles and looks to end the call as the others drift back toward the TV and put on an action film. A loud one.

But Anton doesn't end the call. He steps outside the room, not seeing Sophia, hidden in the shadows. "Father?" he asks. "What changed your mind?"

His father laughs quietly and says, "I like how you kick the balls of that cheating liar, Prescott. Smart."

"Prescott?" Anton asks, confused.

"Together we will make him pay," says Vladimir, chortling. "Again."

"I'm not sure what you mean," Anton says carefully, unwilling to give too much away.

"It was good, this information you give to Mr. Linden, about these mines in India. Very discreet."

Anton freezes. Searches for something, anything, to say.

"Anton?" his father's tone now darkening and suspicious. "I am right to say you did this, no? Such a man who does this deserves my respect. And ComEx." He pause for a moment, "You did this, son? Correct? For ComEx?"

Anton squares his shoulders and tenses his jaw. "Yes. Yes, I did."

A pause while he swallows hard and squeezes his eyes closed. "For ComEx."

Sophia stumbles away, muffling her sobs. I bet she's wondering how she could be so stupid.

Anton returns to the TV as the images fade.

I sigh. A good day, on balance. I light a cigar.

———————~———————

A bit later, I am enjoying a late-night liqueur in my armchair when he burst into my office. One look at his fiery little eyes all ablaze in outrage and I realize there is no need to dance around it.

"I told your father you were ready," I tell him. "Still, he needed a little push." I take a sip and roll it around my mouth for a moment. "I obliged."

"Sophia will never forgive me."

Did the little shit actually *just say that?* I'm tempted to leave him to it – that anguish is so much worse than anything I could devise – but it's always accompanied with soul-searching that has the potential for real transformation, and I can't have *that*. I've invested a great deal in him.

"So she won't forgive you, so what?" I ask, wishing I had saved the cognac for an evening without these kinds of irritating interruptions. "Think about your father! He's so *proud* of you!"

"But I didn't *do* anything," he whines.

No. I did.

"Anton," I say with remarkable patience, "that doesn't matter. He thinks you did."

The boy starts pacing. "I had everything under control!"

"You were going to lose ComEx. This I can assure you."

He stops and glares at me, the arrogant little prick. "How did you know about the Californuim?" he demands to know. "I never told you."

"Unlike you, some people keep me informed around here," I say pointedly, and fight the urge to pout a bit. He should know better than to keep secrets from me. "And I distinctly remember you saying ComEx was your highest priority. Now prove it."

He remembers saying that, too. His face collapses in defeat.

I swirl the last of my cognac around in my glass and stare into it with a touch of sadness. "And here I thought you'd come to thank me. To *celebrate*."

CHLOE

I'm going to scream at the top of my lungs. I have to break something or else *I'll* break in two. This movie I'm watching isn't doing a thing to take my mind off it, even though I have it up to full volume. I look at the actress with her fluffy hair and perfect body and imagine what her face would look like if I ripped her cheeks open with my fingernails.

Suddenly my door is flung open. Richard hurries in. He relaxes, relieved, at the sight of me. I yank off my headphones. "Knock!"

"I *did*!" he says. "You didn't –" He gestures to the headphones. Then quietly: "I was worried."

"Oh, get over yourself. I don't need a baby-sitter." Before he can peer into the connecting room, I answer his question. "And Sophia's off practicing her speech, so you can go now."

"Didn't you hear? Sophia's dad pulled out of her charity."

"Oh?" That was fast. I laugh at the thought of Sophia not getting what she wants for once. "Sorry, not sorry!"

"I told you Anton would screw her over *again*," he says matter-of-factly.

"You knew that would happen? So now you can see into the future?" I ask, hoping he hears the sarcasm in my voice. "Is that something Dr. Browning taught you?"

He just looks at me sadly, like I'm some big disappointment he'll never be able to fix.

"I bet you can you predict what will happen to me, too?" I ask, all wide-eyed and sweet.

"Chloe, stop –"

I get up on my hands and knees on my bed like a good little girl, like I'm sure Sophia does. "Tell me what you see!" I beg him. "Pwease! Tell me I'll find a boy-fwend who will lose his mind whenever I do this." I toss my hair over one eye and pull my shirt off my shoulders.

He winces like I'm hurting him, which just makes me want to do it more. I twist my shirt into a knot so he can see my belly ring.

"Tell me I'll find someone who will say, 'Gee whiz! I *really love all* the dark corners of your soul, Chloe!'" I'm so angry I'm practically growling. "'I adore every rotten part of you, Chloe!' Will I find a guy like that, do you think?"

"Chlo," Richard says, and I can hear the pity in his voice. I want to hit him. Who is *he* to pity *me?!* I have three Vogue covers!

"Will I ever get that lucky again?" I ask.

"I hope so," he says quietly, looking down at the ground.

"Hah!" The angry tears spill down my cheeks, but I don't care. I want to slap that look off his face. He doesn't understand how this feels, he doesn't understand a thing.

"Get out!" I scream. "What good are you if you can't see my future?!"

"Chloe, you're way too into a guy you only hooked up with a couple of times."

"Shut up!" I never should have told him about James. I never should have told him *anything.*

"And he's not coming back."

"You don't know that!"

"Come on, Chloe. Stop – "

"— James belongs with *me!* And when he comes back, he'll come back *to me.*" My throat aches. I can't live like this anymore, trapped in this place.

"No, he won't, Chloe," Richard says in a loud, calm, careful voice that reminds me of the staff at that place they sent me to when I was little. I hate him. I hate him with a desperation I can't describe.

"GET OUT!" I scream, totally raw, and throw my iPad at him. He deflects it with one arm. I reach for the lamp at the side of my bed but Richard runs out of the room, slamming the door behind him.

I have to get out of here. Tonight.

By the time I've finished packing a small bag, my breathing is normal again. All I can think about is escaping. But there's something I have to do, something important, before I do.

In the bathroom, I yank open the medicine cabinet and pull

out several pill bottles, carefully selecting Sophia's favorites. I line those bottles up, labels out, in the dressing room, right next to her mirror. I give them a little pat.

Sorry, not sorry.

CHAPTER FOURTEEN

PETER

I haven't had a real night's sleep in three weeks. It feels like I haven't closed my eyes once, and I'm totally sketched out. It's really hard to concentrate.

"Do you see the file?" I ask, forcing myself to focus.

I'm on FaceTime with Zach, giving him final instructions. He nods. I strap James's watch onto my wrist and synchronize it to the time on my computer.

"Upload the file to The Academy mainframe at exactly 10:30," I tell Zach. "It should take me that long to get to his office."

"No problem. I can do it in my sleep. In fact, I just might," he adds with a laugh.

I'm so tired, I don't even smile. "Come on, Zach –"

"Relax. I got this, buddy." Zach gets serious for a second. "Are you *sure* you want to do this?"

"No," I tell him, and it's the truth. "But I have no choice."

"Ah, the no choice defense. So when you get caught and your mom kills you, I've got first dibs on your bike, right?"

I take a deep breath and bury my head in my hands. I know Zach is trying to cheer me up, but this whole thing is just too much.

"Ease up," Zach says. "We've been doing this since sixth grade, remember? Text me when you get out of there." He shuts down his FaceTime.

I sneak out without any problems. I figure once I have the stones, Charlie will be back and I can ask him how to find the Tree. The night is quiet and cool. I'm hurrying toward the library when someone turns a corner and smacks into me. Chloe!

"What the hell are you doing out here?" she asks in a loud whisper.

"You first, Princess."

It's interesting, seeing Chloe shocked and not so put together. She pulls her black coat tighter and looks away. Her cheeks are wet. Has she been crying? Is that even possible?

"Seriously," I ask. "Are you alright?"

"I'm going for a walk. Fresh air."

Yeah right. "Me too."

She looks me for a moment and finally says, "You didn't see me, Foster. And I didn't see you," and then disappears into the darkness. I check my watch. That's forty seconds I won't get back.

There's an underground tunnel that connects the library to the administration building. I noticed it my second day at The Academy, when I got lost. Someone told me it was for the professors, so they wouldn't have to walk outside in the winter. I remembered it when I was trying to figure out how to get into Dr. Browning's office.

The first thing I did was check out the security for that building. All of its outer doors are controlled by key cards, just like the library. But once you're inside either building, no key card or security code is needed to get to the other via the tunnel. I sign in on the iPad at the entrance of the Library.

The night guard looks at me for a moment. "Kinda late, no?"

"Ten minutes. Left my phone," I tell him. I hurry down a corridor to the back of the library where the tunnel door is. I can see a few seniors studying by the fireplace; the library is open all night for upperclassmen. I figure I can get in and out, and no one will know anything.

I hurry through the tunnel into the Admin building using the flashlight on my phone. I crouch in a darkened alcove. I'm just down the hall from Linden's office and I can see the light shifting as he moves around in it. I look at my watch and silently count down 5, 4, 3, 2, 1 …

Nothing. The silence stretches. Damn it, Zach! What the –

And then the fire alarm goes off. The old-fashioned bell startles me as it clangs right above my head.

Thirty seconds later, Professor Linden walks out of his office, sniffing the air, looking for smoke. When he disappears around the corner, I pull out my phone and text Zach: Thx buddy

When I look up again, Cole is hurrying down the corridor toward Linden. Both of them have to shout over the alarm. I can barely hear them.

"Is there a fire?"

"Don't think so. Board says it's your office."

"There's no fire in my office!"

"Could be a short."

"Well, shut the damn thing off!"

Cole starts unscrewing the fire panel. I take a deep breath and hurry toward Linden's open office door.

Inside the office, coals glow in the fireplace. The walls are lined with floor-to-ceiling bookshelves and ancient artwork depicting all these war scenes.

The alarm cuts out, but the ringing still echoes in my ears. I know I don't have a lot of time before Linden returns, so I quickly look through his desk and the bookshelves, wishing I had more time because some of this stuff looks really interesting. But I better step it up. Linden's office is crammed. There are a thousand places to hide something.

Suddenly James's watch plays that melody again, but really faintly. I can barely hear it, so I'm not too worried. And I don't have time to mess with it, so I keep searching. I hurry to the other side of the office.

When I get to the credenza by the window, the melody stops. I keep moving and it starts to play again as I get near the dioramas. *Holy shit!* The watch is reacting to my location in the office!

Just to test it, I get up close to the dioramas: the Peloponnesian War, The Civil War, The Crimean War. As I get closer to a smaller diorama, the melody gets louder and faster. I worry that Linden will hear it. I peer into the glass box. It's The Academy campus. I recognize the buildings, the Chapel, the quad, all surrounded by a huge forest.

In a clearing in the center of the woods is this huge oak tree, and it looks so familiar. The watch is practically vibrating on my wrist now. I take a closer look. On the oak tree in the middle of the diorama is the three-pronged symbol! When I reach out to touch it, the melody becomes *one dinging note, over and over again.*

The oak tree is cold. Plastic. But it *moves.* It's not glued to the diorama's base! I lift it up. Underneath it is a black stone, almost pulsating. I grab it.

The watch goes quiet. I can hear Linden in the hallway.

"Do you have any idea how many priceless books I have in my office?" he asks.

Silence. I go as quietly as I can toward the door.

"This is ridiculous!" Linden continues. "That alarm hasn't gone off for –"

"-- since 1972," Cole interrupts. "I remember."

"Shut up. That wasn't *my* fault. Just fix it!"

I can hear Linden's footsteps in the corridor. He's coming back to the office.

There's no way I can make it out without being seen. I have no choice. I move backward into the shadows and crawl underneath one of the dioramas.

The second I do, Linden appears in the office, muttering to himself. I can see him down the last of his drink. He grabs his reading glasses off his desk and looks like he might go back to his book, but then he pauses. Something's wrong.

He knows I'm here. I can tell. My hands are shaking but I pull out my phone. It's only inches from my face, but I push a few buttons and then, a second later, I can hear the slight SSSSSSST of the sprinklers in the ceiling hissing and gurgling. A light mist falls.

Then huge drops of water start soaking the carpet.

"COLE!!" Linden storms out of the office, and I see my chance.

DR. BROWNING

The fire alarm actually made me jump. I know, without thinking too hard on the matter, who is responsible for it, who is always responsible for division and chaos.

I was preparing to leave for the evening but the clanging bell (and then its sudden silence) has piqued my interest, so I grab my pale, white stone and gaze into the painting. I brace myself.

The first image is Peter racing down a hallway. I can't quite see which hallway but I'm certain it's Peter. Where could he be going in such a rush?

I'm thinking on that when the canvas starts to blur again and my attention is dragged to Sophia's room. She wears her riding jacket and her hair is still up, but she's pacing, and trying not to cry. *What's going on?*

Her cell phone rings. She grabs it. "Daddy!"

I imagine Michael Prescott at the other end, settling into the leather seat of his private jet. Michael is a good-looking, prematurely grey, well-groomed man in his late fifties. Plenty of women find him irresistible. I don't.

"Sophia," he says, his voice strong and deep.

"Daddy! Oh my God ... I've been calling you! What happened? Why won't you –"

"What happened is that my daughter, in keeping with her self-centered nature, couldn't keep her mouth shut."

Sophia is stunned into silence.

"We had an agreement, Sophia," he continues. "I thought you were adult enough to honor it. My mistake."

"But –"

"-- and in the real world, when agreements are not honored, do you know what happens?"

"Daddy, I'm telling you! I didn't say anything to Anton, I swear it. It wasn't me –"

"DO YOU KNOW WHAT HAPPENS?!" The voice erupts from the phone and even I wince. Sophia holds the phone a few inches from her ear, her mouth hanging open in disbelief. "You were never the sharpest tool in the shed, Sophia, but I never realized you could be so stupid. Volsky is laughing at me. Why? Because my daughter exhibits the intelligence and discretion of a two dollar whore."

Sophia drops her phone onto the bed, her breaths coming short and fast now. "I can't believe it! You couldn't keep your mouth shut for seventy-two hours!" His voice drops in disgust. "Just like your mother ..."

Sophia stares at the phone as if it's a snake about to bite her. She backs away from it. But the voice continues. "... And if you think I'm going to spend my hard-earned money and *reward you* for being such a fucking idiot -"

I hear the rest of his diatribe before he hangs up in disgust, but by then Sophia has already fled the room and gone looking for her best friend.

"Chloe!? Oh my God, Chloe!" She's so distraught she doesn't notice that Chloe isn't even there. "Everything is ruined! Chloe?"

Sophia checks the bathroom. Chloe isn't there either. Realizing that she is utterly, terribly alone, she lifts her face to the mirror and takes in the sight of her own tear-streaked misery.

———— ∿ ————

Then poor, broken Sophia opens Chloe's medicine cabinet, and there, right in front, is a gleaming row of pill bottles. They look enormous, shiny, gorgeous. Sophia takes a deep breath and quickly shuts the cabinet door.

Good girl.

But as she walks through the dressing room between Chloe's room and hers, she spies the second row of pill bottles neatly arranged in front of the mirror. This time, she stops. She runs a finger over the row, like a child in a daze. Like she thinks there's special meaning in them being there, like that, when she needs them most.

My heart falls. There is nothing I can do.

Or is there? I can't very well sit here and stare at a painting! Not when she needs me! I know in a flash that I would rather defend my own actions than mourn the loss of another student. *A student I can save!*

I race from the room and down the corridor, running as fast as I can, hoping no one can see me. I push open the heavy door to the stairwell and hurry down the stairs, counting the seconds in my head, wondering if she has the lids off the bottles yet or –

I reach the bottom of the first floor expecting the dorm foyer. It's not there. Instead there's another brightly lit corridor that's familiar – it's definitely an Academy hallway – but *where am I?*

I can't think about that now. I run. I run as fast as I can but the hallway floor suddenly tilts to one side. I throw my arms out for balance and call out. "Sophia!"

I turn the corner and run to a door marked EXIT. I throw it open but it's not an exit at all. It's another stairwell! I turn around to retrace my steps but the hallway I expected isn't there – I nearly fall off a balcony ... *where there wasn't a balcony before!*

I turn. I'll run, I don't care which direction! But suddenly Cole appears a few feet away. He stands there, glaring at me. I'm about to run the other way when –

"Don't," he says with a sigh of exhaustion. "Dr. Browning, just stop."

"It's her *life!*"

"I know."

"*Please!*" I have to make him understand. "This isn't her fault, you have to see that. She wouldn't do that, ordinarily. Chloe left the pills there --!"

Cole shakes his head. "It doesn't matter now," he says sadly. "I told you. Everything comes at a price."

I'm shaking with frustration. I will not give up. I will not leave her in the clutches of self-loathing and evil. I *won't*. But what can I do? *Think.*

Suddenly I remember the sight of Peter racing down a hallway very much like this one, and I get an idea.

"We must let the students' true natures prevail," Cole is saying.

I nod as if paying homage to an ancient sage, but I'm thinking, *Must we?*

PETER

I make it out of the west building without anyone seeing me. One down and one to go. I pat my pocket where the stone is hidden.

I hurry to the other side of the building and slow down as I approach Dr. Browning's office. I didn't feel too bad sneaking into Linden's office, but I'm not feeling great about doing the same thing here. I really like Dr. Browning. I've already disappointed her once and I really don't think she is going to let me slide twice.

And I wouldn't blame her.

Her office is dark but the door is wide open. There's not even a lock on it. I walk in quickly. Suddenly a light goes on and my heart freezes. It takes me a moment to realize the light is motion-activated. *Thank God.*

I move around the office with my wrist out, hoping the watch will help me find her stone like it did in Professor Linden's office. It doesn't make a sound. I shake it a little. "Really...?"

I give up on the watch and start to go through her desk. There isn't much in it. Then I go through the bookshelf, the row of plants, and even the coffee table magazines. Nothing. Other than plants and paintings, there isn't a lot of stuff in her office. I should be able to find a *stone.*

After a beat, the office light goes off. Then something glows on the other half of the office, where all her painting supplies are. As soon as I move toward it the light turns back on but I can still make out the glow; it almost looks like a super-flat screen TV. But it's not. It's the huge painting Dr. Browning has been working on! Blurry images start to wave across it.

Suddenly the colors sharpen. Two people are standing in a hallway. It's Dr. Browning and that janitor, Cole. *They're just standing there.* I swear I could put my hand through the painting and touch them.

And then I can hear them talking.

"You won't argue the point, I assume, that Sophia needs my help right now. Right at this very minute," Dr. Browning is saying. She sounds like she's shouting, even though Cole is right there.

"I'm afraid it's not your place to decide, Dr. Browning. It's hers." That's the most I've ever heard Cole say. At first I wonder when this was recorded, but then it hits me. Sophia needs help? Now?

"I'm not insisting that *I* be the one to *help Sophia*, Mr. Cole."

"As I said," Cole says, "accounts are now reset. You forgot the rules governing the campus grounds. So I'm here to ensure that you obey the rules. You *will not* interfere with a student's free will again."

What the hell are they talking about?

"None of us makes choices in a vacuum, Cole! Or would you prefer to harness me and give Linden free rein?!"

Cole runs a hand over his face and I can tell he isn't happy. "What I'd *prefer* is a hot bath and a good book," he says. "Soon Sophia will make her choice. Then you'll be free to go."

"And if it's too late?" Browning asks, really loudly.

The image blurs and the sound drops out, then it focuses in an instant.

There's a girl in a room, leaning up against a wall. Mirrors everywhere. Is that a bathroom? I look closer. That's *Sophia!* She's looking at pictures on her phone. Tears run down her cheeks.

She sits down on the floor now, and I can see a row of pill bottles next to a glass of water. She drops the phone and grabs one of the pill bottles. She pours some pills into her hand.

"Sophia..?" She's wearing her riding clothes. The same clothes she had on tonight at dinner. *Holy shit, is this happening right now?!*

"Hey! Sophia!" I yell. She doesn't react. She can't hear me.

I watch, horrified, as Sophia lifts the glass to her lips. I run up to the painting and bang my fists against the frame. She flinches and turns her head toward me. *She heard that!*

But she can't see me. Is she looking into another mirror? She looks surprised and a little guilty. I stick my finger into the painting and try to write on it. Three big letters, in reverse order, so she can read them: W T F?

Sophia just stares. I can tell the image clears because her eyes focus, first on the letters and then on me. I see my reflection in the mirror behind her. Her eyes widen in surprise.

I write more. S T O P !! I see her read each letter. I grab the frame and scream as loud as I can, "Sophia? You hear me? *I'm not walking away?!*"

She looks at me and then stares at the pills in her hand. Suddenly she throws them on the floor, violently, like they burned holes in her flesh. They scatter and roll across the floor.

The image fades. The canvas goes dark, except for something white in its very center: a stone. It's like it's floating there. I pull it from the painting, and the second I do, the painting returns to its original form. Two dimensional swirls of color. Normal.

Ten minutes later, I'm climbing the stairs to my dorm. My phone dings. It's a text from Sophia.

Thank you

CHLOE

I like Richard's Ferrari, but it's hard to be low key in it, I'll just say *that*. Tonight I park it on a side street in Thomasville, a town forty miles from Providence. No one here works at The Academy, and no one is ever out this late.

I walk the two blocks to the bus station and find what I'm looking for: a cab parked across the street. There are only two cabs in town, but this is the only one that matters to me.

I open the door before the driver sees me coming and slide into the back seat. He was dozing. Now his eyes widen in recognition.

"Hi, David."

"*Victoria.*" He straightens in his seat, saying the name like I'm the last person in the world he wants to see. I would be insulted by his manner. But that would mean I care … and I don't.

He looks at me in the rearview mirror. "You should get another cab."

"There *are* no other cabs," I say, rolling my eyes. "So get this shit show moving."

He swallows hard. He doesn't even turn around to face me. "You're not hearing me. I'm not doing that again."

Yeah, sure. I crumple up a couple hundred-dollar bills and toss them at him. They bounce off his face and into his lap. He looks at them and sighs.

"Just drive. *David.*"

He starts the engine.

In the backseat, I hunch over a little to pull off my blouse and undo my bra. I catch David stealing glances in the rear view mirror.

Our eyes meet. Each time, David looks away but he hesitates a little before he does. The cab zooms along the highway; I don't have much time. I put on the gold sequined tube top and black leather mini skirt. Then I lace up my thigh high black boots. Looking into my compact, I trace my lips in liner and then fill them in with shiny, pink lipstick. I do it super slowly.

"Why don't you let me take you home?" David asks.

I smile at him lewdly and rub my lips together.

"I meant *your* home," he says with a sigh. "Wherever it is you belong…?"

I slip a jet black wig over my head without answering. After tucking in a few blond strands, I fan the bangs across my forehead to make my kohl-rimmed eyes pop.

We're almost there. I can see the glow of the fluorescent lights. Excitement builds in the pit of my stomach.

David turns the cab into a lighted area and parks. He turns to me. "This is … I don't hardly know you, but you gotta listen to me. This is *wrong*."

"You're right." I lick my lips. "You don't know me."

David un-crumples the $100 bills and holds them over the back seat. "Come on, whatever your name is. I'll take you back. No charge."

I laugh. He's practically pleading with me. Men.

"Keep the meter running!" I say with a smile and climb out of the cab.

It feels good: the boots, the skirt, the wig. The cool night air on my thighs. My sticky wet lips. God, I love it! The adrenaline rushes through my blood; I can practically feel it, like liquid gold, pushing me higher. *I'm finally free!*

And this is the closest to happy I can be.

As I pass a parked car, I catch my reflection in one of its windows.

The image twists and distorts, reflecting the neon sign illuminating the parking lot: *Empire Truck Stop*

CHAPTER FIFTEEN

DR. BROWNING

I look up at the night sky on my way to the Chapel. The stars are spread like diamonds against black velvet. I imagine what I can't see: galaxies, made up of millions of stars, shimmering in a sea of black calm. It might be too much for the human brain, which isn't hardwired to consider the endlessness of space and understand a universe of infinite possibility. But it still fills me with awe, and I draw strength from it.

I have been called to a meeting, and I know I'll need that strength.

Inside the Chapel, Professor Linden lounges in a pew, gazing at the Chapel's decorations with obvious contempt. "You heard about the break in, I assume?" he asks without turning.

"I did. Was anything taken?"

"Indeed. The same thing that was stolen from *your* office, my dear

Charlotte. You know by whom. And you know why."

Professor Linden turns to glare at me as if I had something to do with it.

"We have to come to some kind of understanding, and *soon*," he says.

"Yes, we do," I agree, noting this is the first time in over a century he has addressed me by my first name.

"Then we agree. We both need that manuscript. Unless you wish to be exposed to the whole world..?"

He knows I would rather not operate in the shadows the way he does, but I do what I have been instructed to do. Still, I frown at the implication.

"Me either," he snorts, assuming by my silence that I agree.

"Afraid of what might happen if people knew you were tied to every misery from the Potato Famine to the Ebola breakout?" I ask.

"Yes. And if they discovered you couldn't stop any of it."

I flash back to both of those failures, and others. So many lives lost by not stopping Linden's manipulations in time!

"You prey on human weakness and consider the resulting chaos an accomplishment!" I snap at him.

"And you consider human despair your greatest opportunity!"

"I don't exploit personal tragedies to advance my own agenda," I say with a groan. "I simply help those in need. I have nothing to apologize for!"

"Of course not! Except that you benefit so profoundly from your own benevolence," he sneers, peering at me with red-rimmed eyes. "At least I am honest enough to never hide my true intentions. James could have told you that."

I look away. He is a lizard of a man, and deserves only to crawl back to the mud and muck where he came from.

"It will be a magnificent fire, Professor Linden." I say.

He frowns, confused.

"The one that destroys you," I tell him. "And I will not turn my back or shield my eyes. I will watch you burn."

My words still hang in the air when it hits us: a thunderous explosion followed by a shock wave that shakes The Academy to its core. The entire chapel vibrates and a second later I can hear the cacophony of car alarms from the student parking lot. Several of the candle stands near the altar fall over.

It takes us a moment to get our bearings. We rush out to make sure the campus hasn't sustained any visible damage. From the Chapel steps, everything seems to be in perfect order.

Professor Linden and I realize it at the same moment. We look up into the heavens, where the planets roll gently in the blackness, floating closer to each other. Suddenly he points and I can barely make it out.

The planets now form a perfect line.

Only the most dedicated astronomers and those in the know would see this line of planets shift into the three-pronged symbol that decorates so much of our campus. Fewer still would understand its larger meaning.

The time has come. We are entering a period in which real change can occur. Both Professor Linden and I know exactly what this means. We just didn't know exactly when it would occur.

"So there it is!" says Professor Linden, a touch breathlessly. "The signal we knew was coming." He turns to me, obviously concerned. "And Peter has rendered us *helpless*! Without those stones, we are as blind as our students."

So that's why he's so anxious.

"I rely on faith," I tell him. "Not stones."

"Faith is delusion. The *reality* is this: without those stones we stand no chance at finding the Manuscript. And if we don't get it *and James* soon, we lose everything –"

"-- you want me to place a manuscript *above the life of a child?*"

Somewhere far away, a bird chirps, breaking the silence. It's nearly dawn. The campus is awakening. In the Chapel garden, flower petals float to the ground. Beetles crawl over the white blossoms.

Linden pulls up the collar of his jacket. "The Tree will consume whomever it consumes, Charlotte," he says, before walking away. "But it must be fed."

PETER

Sophia!!

My eyes snap open. It was just another nightmare. I couldn't stop her this time. I watched her take the pills as I bashed the painting with my fists and yelled for her to stop. It's been so long since I have felt that helpless.

It's been two days since that night in Dr. Browning's office and I can't stop thinking about Sophia. Now I get why she puts on that front, like she doesn't care about anything. It's this place. It changes people. To survive here, you have to become someone else, someone who can never be seen as weak. I wonder what Sophia was like before all this, before The Academy.

It's not like I forgot what she said at the stables. I know she half expected me to walk away that night. But I couldn't. I just couldn't let her take those pills and do nothing. I've been lying in bed for hours, drifting in and out of sleep, thinking about how hard it must have been for her to get by all these years, with no help from anyone, never knowing who to trust. I look at my phone again to see the "Thank you" text. Just seeing it makes me feel–

BOOM!!

What the hell?! My entire room shakes like it's in a paint mixer. Then everything quiets except for the car alarms in the student parking lot. I look out my window, expecting to see a huge bomb crater in the quad. But there's nothing like that.

The sky catches my attention. It's alive with colors. I know what they are right away: the East Coast Northern Lights. I bet they have something to do with that big explosion, or whatever it was.

I turn on the TV and get on the Beast to see if there's any info. I can't find anything, so I check out the Tunnel. There's nothing about an explosion yet, but the main headline is, "Fall from Grace: Daddy Prescott's last-minute pullout from Sophia's Pet Project."

So that's why she went off the rails.

I text Sophia, *You alright?*

She texts me back immediately. *Fine! Wow that was loud*

I wish she'd write more but she doesn't.

As I'm brushing my teeth, I hear the news anchor on TV. "*... take you to Japan, where an inexplicable storm surge threatened the island of Hakkaido before subsiding. At the same time, miles away in Tanzania, Africa, eyewitnesses report an entire lake rising into the air in broad daylight and then falling again.*"

Too bad they don't have footage of *that*.

"*In what might be a related event,*" he goes on, "*sources say that at approximately 3:57 this morning, the entire eastern seaboard of the United States suffered an electrical blackout.*"

I grab my backpack, which was hanging on the door connecting my room to Charley's. I knock on it. "Charley?"

I want to tell him that I got the stones, and ask him what I have to do next.

"Power has since been restored."

There's no answer. I open the connecting door. The room is empty, bed made. Charley never made it back last night. Maybe he stayed late at the event?

"It's still unknown, whether that blackout is to blame for the mysterious disappearance of three aircraft in the New England area ..."

———

Dr. Browning steps up to the podium to address the student body, all assembled as requested by text early this morning. She glances at me before she starts.

"Good morning. Please settle down."

Everyone goes quiet. I'm trying not to look as worried as I feel. *What if someone saw me last night?*

"I begin by assuring you that last night's fire alarm was set off in error. There was no fire," she continues.

I look straight at her, poker faced, as relief floods my whole body. Looks like I won't get busted. I have to remind myself not to smile. *I did it.*

"I take this opportunity to remind all of you that if you park for any reason in the clearly marked fire lane, your car will not be towed. It will be crushed into scrap metal and you will not be allowed another until the new year."

The students groan. Dr. Browning waits for them to quiet. "In more distressing news, I've learned that the Mercer family helicopter went missing early this morning. There is no further information available yet." Her gaze travels over the now solemn group of students. "Please say a prayer for Charley and his family," she says, forcing an optimistic tone. "Let's hope for the best."

My mind races, and the lightness I felt seconds ago vanishes. *Charley's gone missing? I just talked with him!* Everyone else is whispering, and Sophia catches my eye. A second later, I get a text from her. *Wait for me outside.* I nod.

"I'm sure most of you felt or heard the planetary alignment early this morning," Dr. Browning is saying, and I make myself concentrate. "Our location allows us a rare view into the East Coast Northern Lights. It's just a reflection of a rare planetary alignment. Happens every decade or so. School tradition dictates that we host a special dance to mark the occasion – "

The students applaud and whistle.

" – so please sign in to Bradley Hall *in costume* no later than 7:30 Friday evening. The theme will reflect The Academy's founding fathers. That will be all."

The students leave the hall in groups and I hear bits of conversation as I pass. Some are worried about Charley. Some are excited about the dance. A lot laugh about what they did when they heard that loud bang early this morning.

And every so often, I'll hear something about a "stone arch." It's talked about in hushed whispers. After hearing it three or four times, I would usually ask about it because obviously it's important.

But at this point, I can't make myself care. I've got too many other things to worry about. Like what happened to Charley? And what do I do with the stones? And how am I going to get James out of the tree ... and out of my head?

I finally see Sophia half hiding in a bay window, waiting for all the others to pass. Some guys pass her and start laughing, and it's not hard to figure out why. The humiliation is all over her face. I sit down next to her as the last of the students walk out of the assembly.

"I'm sorry about Anton," I say.

She nods and smiles, but it's a sad, tired smile. "Can't blame a snake for acting like a snake, right? Like my dad said, I should have known better."

She stares out the bay window. Obviously I'm not the only one with a full plate right now.

"I hope Charley is alright," I say.

She smiles a little. "I wouldn't worry too much, Peter. Seriously, he's done it before. He disappears, everyone freaks out, and then he shows up a week later with a great story."

"You think he faked it? How? I even heard something about it on the news. And Dr. Browning said ... "

"Last time his yacht disappeared during that volcanic eruption in Iceland."

I nod. Nothing about this place surprises me anymore and I like Charley. Hell, I *need* Charley. I hope he's okay. Who else can tell me how to find that tree?

Sophia stares out the window. "I totally understand how he feels. Sometimes I just want to disappear, too."

"Like last night?" I ask, taking a chance.

She turns and her eyes search my face. I don't know what she's looking for, or what she's afraid of finding, but she relaxes when she sees I'm not making fun of her, and nods.

"I wanted to say thank you for that," she says. "For not walking away." She shakes her head. "Especially after what I said at the stables."

"No worries," I say. "I'm just glad you're okay." I want to say something else, the right thing to make her feel better, but I can't think what that might be, so I just end up saying, "If you ever need someone to talk to…"

"I'm fine. But thanks," she says. "It's just…"

She stares out the window again, looking completely untouchable. Like whatever is going on inside in her life is too much for anyone to handle, and she's totally on her own.

I know the feeling. I want her to know she isn't alone.

"Last year, I totaled my bike," I tell her. "My back tire blew out in a turn. Had a really bad head injury, a punctured lung, broken pelvis. I was in a coma for three weeks. They said I died and came back."

Sophia's eyes widen and I shrug.

"All I know is that I didn't think anything could hurt that much. I was so tired, I just wanted to sleep and not wake up. I never thought I would ever recover. I was so weak. Eventually, I figured that the only way I was going to make it was to pretend to be strong."

I nudge Sophia a little with my shoulder.

"I think that's all it is, really. You *pretend* to be strong. Every day it gets a little easier and then eventually … you *are*."

Sophia just stares at me a moment. "My dad pulled out of my charity. You probably know already. Everybody does." She looks down. "Building that charity was the first thing I've ever done in the real world that meant something. I was finally good at something."

I want her to keep talking, so I just nod.

"After I talked with him, I felt like such a failure, a total joke. Like everyone would be happier if I was just *gone*. If it wasn't for you, I would've -" her voice begins to shake. "-- I would've made the biggest mistake of my life."

"You're *not* a failure."

"Tell that to my father."

"Your goal was to help those people in the village, right? And you *did*! Who cares who gave them the money? They got it, thanks to you, and now they'll have what they need. Their lives are better because of you."

We sit there quietly for a while.

"I never really looked at it that way," she finally says. "My father ..." she stops. "Everything got stacked up on me and I just wanted to escape, get smaller and smaller and just disappear for a while." She takes a deep breath. "The pills just seemed ..."

"Sophia, look at what you've already been through, what you've already done. I mean, everyone else I've met here is only interested in themselves, what *they* want, what *they* need. You're the only one here who even thinks of other people."

She looks down for a moment. I wonder if I went too far.

"You know, everyone at The Academy only knows me as Michael Prescott's daughter," she says.

"Who?" I ask, and she laughs.

"I'm serious. You talk to me like I'm my own person." She takes a deep breath and looks at me. "I don't think there are words for that, really. To thank you for seeing the real me, or at least the person I want to be."

"You don't have to pretend to be strong, like I did," I say. "You already are."

We stand there smiling at each other for a beat. She looks so vulnerable, and I know there's a connection here. One I haven't felt before. She doesn't seem in a hurry to run off, so maybe she's feeling it, too.

Then, in the distance, a bell rings.

Sophia breaks the silence with a sad shrug. "Back to reality."

CHLOE

I see Peter and Sophia sitting in the bay window. *How does she do it? Was she born with this weird super-power to bend men's brains?* She really has that "rescue me!" bit down. And by the looks of it, it's working yet again.

I'll just go break up their little tête–à–tête, Nothing good can come of it and besides, Peter needs to be reminded that he didn't see me last night. I admit I came home a little disappointed, mostly because Sophia was there in bed, sleeping, instead of off in Overdose Paradise.

I get up but suddenly Dr. Browning steps in front of me, blocking my path.

"Chloe," she says to me, as if we share a secret. "You must be pleased that Sophia sustained such a major blow last night without relapsing."

Yeah, I'm thrilled. I quickly rearrange my features into what I hope is the picture of innocence. "Of course I am! She's my inspiration."

Dr. Browning looks at me coolly, adding things up in that little saintly brain of hers. "I'm sure. Still, I can't help but wonder what kind of person treats a friend with such reckless cruelty?

What the hell is she implying?

"Perhaps someone who treats *herself* with such reckless cruelty?" asks Dr. Browning, looking sadly off into the distance. My mind is going a million miles an hour, trying to figure out what she knows. The pills? The cab ride? The truck stop?

She leans in closer and I fight the urge to step back. "The real question of course is why?" She looks at me carefully, like she's checking out my makeup.

"I'm worried about you, Chloe. I see less and less light in you."

I raise my eyebrows. I don't even know what that means.

Then she almost whispers. "When you look in the mirror, *do you like what you see?*"

That floors me. I toy with several different very clever and inappropriate responses, including a few about liking the paycheck I earned for last year's Vogue cover. But by the time I've sorted through them all, Dr. Browning has walked away. *Nice.*

I'm still standing there, fuming, when Professor Linden passes.

"Hello, Chloe!" he says brightly. "You look quite radiant this morning."

There's no way in hell I'm going to be trapped into a conversation with him, given what just happened. So I give him a quick wave and hurry to the restroom. I need some alone time.

Inside the restroom, I check my cuticles and wash my hands. I spend a few seconds oiling them up, remembering mother's lecture on dry cuticles and wishing I didn't. What did Dr. Browning *mean* by that? Does she know something or was she just prying? I think of everything I've done in the past few days and assure myself that I have total deniability! It's not like I *gave* Sophia the pills.

I finish oiling up my hands and lean into the mirror above the sink to check my lipstick. I jump back, horrified.

I can't see my face.

I look back in the mirror. I can see my hands. My neck, my dress. I can even see my hair. But right there, where my face should be ...

... there's nothing. Nothing but a gaping hole. No nose, no eyes, no mouth. Just a brownish smear, like a finger painting. I touch the mirror. I touch my face. Maybe it's a flashback from last night at the truck stop? There's pretty wicked stuff there.

But everything feels normal. *I just can't see my face.* The new *face* of Ford! I want to scream.

Oh. My. God. I move my head. My image moves. *What happened? Who did this? WHERE DID I GO?* I can feel the tears drip down my face. I can even wipe them away; they're real tears! But I keep searching the mirror for my face, for me, and it's not there. I'm not there.

Five minutes later and I have calmed down a little. For once, I'm a teeny bit grateful for Richard's predictability. He is practicing his idiotic martial arts moves in the same grassy space he always practices in this time of day.

I wobble up to him, barely noticing that my new MiuMiu boots are sinking into the grass. I have to know if it's just me – or is this how everyone sees me? And *why?* Still, I can't let him know how freaked out I am because the last thing I need is another bloody lecture on the dangers of excessive drug use.

I stand there, waiting, forever. For, like, thirty seconds. Richard continues to play Zen master, hacking at the air, refusing to break his concentration.

"I need to talk to you!" I shout at him. "*Now!*"

He won't turn to look at me and instead does a few more stupid moves.

"So talk." He kicks out at the air in front of him.

"Richard!" I say, with exaggerated patience. I need his *attention*. "Do you notice anything different about me?"

Richard rolls his eyes. "Narcissist, table for one?"

"*Richard!*"

He finally looks at me, really quickly, and then scans my outfit. He shrugs. "New lip gloss?"

Then he starts his maneuvers in the other direction, turning his back. He doesn't see me exhale in grateful relief. So I have a face.

I just can't see it. *Why?* I remember what Dr. Browning said. Does she have something to do with this?

"Richard? Do you think I'm cruel? Be honest."

"Cruel as in vicious and unfeeling? Yes. Next?"

My eyes narrow. *Very funny.* "I'm serious."

"So am I. You haven't helped another human being, or done something kind, or thought about someone else's good, since you were about, oh, six."

"That's not true!"

"It's the truth, the whole truth and nothing but the truth, so help me –"

"Stop being such an ass!"

Richard drops his arms and turns to me. "Chlo," he says, thinking I'm ripe for a lecture after all, "you spend all your time looking in the mirror, but what do you really see?"

Not this insufferable bullshit again. "What are you talking about? Do you know something about this?" I ask, tapping my face (gently).

"There's only so much I can do for you, Chloe. You've got to figure out that what you look like isn't the most important thing about you."

Like I believe *that.*

"Is this just another jealous tirade of yours?" I ask. "Because I don't need it."

"What *do* you need, Chloe? More drugs? More nights at the truck stop?" He comes at me now, wiping the sweat off his forehead with his arm. I want to push him away but I'm frozen. *How the fuck does he know?*

"Has any of that made you happy?" he asks, being a total bully, and really mean. "Made you better? Made you whole?"

I finally find my feet and storm off. I can hear him calling after me. "Don't you even *want* to be better than that?"

CHAPTER SIXTEEN

CHLOE

I want to die.

There's no reason to carry on. There's no reason to get out of bed, even. I've made a mental list of people I'm going to give my things to (dresses, some jewelry). I've even begun to feel a little more kindly toward Richard, because he'll probably be the only one crying at my funeral.

He came to see me last night, all worried, and I let him feel my forehead to see if I had a fever (I don't, *duh*). He said I looked pale.

Of course I look pale. I'm not wearing any bronzer because *I can't see my bloody face!*

Why? Why *me?* If Richard couldn't see his own face, if *Richard* couldn't be sure he existed, he would know how this hurts. Of course, he doesn't have that great a face, to be brutally honest. But mine is everything to me! This face is *who I am*. People see me and stare. They whisper my name. Men pause in admiration. Women look at me sideways, all jealous and mean! I love it! All my life, people's eyes used to linger on my face, taking it all in.

The truth is I knew from the age of six that beauty is the most powerful thing in the world. And I've got it.

Or at least I *had* it. People aren't looking at me the way they used to. Now they glance at me, in like half a second, and then move on. I'm invisible. No one says anything but I know something's missing. What did I do to deserve this? There's nothing – *nothing* – in this world that can make this bearable. First James and now this. It's no exaggeration to say I've lost everything that matters to me.

I might as well be dead.

I stop sobbing long enough to turn over. I didn't think I had any more tears left, but I guess I do. I'm not even mad anymore at Richard for emptying my entire medicine cabinet and basically *stealing* my collection of pharmaceutical friends. Who cares? I'll just lie here and stop breathing. People die from broken hearts all the time.

Then I hear a click. A lamp goes on in the next room; Sophia moves about the dressing room, taking off her shoes and hanging up clothes. I'm not dead yet; I still have the strength to hate her, after what she did to James and me.

She pushes open the door to my room and calls out softly, "Chloe?"

"Go away," I say.

She doesn't because she is determined to kick me when I'm down. That's the *real* Sophia – she hates me, too. I'm half tempted to get up and kick *her*, but then I remember: I don't exist anymore.

Sophia sits down on my bed and starts stroking my hair.

"You're not really sick, are you?" she asks.

My impulse is to mock her for being so freaking observant, but I don't. I just lie there. Pretending I have a face, an identity. Pretending I'm still worth something.

"Your just really sad, aren't you?" Sophia asks.

I want to snort in a don't-be-ridiculous way but instead, I just shake my head. Why is she even here? And why is she being so nice? No one's watching. It's not like she's going to get anywhere pretending she cares about me. As if I'd fall for *that* anyway.

"I don't know why you feel this way," Sophia is saying softly, "and you don't have to tell me. But I've been there, Chloe. I know how pointless everything seems."

You have to hand it to her. She's doing a pretty good job pretending to care if I live or die. She keeps stroking my hair the way a really great nanny would, and it feels nice, actually. Or maybe this is just how things seem when you're about to die. I almost smile. Then I think that this is probably the hand she touched James with, and I flinch. She pulls away.

"I know you don't believe me, Chloe, but this is going to pass. Whatever it is. It feels really bad now, but it will get better. I promise. If you can just hold out."

She takes my hand through my duvet, and I let her. I even grip her fingers with mine a little because, I don't know. I don't believe her, but …

"It'll pass, Chloe. You'll feel better soon." Then she leans down in whispers in my ear, "I love you."

I start to cry again. I don't know why, maybe because I'm so surprised. Tears just run down the side of my face. She actually sounded like she meant that and maybe, for half a second, I almost believed her. Then my muscles relax, and this warmth rushes over me, and I close my eyes.

I figured Sophia would see that I'm sleeping, or trying to, and leave. But she doesn't. She sits on the bed, pulling my blankets up, making sure my pillows are all around me, patting my arms as if she's comforting a child. She does this forever, and then she goes back to holding my hand. And I keep wondering *why*.

I guess I fell asleep pretty fast. I never saw her leave. When I get up just before dawn to use the bathroom, I stop and stare. There's Sophia, wrapped in her bathrobe, asleep at the foot of my bed. She's curled up like a kitten, her head on one of the lounge cushions.

She stayed with me all night. I don't think anyone has done that for me, ever.

PETER

It's morning but I'm exhausted already. I was up all night trying to figure out what to do next and leaving messages for Charley.

Now I'm FaceTiming with Zach, but I have to be careful what I tell him. The last thing I want is for him to end up in a wheelchair like Charley. I point at the closet door.

"See James's name?" I ask. "It showed up a couple of days ago and now it's fading."

I turn back to the computer monitor to see if Zach is paying attention. His FaceTime image squints.

"Yeah, dude, I think I can see it," he answers.

I had to show Zach the name before it disappeared completely.

I am hoping he sees something I don't and he agrees: I'm not crazy. So *that's* a relief.

When I trace James's name so he can see it better, I snag my finger on the edge of one of the letters.

"Ow!" A bead of blood oozes from my finger. "What I don't get is what these symbols mean," I tell him, wiping my finger on the corner of the door. I look at the camera, and turn my back to the closet to say. "And Charley isn't here to tell me."

Zach doesn't say anything. His eyes open wide. He's looking behind me, stunned.

I turn around to see the thin red line of blood moving! Gaining speed, it starts zooming across the surface of the closet door from one engraved symbol to another, filling them, encircling them. Soon the movement is so fast, it's a total blur. The entire door shimmers. I stare, speechless, as one set of numbers repeats over and over on the door.

42. 54. 72. And 61.

"What did you do?" Zach stammers.

I look down at my finger. Then I stare at the door again, where James's name seems to darken. I follow the numbers that keep lighting up. They keep repeating a certain sequence, and I remember it: it's the same sequence that unlocked James's laptop! I grab a pen and start to copy the sequence in the order they light up.

"It's a message!" I say.

"From who? And what the hell does it say?"

I stop. I don't know yet. But I know where I should look. Zach stares at the closet door. For the first time in Zach's life, he's speechless. But I don't have time to tell him what I'm about to do.

"Gotta go! Call you later!" I say and close the screen.

I race across campus to the library and barrel through the door. I elbow past some of the other students waiting for Mrs. McCarthy and slap the wrinkled page on the counter in front of her.

"Peter. The line is –" She stops as she looks at the numbers on the page and I realize some of my blood got on it because I was in such a hurry. Then she looks up at my face and shakes her head.

I can hear the students in line behind me whispering. I must look manic. I try to pull it together a little. I run my hands through my hair, which doesn't help much.

Mrs. McCarthy hasn't said a word. *Come on.*

"I think they're some type of Masonic code," I tell her. "I need to see the books James Harken researched before he disappeared."

Mrs. McCarthy's expression darkens. She folds the paper over so no one can see the numbers on them and shoves them back across the counter at me.

I'm about to beg her to help me when she gestures to another librarian to take over for her. Then she waves for me to follow her past the stacks.

The stacks are twelve-foot high shelves of books and boxes. Each shelf, each box is dated. Some look really old. We walk toward the back of the library to a door without a sign on it or anything. Hanging on the wall are old framed blueprints of campus buildings and some old county maps. She presses a few buttons on a keypad and the door clicks open.

The door leads to a room that's a little darker, and noticeably cool. It's mostly shelving but there are a few desks with low-wattage LED lamps against one wall. I can feel my heart beat faster.

"Part of The Academy's archives are kept here to ensure their preservation," she says, giving me a look. "I shouldn't have to lecture a librarian's son on the importance of caring properly for museum quality books, especially hand-written ones that predate the printing press."

She unlocks another glass case. Inside are old bound books. She lifts the lid and the seal parts, making a sucking sound like a refrigerator.

"We control the temperature and humidity at all times," she says. "These books are never to leave this room for any reason and must always be handled with gloves."

The ancient leather bindings of these rare and valuable documents look out of place in such a modern room.

Mrs. McCarthy looks at me sternly. "I'm not sure I know exactly what you're looking for," she said.

I shrug weakly. "Neither do I."

She hands me a pair of thin white cotton gloves, and puts on a pair herself. Then she removes several volumes from the case and nods at a desk.

"You may sit here to examine the books. But student access to this section of the archives is limited to one hour per month."

She looks at me sternly, as if waiting for me to protest. I don't.

"James was looking for Masonic symbols and codes on campus," she says, pulling books from various shelves. "The following volumes are a good place to start: Astrology. Templar Knights. Bloodlines. Commencement Rituals." She picks another book from a different section. "This was the last book that James was researching."

She hands me the book. It's called *Masonic Symbols: Myths and Legends*. Then she points in different directions all over the room.

"Constitutional Law of the Original Colonies here. Scripture and Theology over there. Astronomy. Agrarian Records dating to 1680. The rest of the records you should be able to find on your own."

"Thank you." I nod, a bit dazed.

She peels off her gloves and pushes her glasses back onto her nose. "And the filing system goes by Section, Shelf and Book number. This is as much time and help as I can give you, Peter. Good luck. You have fifty five minutes left."

She pauses when she gets to the door, like she has something to say. I wait.

"Peter," she finally says in a quiet voice. "Think beyond the box." She pulls the door shut.

Beyond the box? What the hell does that mean? I sigh. Whatever. I now have less than fifty five minutes left.

I go through the books as fast as I can, making small notes on the paper with the numbers on it. I don't find anything useful and I save the Masonic Symbols book for last. Finally, I think, I've hit pay dirt. Its pages are old vellum, yellow with age. I remember James scanning pages that look like this in the video! I bet the scans are on the hard drive!

I flip through book, figuring maybe he left something in it for me. But there are no loose pages. I start to dig.

I first go to pages 42-54-72 and 61, but they have headings like "All-Seeing Eye" and "Eagle, Double-Headed" and nothing there looks familiar or useful.

So what do those numbers that lit up mean?

I find the Table of Contents and stop at "Tree of Souls pg. 135."

The Tree of Souls

(Souls, Tree of): A mystical oak revered as a symbol of strength, integrity and balance between the forces of Dark and Light.

- *Location : Unknown*
- *History: Said to be the product of a compromise between those from above and those from below. Created by combining a small drop of opposing life forces.*
- *Purpose: To mark the place where total neutrality is maintained in the battle for human providence. The Tree of Souls is breached by human souls bearing stones (see Stones, Light and Dark). One myth states that the souls it consumes are gone forever, however eyewitness accounts vary. Scholars believe that the Tree's power can be unlocked by a set of specific and miraculous stones, rarely seen together, possible two (2) or three (3) of differing weights and colors. These stones, it is said, can be used to access, communicate with and possibly free still-functioning souls inside the Tree during rare incidents of planetary alignment (See Planetary Alignment) by*

I start to turn the page, trying not to freak out. Possibly free still-functioning souls?! During the Planetary Alignment?! Like … *tonight?*

I flip the page, desperate for more information, but the next page starts with the definition of "Triumvirates." What happened to the rest of the "Tree of Souls" entry?

I open the book wider. The next few pages are missing. Someone carefully cut them out! I don't know why, but I can guess who.

I pull out my phone and hit speed dial. I leave him a voicemail.

"Zach? I need that hard drive I gave you. Now."

I check the clock on the wall. Twenty two minutes left.

The stones are going to be useless if I can't find the Tree. I was hoping the books would tell me. Am I going to be wandering around that forest all night, totally clueless?

I look at the numbers on the paper again. Now it has three-pronged symbols all over it; I drew them on there without even realizing it. I stare at the numbers and symbols. I have the stones. And the planets are aligned, so I have to get into that forest *tonight*. But how do I find the Tree? What am I missing?

I sigh. I've got a bunch of books spread out on the desk. What a mess. I figure I better start putting this stuff away before Mrs. Mc-Carthy comes in here and blows a gasket.

I put the oldest books back in the case, and then replace the others on the shelves. I squint at the little placards set above the shelving and notice that the upper row of shelves has a completely different numbering system. Instead of starting at 1, it starts at 4 ... and goes to 72.

I freeze for a second. 4 to 72!

There's gotta be a thousand volumes in that upper shelving! I know I don't have time to go through all of them, but maybe the numbers are actually call numbers. I find Shelf 42, Section 547 Book 261. Nope. There are only 300 sections.

Desperate, I start writing the sequence of numbers over and over on the paper, always in the same order but with a different starting point. 42- 54- 72 and 61 ... 54- 72- 61 and 42 ... 42547261 ...

54726142 …72614254 … None of them leads me anywhere.

I put them back in their original order … 42-54-72-61. Then I write them down backwards … 61-72- 54-42. *Think!*

61 minus 72 is *-11*. 72 minus 54 is *18*. And 54 minus 42 is *12*.

Maybe the book I need has the number 11.18.12.

Section 11. Shelf 18. Book 12.

I get on the ladder to find the book. It's this huge, old volume with a weakened binding that's about to fall apart. The title is written on the spine in ancient lettering, and it's really faded. I pull it off the shelf and stare at the cover: "The Life of St. Norbertus, founder of the Premonstratensians."

This isn't it. This can't be it. I want to punch something.

Instead, I just sit there on the ladder. Five minutes left. I have to accept the fact that I couldn't do it – I couldn't figure out whatever it is James wanted me know. And if I don't figure this out by tonight, James is stuck in that tree and in my head until the next alignment! In ten years!

I failed. I realize the door will open any minute and Mrs. McCarthy will ask me to leave.

So much for thinking outside the box. Wait, she said "*beyond the box.*" Why did she say it that way? There are no boxes in this room. That was the first thing I looked for when she left. *Think.*

I look around the room. This room, *this room,* is basically one big box. Maybe she was talking about the room and *if I'm thinking beyond it,* then I have to imagine something … just outside its borders.

The maps on the outside walls.

Holy shit. The maps! I yank off the gloves and drop them on the desk. When I pull open the door, I'm surprised at how heavy it is.

And when it clicks shut behind me, I realize I won't be able to get it open again anytime soon. I better be right.

I hurry past the blueprints on the wall and I see what I'm looking for: a map of the entire County. I left my papers inside, but I know the numbers by heart: 42. 54. 72. 61

I trace the latitude line to 42.54. Then I mark at the longitude line -72.61 with my other finger and my heart stops. 42.54 by -72.61 is located directly in the middle of the forest, about five hundred yards northwest of The Academy gates and three hundred yards inside the forest.

That's where the Tree of Souls is.

I can't believe it. They were longitude and latitude numbers. And I had them the whole time.

I take a quick picture of the map with my phone and race out of the library. I have to get that zip drive from Zach *today* and find out how to free James.

I'm halfway to the dorm when I see my mom, her purse unzipped and flapping, her hair coming out of its ponytail. What is she doing here? A second later, she sees me and hurries toward me.

"Peter! Peter!"

"Mom? What's the matter?"

She looks like she is having another one of her panic attacks. Everything I was just thinking about flies out of my head.

"Are you okay?"

She hugs me really hard. "I -- oh my God. We're going home. *Now*."

She pulls me by the arm toward the parking lot. Practically dragging me. Some students stop talking to watch.

I can't leave now!

"Would you stop for a second and tell me what's going on?" I pull my arm back.

She catches her breath and stares at me. "A month ago, you couldn't wait to get out of here."

"Yeah, well, a lot has happened," I say. "Ma, you can't just yank me around. I'm not some *kid*."

She takes a long look at me and hugs me again, as if she hasn't seen me in years. I put my arms around her, and it feels good. I hold her tighter. I can feel her shoulder blades; she has lost a lot of weight.

I want to tell her that I'm doing okay. That she's probably breaking a hundred rules just being there. And that I don't want her mixed up in whatever mess I'm in.

"Mom, listen. I can't talk now. Let me walk you back to your car, okay?

"Peter – "

"– Because there's something I've got to do. Something important."

"You're not safe here anymore."

Safe? "What?!"

"There are some things I didn't tell you about The Academy. Okay? Just trust – "

"Wait, what are you talking about?" I ask.

"After your accident – remember those visions you kept having? All those questions you asked?" she sighs, and suddenly she looks so tired. "I couldn't answer them! I didn't know what to do. I thought you'd be safer at The Academy! I was wrong, Petey – "

"All this time, you knew the truth about The Academy *and you dumped me here anyway?*"

"I knew just enough to be afraid," she says, pleading with her eyes. "I couldn't protect you anymore."

I look away. I've probably got a thousand things processing at once, everything I've seen, everything that's gone down here. All this time *she knew what I was going through?*

She sees the look on my face. I don't want to be here now, having this conversation. I want to get as far away from her as possible. I don't know when I'll want to see her again, since she has basically lied to me since day one.

"Why *now?*" I ask, but I don't even know if I can accept her answer, whatever it is.

She holds out a photo, and I make myself look at it. It's a picture of her as a teenager, standing next to a guy that kinda looks like me. Behind them is a huge arch with a banner on it, and on the banner is "Alignment Dance 1998".

I stare at it. There, in the corner of the banner, is the three-pronged symbol connecting a row of planets.

"Because I know that when the planets align, terrible things happen," my mom says, her voice shaking. "And this morning, I heard the ...."

"What kind of terrible things?" I ask.

"People disappear and never come back."

My mind reels.

"Seventeen years ago, the night of the Alignment Dance here at The Academy," she says, swallowing tears, "I lost the love of my life. Your father."

CHAPTER SEVENTEEN

DR. BROWNING

There's Diana, trying not to cry. Judging from the shock on Peter's face, she has already said too much.

"Diana!" I call out.

They both turn. Diana looks terrified. She grips Peter's arm fiercely.

"I know what you're going to say," she says to me, "but –"

"You can't, Diana," I say, as gently as I can. "And you know why."

She holds my look, but I know the tears are coming.

"She can't what?" Peter demands to know.

"I just want to take him home," Diana says. "*Please*, Dr. Browning. He's my son."

I have enormous compassion for Diana. I know the kind of worry that is tearing her apart.

"Remember what happened to his father!" she wails.

"Which is why you brought him *here,*" I remind her.

"What happened to my father?" Peter interjects, raising his voice. Both of us ignore him.

"Go home, Diana," I say, firmly. "*He cannot leave.*"

Diana chokes back the tears. She nods. She knows it's true.

"Mom...?"

Diana squeezes his shoulder. "She's right."

Peter looks at me. "*I can't leave? Why not?*"

———— ~ ————

Fifteen minutes later, we walk Diana to her car. She hugs her son and drives off. I say a quick prayer for Diana's comfort and peace of mind ... because even if I can't imagine what form that comfort might take, I have faith that it is there, if only we ask for it.

Peter watches her go, dazed and angry. Then he turns to me.

"What *are* you?"

"You've known since the day we met, Peter. Consider me ... a *guide.* To help you navigate your way through The Academy." I gesture for him to follow me as we move around the back of the school, through alcoves and back ways, far from probing eyes.

"Seriously. What *is* this place?"

"Well, it was *supposed* to be an oasis in the sea of depravity that is the modern world –"

"-- Oh, it's got plenty of depravity," Peter counters, and he's not wrong. But how to explain?

"... it was designed to be a place where free will is honored above all else."

"Free will?" Peter frowns. "Are you kidding? I get ordered

around here all the time, and no one told me what to do at Providence High!"

"There was a great deal of outside influence there. Influence you never really saw. You had already internalized the social dynamics, and ..." I stop. That's not the explanation he's looking for and I have only a few moments to explain so much.

"Peter," I say. "Let's just say that the decisions you made outside The Academy gates were subject to a great deal of influence. Have you ever lost control of yourself and just for a moment done or said something that you would normally never do? Something you instantly regretted? Ever felt as if you were driven by some deeper force to step outside what you would normally do?"

Disbelief clouds his face.

"Outside influence takes place everywhere," I continue. "*Everywhere but on this campus.* That's true whether you recognize it or not."

"You're saying that every choice I've made in my life was controlled by –

"-- no, not controlled." I drop my voice to a whisper. Anyone could be listening. "*Influenced.*"

"By who?" His voice lowers as he tries to grasp what I just told him.

"By those who push people toward the Dark ... or, like me, Radiants, who guide them into the Light."

Peter's expression changes. "Magnus Novus Orbis. A new world order!" he says softly, more to himself. "Creating 'the world's next generation of leaders!' James wasn't crazy."

"No, he wasn't," I say, although the mention of James pains me. "Each Academy student is incredibly important. They're more important in terms of authority, and the ability to affect change, than most. You see, one day, the choices they make – ”

“-- will influence *millions.*” Peter finishes my thought.

He gets it now: the money and power contained within these walls defines the future of the world. It chooses whose music defines a generation, which war gets funded, what's regarded as high fashion, who is chosen to explore Saturn and what is revealed about the mission. It decides which dusty villages survive and which ones suffer famine and genocide. Yes, Academy graduates decide which cultural influences will pervade society – that is, which movies, trends and celebrities will degrade it further, and which ones will elevate it. They will decide everything about this world, except the weather, and that may change soon.

“And every decision made by Academy graduates,” I say, “affects the balance between The Dark and The Light. And this balance must always be maintained. This campus is the only place where it is truly enforced. Now do you see why your mother wanted to take you home, and why she realized you're safer here?”

We walk for a long, long time in silence.

Finally Peter stops and turns to me. “You couldn't just *tell* me all this when I got here?”

“No, Peter, I couldn't,” I say with a touch of sadness. “Explaining everything would rob you of your most precious gift.” I smile at his confusion. “*Faith*, Peter! Faith in the basic goodness of others. Faith that the Light will be there when you need it. Each choice you make is an expression of that faith, or a lack of it. And that's how one builds a life … one choice at a time.”

Peter takes a second and sits down on a nearby bench, his head in his hands.

"I wish I could have told you sooner," I admit and sit down beside him. "But only when a student seeks my counsel, when he asks me questions, am I permitted to guide him. Not before." I lower my voice, trying to help him assimilate all this new information into something manageable. "The Academy has guided those in power for centuries."

" 'Those in power,'" he snorts. "Nice. We don't even own our house."

"Not all power is derived from wealth. You know that."

"But there's 'influence' here!" he says, his eyes darting about. "I wasn't going to go into that forest, I knew I shouldn't go into that forest. But then I heard someone calling for help, and I wanted to do the right thing, so – "

"First, you weren't on campus. And second ... not everyone plays by the rules," I reply, a little too pointedly.

"Linden?"

Just then I see Cole watching us from across campus. I can tell from his body language that he is *not pleased*. I stand, quickly.

"Walk with me, Peter. We don't have much time left."

"So if you're a 'guide for the Light,'" he says, hurrying after me, "Professor Linden is ..."

"... a subject I cannot discuss with you."

"Right. Of course not." He thinks a second. "No offense, but things aren't exactly working out for your side. Watch the news lately?"

It's time to say good-bye. I'm reluctant to do so. I care so much about Peter, his lively mind, his open heart. He has no clue of the power and responsibility that has been bestowed upon him. It's my job to make sure he reaches his potential, but I can only tell him so much at this juncture.

"It seems like there's nothing but darkness out there, I know," I tell him. "But that's because those who do good so rarely advertise. So much of it is unseen, unexplained, uncredited. And deeply personal. But ... *it's there*. I promise."

I pat him on the shoulder and look over to where Cole was standing. "I have to go now."

"I'm the only one who can get James out of that tree, aren't I?" Peter asks quickly. "And find whatever journal thing he had."

I stiffen. "It's a manuscript. And James had no right to take it!"

"Why? What's in it?"

I take a step closer him and whisper. "Mr. Cole documented the history of The Academy and its students." I step back. "It's not ... meant for the outside world."

"So James has it?"

"He knows where it's hidden." I have said too much. I cannot cross any more lines. "But that is not a wrong you are obligated to make right!"

I leave him there, confused and afraid, a little dazed, and overloaded with powerful new information.

When he remembers he's holding the photo of his parents, he calls out after me.

"Wait! Did my father go here? What was his *name?*" Peter comes after me but suddenly stops, eyes wide.

There's Cole, standing right there in my path, so close I nearly bump into him. And twenty seconds ago, he was a hundred yards away *on the other side of campus.*

Cole's eyes are fixed on me, and dark with warning. Peter knows enough to stay quiet.

I shrug. I will not be intimidated. I have done nothing wrong.

"He asked," I say.

Cole waits in the silence, letting it stretch, as if that and his glare were enough to cause me to confess a deep, dark truth.

But I have nothing to confess. I simply raise an eyebrow.

"He *asked*," I say again, louder.

Then I walk around him in a wide circle and continue on my way, chin up.

PETER

I stumble back to my room, past workers and waiters setting up for the party tonight. I'm so tired, everything hurts. But I doubt I could sleep if I tried.

My father went to school here! My mom knew this and never told me. *Who was he? What was his name?* Did he know he was going to have a son? I have too many question and no answers, and I'm so pissed at my mom I can't think straight. I call Charley again. I get his voicemail.

"It's Charley. Yes, I know it's you and I'm ignoring you. Do your thing."

I leave my eighth message after the beep. "Dude, it's me. You picked a shitty time to go missing. I ... I really need to ask you ... Just call me."

Shit. I gotta figure out what to do next, but an alarm goes off on my phone. I have exactly two minutes to get across campus for my last class of the day, Global Economics. I break into a slow run.

I hurry across campus but everything takes longer because there are people everywhere. Caterers in aprons carry huge vases of flowers into a courtyard, where tables are covered with silk table clothes. I'm practically run over by a moving clothes rack, which turns out to be dozens of dresses with enormous skirts and formal outfits for the guys, covered in plastic, being rolled into the dorms. I guess that's what we're supposed to wear tonight.

When the rack finally gets out of my way, I hurry to the Forbes building. I turn the corner and stop: there's Zach right there! Talking. With *Linden*. I'm too far away to hear what they're saying, but …

They look up to see me coming and Professor Linden tosses me this quick wave and hurries away. Zach stands there, hands in his pockets, with a visitor's badge on his shirt. He sees me and smiles.

"Hey buddy!"

"What was that?" I ask, "You know Professor Linden?"

"Who? Him? Nah. I just asked him where to find you." Zach looks around and grins. "This place is... plush."

He holds out the hard drive but I push his arm away.

"Not here!" I look around. I know I'll be late to class. Screw it. I'll say I had stomach pains or something.

"Put it away and follow me!" I say to Zach, and he shoves it back in his pocket. I take him to the garden behind the Chapel, the same one Chloe took me to after I woke up by the fence. No one seems to come here, so it's perfect.

"Give it to me."

Zach does, reluctantly. "You sure this is a good idea?"

"It's my *only* idea," I tell him. I can see by the look on his face that he's seriously worried about me. And I haven't even told him everything.

"Don't worry, I'm fine," I say, although that's mostly wishful thinking. "Planets aligning, nightmares, and I haven't slept for a month. No big deal."

"What can I do, man? Name it."

I appreciate the offer but I decided a while ago I was going to keep Zach out of this. I shrug.

"It'll be over soon."

"You gonna tell me what you're up to?"

I am tempted. Just telling Zach everything would help me get my head around it. Maybe get some clarity. But I can't.

"It's safer for you if you don't know anything," I tell him. And then I realize this is exactly what James told Charley before he disappeared. Shit.

"I could maybe come back and –"

"I gotta go get some stuff ready," I say, stepping out of the garden and back onto the path, nearly crashing into Chloe, who is also about to be late for class. She looks like she wants to bite my head off just for being in her way, but then she notices Zach behind me.

Chloe's expression goes from vicious to faux-friendly in a millisecond. She sort of swishes her hair around and turns a little.

I can't stand her but I have to admit, she's really hot.

Zach gives her a quick look and then looks back at me.

"Call me, yeah?" We bump fists and he leaves without another word, heading toward the entrance arch and the parking lot. I'm a little surprised he didn't give Chloe a second look. Just about everyone does.

I see this snub wasn't lost on Chloe either. She looks like someone slapped her.

"Get out of my way," she snarls and barrels past me.

I decide to cut class. I gotta open up this hard drive right away. I'll find the pages James scanned, and they'll tell me how to use the stones.

LINDEN

I sit at my desk, dangling my glasses in one hand and gazing coldly at Chloe. I hate office hours.

"I'm afraid I don't understand," I say.

"He didn't even look at me. I'm *invisible!*"

"That part I get," I say, impatiently. "You've described it six different ways. What I don't understand is what you expect me to do about it." I lean forward. "Maybe a therapist would be better qualified to help yo-"

"I don't need a fucking therapist."

"Allow me to assure you: you are *not* invisible. I can see you just fine. In fact, you look … quite lovely."

She heaves a sigh for the ages and stifles tears. "No. Something changed. Men act like they can't even see me. *Me* of all people!"

"What about the dance tonight?" I ask. "If it's attention you're after, I'm sure you'll get lots of it there."

"That's not what I am talking about, and you know it!" Chloe snaps back at me. "After all the information I've given you the past few months, the least you can do is fix this for me."

"This delusional loss of your sexual appeal wouldn't have anything to do with James, would it?" I ask, and her demeanor shifts. I knew it would. She's suddenly on edge. "It's a shame, really," I say, "to see you take a backseat - yet *again* - to Sophia."

Chloe freezes at the mention of Sophia. "When James comes

back, he'll come back *to me!*"

"The real question is, is he coming back at all?" I ask.

It's true that Chloe has given me a great deal of useful information these past few months. But she seems to forget what she has gotten away with since then, and I'd be delighted to remind her.

"James *is* coming back," she continues with a pout.

"Anything is possible, certainly," I say. "But the costs associated with getting James out of the tree, not to mention returning you to your former glory will be quite high. So high, in fact, that I doubt you'll be willing to pay them." I lower my voice conspiratorially. "There are quite a few people who stand in between you and your goals, you know."

"What kinds of costs?" she asks.

I smile. I baited my line and the beautiful, vain, predictable Chloe is nibbling at it. She is dreaming, no doubt, of a loving reunion with James, of a world in which Sophia, for once, loses the guy.

I have to set the hook ever so carefully. This is one fish I don't want to lose.

"I have always admired you, Chloe, and your commitment to getting what you want. Most people are hampered by the elaborate myths designed to shame them, beat them down, stifle their very human impulses in the hopes of a mystical reward at some vague future date."

She regards me coolly.

"And then there are those like you," I continue, "who have the strength to resist such nonsense."

"You have a pretty good idea of who I am, Professor," Chloe says slowly.

"Yes I do. And I'm confident you're strong enough to take what belongs to you. Certainly Dr. Browning hasn't offered you any means of getting what you want."

Chloe tenses. Her eyes flick away for a second. She is, no doubt, remembering the brown smudge of nothing she saw in the bathroom mirror.

"Of course I can help you," I say with a smile. "*I'll* go out of my way to make sure that James Harken returns to The Academy. And that you get everything you so richly deserve."

Her expression brightens for a moment, and then settles. She waits. She knows what's coming. This is the part she likes, the part she understands.

But decorum, as well as certain other rules, requires that *she* make the next move. And, finally, she does.

"What do I have to do?" she asks in a voice filled with resolve.

I set my glasses on my nose and peer down at her. I pretend to think for a moment. I know perfectly well what she'll have to do – this was plotted ages ago – and I know that she will agree instantly. Nonetheless, I have found that a well-timed pause offers numerous advantages, not least of which is the pure pleasure of victory and the anticipation of more to come.

"How well do you know Mr. Cole?" I finally ask.

CHAPTER EIGHTEEN

PETER

I race to my room. As soon as I figure out how to use those stones, I can get James out of that tree.

I quickly lock the door to my room and the door to Charley's suite. It's quiet. Everyone's in class. I close the drapes on my windows and pull the hard drive out of my jacket. *This is it.*

I look down at the hard drive. *This is almost over,* I think as I hook up the cable to the external hard drive. But it starts to make a weird clicking sound. No! My heart sinks. I click on the drive. It says it's "not accessible."

Hard drive failure!? NOW?!

Ten minutes later, I've tried everything. It's no use. The hard drive is fried.

I scream in frustration, picking up the hard drive and throwing it across the room. I needed that information. What the hell am I going to do?

To hell with it. I'm not waiting anymore. I have to get to that tree. *Now.* There's no way around it. Someone has to save James, and it looks like I'm the only one who knows where he is. I fill my backpack with stuff I might need – a jacket, my Swiss army knife, bolt cutters, my riding gloves. I carefully place the two stones in the outside pocket. What else?

I remember the first time I tried going into the forest. I need to protect myself. I pull out the large black Maglite my mom gave me as a stocking stuffer. I shove it in the backpack and zip it shut.

I'm trying to keep everything straight but my head is swimming. There is so much I don't know, but I'm running out of daylight and can't wait any longer. I put on my sweats in case someone sees me. I'll just say I'm going for a run.

The campus is pretty quiet, except for the people setting up the sound system. I hear bursts of static and a few familiar techno tracks. Passing the side courtyard, I see this giant stone arch that I don't remember being there before but it looks like it has stood there for centuries. It's covered with ivy, and it sort of separates one part of the garden, which is empty, from the other, which has all these tables set up in it.

I pass a group of girls in these huge, round skirts. They have to lean way over to take selfies because the skirts take up so much room. They've got their hair piled really high on their heads and they're all wearing low-cut dresses. Obviously costumes from the 1700s. A few have hand-held masks. The Alignment Dance is starting soon. No one seems to notice me.

I get to the track and pretend to warm up. Then I move down to where it loops toward the back gate. Behind me, the campus is lit by enormous spotlights. More and more students in costume come flooding into the courtyard outside the Hall. When I get to the gate, I hear a few girls shrieking with happiness and surprise, and I guess part of me wishes I didn't have to miss it all. I wonder what Sophia will look like in her costume.

I open up my backpack and take out the bolt cutters. I'm about to cut the lock--

"Careful."

I jerk back and hold the bolt cutter behind my back. It's Cole, standing about twenty feet to my left but staring out at the forest.

"Clouds are rolling in," he says. "See?"

He's talking about the *weather*? Maybe he didn't see the bolt cutters. I pretend to stretch my hamstrings.

"I was gonna go for a quick run," I say, "but I guess I better get in before ... "

"Before the storm hits," Cole agrees. "You don't want to be anywhere exposed. You must protect yourself."

I nod. I grab my backpack and stuff the tools in deep. I swing it around onto my back to leave but Cole keeps talking, so I lean up against the fence like I'm not in a hurry.

"I know Dr. Browning has been telling you things," he says. I don't say a word. "She's very good at her job. As a Radiant, I mean." He grabs hold of the fence with both hands. "But you have to hear both sides of any argument, Peter. Professor Linden would tell you that Dr. Browning reveals only one half of the ..." he pauses. Clears his throat. "... bigger picture."

"I don't understand," I say, because I don't. I seriously don't. "What *are* they, Dr. Browning and Professor Linden?"

"They're different sides of the same coin. Night and Day. Light and Dark."

"But what do they *want with me?*"

Cole says nothing. I notice that the guy never blinks. He looks at me like he's waiting for me to answer my own question. But I mean it. What do they want? Finally, Cole sighs. His unblinking eyes never leave my face.

"Dr. Browning is a Radiant. She wants you to overcome your nature in service of a higher purpose. You know that."

"And Professor Linden?"

"Professor Linden is an Essential. He wants the indulging of your nature to become your purpose."

I think on that. "What's an Essential?"

Cole shrugs. "He would say it describes him, his function. Essential. No one would recognize the light if it weren't for the dark. And he thinks his cause is the most honest reflection of mankind's true nature. So he does what he does."

My mind spins. "How about you, Mr. Cole? What do *you* do?"

For a second, Cole looks like he might smile, but he doesn't.

"I make sure the rules are adhered to, that neutrality is maintained, that no student is subjected to undue influence. That's why I'm telling you all this in the first place. A fragile balance must be maintained between both sides."

He watches me struggle to figure all this out.

"Both sides must be heard, Peter," he says. "Only then can one make an informed decision. Of course, you have two years before you have to make the choice."

The choice? About *what?!*

"Until then, you have to protect yourself," Cole says.

"From what?" I ask weakly.

I have a thousand questions but can't find the words. I look out at the forest, too. It's grey and quiet, a mist rising. In the distance, a gentle waltz plays.

Cole turns his stone-cold eyes on me again.

"The storms. They will come, Peter. They always do."

———— ～ ————

How could I be so stupid? As I hurry back to campus, I realize I should have known they would be keeping an eye on me. He must have seen everything. I hide my backpack under a bench. I'll have to try again later, when Cole and the others are busy at the dance.

I slip through the gate and find a stylist to get a white shirt and black cape. That's what most of the guys are wearing tonight, and I've got to fit in. A few guys are going totally period, but there's no way I'm squeezing into one of those high-necked jackets the color of an Easter egg.

Out in the courtyard in front of the main Hall, students admire each other's costumes, guess who's dressed up as which Founding Father, and hang out. This classical quartet plays, and they sound pretty good to me, even though classical music isn't my thing. Hidden smoke and bubble machines blow bubbles over the entire courtyard.

———— ～ ————

Fifteen minutes later, I see Sophia walk into the courtyard. She's in one of those big dresses. Her hair is all done up and she's got more makeup on than usual, but she looks amazing. She finally sees me and waves with a fan. I go over with my cape over one shoulder and she smiles at me.

I want to tell her how good she looks, but she quickly grabs my arm and steers me to the Hall entrance. There, a guy in a white suit hands us these colored masks.

"Please wear your masks at all times," he tells us.

Sophia and I put on the masks on and glide into the Hall, which is draped in colored silks. Tiered cakes and marble vases holding mountains of colored roses are everywhere. The music is instantly louder and there's this vibe of excitement or expectation in the air.

At least for a few minutes, I'm not thinking about the forest, the Tree, or James.

———◈———

Twenty minutes later, we've taken it all in: the costumes, the violinists walking around in costume playing for students, even the expensive jewelry the girls are wearing. I imagine this is what The Academy looked like two hundred years ago, right down to the candle chandelier hanging from the ceiling.

But now all I can think of is whether or not my backpack is still where I hid it. Should I have put the Stones in my pockets? And will Cole still be out there when I try and get to the tree again?

"You're not paying attention!" Sophia says, tugging on my collar. "You sure you're okay?"

"I'm great!" I say, hoping it doesn't sound too forced. And the truth is that everything here is amazing, I just don't have the time to enjoy it. It's dark out now, and I've got to get to that tree!

She smiles up at me. "You better not be lying, Peter Foster. Because if you are, I'll know. Look where we are!"

We're standing in some kind of line. There are mostly couples in front of us. I figure we're in line for photographs but when I look toward the front of the line, there's no setup, no lights, no photographers. It's just that huge stone arch. Couples wait their turn, and then they go stand under the arch.

There's a couple there now. They say something to each other and then they kiss.

Sophia leans in close. "I'm glad it's you," she says. "Here, next to me."

"Me too," I say quietly, and I mean it.

"No one told you about the arch?" she asks. I shake my head and she continues. "When two people kiss under it, they see each other's true intentions!" I must look skeptical because she quickly adds, "It's just this school tradition. I don't even know if it's true."

We watch the next couple take their place under the arch. They kiss. But then suddenly the girl jerks back and slaps the guy! She stalks off, grabbing at her huge skirts, obviously pissed off. The rest of the kids in line laugh at the guy left alone under the arch, rubbing his face.

If I were anywhere else, I would laugh at them, too, and at the whole idea of "seeing each other's true intentions." But I'm not laughing now. What if this really works?

I know I could kiss Sophia and there's nothing in my head that would offend her (mostly because I'm totally focused on getting into that forest tonight). But what if she's able to see *that*? What if she can see me thinking about *getting James out of the Tree*?

This stone arch mind-reading thing might be total bullshit. But

I can't take that chance.

"I'll be right back," I tell her.

She smiles and nods as I duck out of line.

CHLOE

I've never been to an Alignment Dance before.

So far, I'm not impressed. I don't enjoy these boring school functions, partly because when it comes to a little fizzy, the administration acts as if it's liquid meth. And there are never any interesting men here, men who know what they want and know how to get it. This place is populated by silly boys with underdeveloped brains who try to act grown up. But people would talk if I didn't show up, and I have work to do. So the farce continues.

On the plus side, everyone's in costume, and I have a soft spot for that kind of thing. I like watching people pretending to be something they're not. I can tell a lot about a person by the costumes they choose. Some choose to dress like "proper ladies" and some like slags (called "courtesans" back then), but I can always spot the ladies who wish they were slags, and the other way round.

Another advantage is the era. Although the skirts have so many layers they're a little hard to get around in, they provide plenty of places to comfortably hide a flask. Mine has disappeared into this sea of satin but I can feel it bumping against my hip when I turn. Most importantly, I know it will be there when the time is right. (This particular silver flask was given to me by a very close relative, one better known as the Prince of Wales.)

I lean against a magnificent flower arrangement and check out the other girls. Most of them laugh with their mouths open or stare daggers at everyone else because they have no confidence and no concept of how to fake it. Sophia looks okay, I guess. Her dress is pale green, trimmed with beige lace. Her latest good-girl incarnation means she's going easy on the cleavage. If you ask me, her makeup is much too white (I know it's authentic but who cares about authenticity?) and oh my God, I think she even has one of those drawn-on mole things by her mouth.

She and Peter get their masks and then disappear into the crowd, heading for the other side of the courtyard where the stone arch is set up. They're smiling at each other as if there's no one else around, and it's making me a little sick. Why is she being so nice to the Townie? Before I can scroll through the various possibilities, I see Anton step up to the front of the line now forming at the front of the Hall. Of course no one tells him he's cutting in line, they just let him do it because he's Anton. The guy by the door hands him a mask, but Anton doesn't take it. Instead, he grabs another one from the stack.

One that looks exactly like Peter's.

I can't help but lift an eyebrow at that. Certainly that was no coincidence. I watch closely as Anton follows Sophia and Peter toward the arch. Even from here, I can see the determination (and maybe something else? fury?) on Anton's face. Hmmm.

But twenty minutes later, I fear I've missed my chance. Peter, not wearing his mask, comes hurrying back this way, much too soon. And alone. He slips out of the courtyard and is gone. I sigh and set down my pine-nut encrusted yummy because I'll need both hands to manage these skirts. I follow him.

Curiosity may have killed the cat… but satisfaction brought him back.

Alignment

I move as fast as I can, holding the skirt and the petticoats underneath it, down the length of the courtyard, past a dozen giggling girls. I have to elbow my way through a bunch of freshman all stoned out of their minds. The immature brats think no one notices but it is soooo obvious.

Out on the pathway near the Chapel, Peter is about fifty yards ahead. I can see he ditched his costume and is wearing his normal clothes. He stops at a bench not far from the jogging path and pulls something out from under it. His backpack! Things are getting interesting.

But then Peter doesn't go back to the dorms, or even back to the dance. He trots along the jogging trail and disappears down it until I can't see him anymore. Damn these skirts! Of course there's no point in going any further. I know where he's going.

I stop and enjoy a bit of refreshment from my flask, and then tuck it away again.

I return to the courtyard and grab two champagne flutes filled with soda off a servant's tray (even the servants wear white powdered wigs). Very discreetly, I empty a small vial of liquid into one of the champagne flutes, grateful for these long, lacy sleeves.

And suddenly, there's Peter right by chocolate fountain! Only when he lifts his mask a few inches to throw back a little beverage of his own, I realize it's not Peter at all. It's Anton, dressed just like Peter.

He catches my eye. Busted. I laugh.

"Making mischief?" I ask as I join him.

"Wish me luck," he says with a wink.

"I just saw Peter talking a long walk into the forest, so I'm going to guess," I say quietly, running my tongue over the edge of my champagne glass, "that you're not the one who needs luck tonight."

Anton smiles at me, but it's a greasy, self-satisfied smile.

"That's because I'm not the one stupid enough to go looking for the Tree, now am I?" he asks.

That reminds me. "You haven't seen Richard, have you?" I ask. The last thing I need is him ruining everything.

"As a matter of fact, I have," Anton says. "Face down in the dirt."

I frown. I don't like the idea of Anton laying hands on my brother.

"He's fine, Chloe. Or he will be, when he wakes up. Professor Linden warned me he might get in the way tonight, so ..." He shrugs and gestures to my two flutes of soda. "Just do your thing and don't worry."

He replaces his mask and leaves, and I'm five steps behind him, ready for the fun to begin.

PETER

Thank God, the backpack is right where I left it. I swing it over my shoulder and hurry toward the gate. I feel bad, knowing Sophia is waiting in line for me, but what can I do? I can't tell her the truth, and I can't let that stupid stone arch out me, either, if that's even possible.

I keep telling myself that I have to get this done, no matter what. James is counting on me, and I won't let him down. He did all the heavy lifting with that manuscript and everything, and now I'm going to do my part. And then it'll all be over and I can focus on the stuff my mother told me.

I can hear the music and voices getting quieter as I hurry down the jogging path to the back gate. This time, I make sure no one followed me. I pull bolt cutters out of my backpack and cut the gate's dead bolt. Easy. The gate swings open and I'm on my way.

By now, I know I can't trust anything about The Academy – or anyone connected to it. Not even my mom. Knowing that puts me on guard the second I walk through the back gate.

The Maglite feels comforting in my hands, but I haven't turned it on. It's almost a full moon and I can see pretty clearly without it. I don't want to draw attention to myself. I'll wait until I'm hidden by the trees.

I trudge toward the forest, checking the longitude and latitude on my phone and roughly measuring my steps. I veer northwest from the gate, angling my body just a few degrees. A wind is picking up. It was a clear night twenty minutes ago, but now clouds are rolling in, right across a bright moon.

I cross the tree line and I'm in the forest. I hear droplets of rain on my backpack, and seconds later they stab at my face like cold little needles. I turn on my Maglite as the rain really starts to come down. And it's *freezing*. I slip a few times. I remind myself to slow down.

I take one last look at my phone and tuck it inside my jacket so it doesn't get soaked. The wind is picking up, blowing through me. I can see my breath every time I exhale. It's really dark now and I can barely see with the wind blowing everything around and rain stinging my eyes.

Then I step into a puddle. At least that's what I think it is. I look down, but all I can see is mud. I take another step to get out of the puddle but it's as if the ground has totally liquefied! And now my foot sinks even deeper into the mud, which is splattered with rain coming down so hard, it looks like it's boiling.

I keep at it. It's really hard to move and I've got to go super-slow so the mud doesn't suck my shoes off. I hold my backpack above my head to keep the rain out of my eyes. The mud is now up over my knees.

I stop for a second to catch my breath. My legs are killing me. I'm soaked through, and my teeth are chattering because it's so fucking cold. Then I think of James, the visions I had of him, suffering. No one deserves to be trapped in that tree. I can't quit now.

I take a breath and push on. I make a sharp turn to my right and finally the ground starts to become more solid and I start climbing up a berm. Halfway up, my feet slip and I tumble back, falling and landing hard on my side.

I want to lie there but I have to keep going, so I try again, and this time I'm able to lift myself out of whatever pit I was in. I push on without even turning around.

I can't rest. I'm gulping air but I refuse to slow down.

The forest looks denser, the trees more tightly grouped together. I could swear the branches bend and close around me as I walk by, almost sealing me in. The sound shifts and muffles; the air doesn't rush around my ears anymore. It's still cold, and it smells like moss, but the rain just drips off the leaves. It doesn't pelt my face anymore.

I check my phone to make sure I'm going in the right direction, but the screen is shattered and I can't see a thing. Damn it! I sigh and put it away, trying to figure out where I am. I remember the last screen and turn slightly to my right, like I planned. According to my figures and the coordinates on the map, the tree should be about 150 yards dead ahead.

I walk on, shining the Maglite ahead of me. After a few minutes,

I turn around just to look back. I figured I should still be able to see some campus lights behind me, but I can't. It's like a curtain fell. I see only the outlines of trees.

I keep walking, but what I see in front of me doesn't match what I'm experiencing physically. In this dim light, the ground looks flat, but I trip over roots, and there are all these ditches and mounds. Twigs slap at my face and neck, but when I wave my hand around in front of me, they suddenly disappear.

I hear a faint shrieking, and then this weird buzzing. Something pulls at my hair. Then bites me on the hand. Something small and dark smacks against my cheek. I hear fluttering around my head and brush my hand over my forehead. I catch something. It's hard, like a pebble, but then flutters in my hand. I lift up the Maglite and stare.

Beetles. Thousands of beetles, flying at me, flying *into* me. I cover my head with my jacket and hunch over, shining the light a few feet ahead of me. The beetles slap at my clothes and at the fabric of my jacket, making a racket. I can hear them crunching under my feet. A few fly inside my jacket. They're getting tangled in my hair. A few fall down my shirt and I can feel them pricking at my back.

What the hell am I supposed to do now? I'm trying not to freak out.

When a beetle tries to crawl into my mouth, I realize I can't take much more. Then, just when I think I'm going to have to drag myself on the ground the rest of the way, I stumble out into a clearing. I notice the air first. It's clear and cool and still. No more beetles swarming my head. No mud on the ground. No wind blasting me backward. No rain jabbing my face.

It's so *quiet and peaceful.* All I can hear is the sound of me panting. Then I see it, and I freeze. At the other end of the clearing, apart from the other trees, stands a giant oak with gnarled bark. Its branches are incredibly thick, and they reach up and out into the sky, above all the other nearby oaks. The sheer size of it takes my breath away. I just stare. I recognize it! It's the same tree from those visions.

I found it.

CHAPTER NINETEEN

PETER

I stare at the enormous oak. It's easily sixty feet tall and wide enough to drive a car through.

Standing at the edge of the clearing, I can see the three-pronged symbol on its trunk! Some of the tree's branches bend low to the ground and are hung with patches of moss. I move closer, so close now, I can hear creaking and popping coming from inside it as the wind whips around its canopy.

Everything is misty and grey, yet it all feels weirdly familiar. I have to remind myself this isn't a dream or one of those visions. *I'm really here.*

I pull the stones out of my pocket. The symbol looks as if it's pulsating, as if something is radiating out of it. I'm drawn to it, like there's something that makes me want to get closer to it. Can it know I'm here? Is that even possible?

The way it's pulsating reminds me of my closet door, that time I got my blood on it. I try to guess where to put the stones. If only I hadn't relied so much on that damn hard drive! I set the paler one on the forest floor, on the oak's right side. I take a step back again, just to be sure. Everything is quiet. So I set the darker one on its left side.

I stand there for a moment but nothing happens. What if I came all the way out here and it doesn't work? *Maybe I forgot something? Maybe I need that third stone?*

I keep looking at that symbol, and the way it's gently glowing reminds me again of my closet door, and how I got lucky with it when I cut my finger. The blood did the rest of the work. That's when it hits me. *My blood!* I take my knife out of the backpack and cut the tip of my finger. As soon as a bead of blood appears, I touch the symbol and it immediately starts to shimmer! I step back, freaked out.

The blood races around the three-pronged symbol, over and over, turning it rubbery until it seems to boil and stretch in the center. A wave of heat comes off it, so hot I have to back up some more. Now there's a grey four-foot wide circle bubbling in the middle of the tree!

Suddenly something moves in it, like a giant bug caught in hot wax. Only it's not a bug. It's a finger! It presses against the rubbery part of the tree, the thin grey membrane lined with tiny roots. Then it becomes an entire hand – and then *two hands!*

They seem to be searching for a break in the membrane but then starts scratching and tearing at it frantically. I freeze for a second, unsure of what to do next. The hands tear the membrane and then there's James's head, right in front of me, pushing through the opening in the tree and gasping for air!

It's just like the dream! I stumble back. James's faces pushes out further. Then one of his arms reaches out and grabs hold of the outside of the tree! Two eyes, covered in grey slime, open half way.

He looks at me for a moment and then his cracked lips move.

"Help me!" he whispers.

CHLOE

The liquid I poured into one of the champagne flutes bubbled a bit at first, then stilled. It's invisible and tasteless. Perfect.

I sip from the other one and watch Sophia, alone at the front of the line for the stone arch. She looks around. I can only assume she's searching for Peter. I consider telling her that he is long gone, and I imagine the fun of seeing her crushed after being abandoned and rejected.

But before I can enjoy that particular pleasure, she brightens. A masked Peter walks up to her and she pulls him happily under the arch.

Now I know perfectly well that this is *not* Peter. But Sophia doesn't know that, so I sit back to watch the fun, hidden under a mask of my own.

Under the arch, "Peter" bows to her.

"Impressive," Sophia says, as if the Townie thought that up all by himself. She leans closer to him and says something I can't hear, but it's obviously flirty because "Peter" slips his arm around her. And then they kiss.

It's a soft kiss, and it's over as soon as it starts. Sophia stops and her eyes fly open, as if she just got a jolt of electricity up her skirt. She pushes "Peter" away.

"Anton!! You son of a bitch!" She wipes her mouth and looks like she wants to spit.

"I love you!" Anton says, pulling off his mask. "Everything I did, I did for you. Can't you see that?"

But Sophia's not listening. "What have you done?" she gasps, staggering backward. She pushes herself through the line and flees.

Anton races after her. Grabs her arm. She pulls it free and runs off again. Anton looks as if he'll go after her –

"Never thought I'd see Anton Volsky chasing *anyone*," says one of the girls in line, and suddenly Anton stops. He straightens his jacket and runs a hand through his hair, his pride stung. He eyes the girl coldly.

"And you never will," he says. He turns and walks back to the party.

I would very much like to see how this all plays out but I can't stay. I have a promise to keep and a job to do.

I find Mr. Cole in one of the side gardens, staring off into space like a zombie. He gawks at the night sky with such concentration, I want to ask him if he's in charge of the planets this time of night.

Instead, I concoct a beautifully detailed sob story about my love life, describing how lonely I am and how my heart has been broken yet again (sniffle). Men hate to see women cry. They're so predictable.

So I'm not at all surprised when I ask Mr. Cole to drink a toast with me "to a happier tomorrow!" that he takes my other champagne flute.

"I would be honored, Lady Winters," he says.

PETER

James lies on the forest floor, damp and trembling. His eyes flutter open. His whole body shakes. I run over to him. His face is waxy.

I want to help the guy but I'm trying not to freak him out.

I touch his shoulder, "You okay? I mean, holy –"

James pushes my hand off his shoulder.

"D...Do...Don't ... touch me," he says in this weak, raspy voice. What the hell am I supposed to do? I step back, giving him room, as James gets slowly to his knees. I go to help him again but he waves me off.

James gets to his feet, breathing really hard. He wobbles but I don't touch him. His hair is long and stringy, and he is covered in that grey slime. His eyes are rimmed in red, and glassy.

With a shaking hand, James points to the stones. I scoop them up and drop them into my backpack. James watches me for a beat, and then holds out an arm.

"Let's get the hell out of here," he says with a weak smile.

I put his arm around my shoulders. There's nothing I want more than to get back to campus. I finally feel like everything is going to be alright. I got the stones! I found the Tree and got James out!

He leans on me and we hobble from the clearing, hurrying as fast as we can through the forest. His skin is damp and gritty, and he smells like sweat, but I don't mind. *I did it!* And he'll be able to answer all my questions. I can think of a dozen right now, but I remind myself: there will be time for that later.

———— ∿ ————

Five minutes later, James is already stronger and doesn't need to lean on me anymore. He is walking by himself now, and I've been letting him ramble like a maniac. I slow down a little, stunned by what he just told me.

"Why would you hide the manuscript *there*?" I ask, because I have to know.

"Isn't it obvious? It's the last place they would ever look," James tells me with a big grin. Suddenly energized, we hurry through the forest and soon James is out ahead of me. Near the edge of the forest, James stops in his tracks.

"Listen," James says with a little smile. "I've missed that."

I listen to the rising breeze. Leaves flutter all around us. James closes his eyes and seems to soak it up, and I take the opportunity to get a good look at him. He's a little taller than me but so skinny he looks smaller somehow. The skin on his face is pulled really tight. His clothes are ripped and he needs a shower, bad. James catches me staring at him.

"Listen, man," he says, "don't think I can't appreciate how rough this has been on you. Getting out here, helping me."

I nod.

"I mean, everyone wants to be on the winning team, right?" He shakes his head. "The pressure this place puts on you! Makes you do shit you never thought you would."

"Like steal a book?"

He throws me a look. He wasn't expecting that.

"I tried to expose the truth," he says. "But every tech company, every newspaper, every frigging news outlet in the world ... is run by alumni. Get it?"

"You could have walked away. Left me the hell out of it."

"It's not like I had a choice," James says, "It had to be you."

I stop walking again. "What does *that* mean? There are like three hundred other students at The Academy."

James narrows his eyes at me, impatient to keep going. "But they don't have what you have." He sighs.

I'm obviously missing something. But what?

"You think Anton's blood would open that tree? Or Charley's or Sophia's? It had to be someone, anyone, from your family line. And that means *you*. Get it?"

I can't believe it. "This is about … my *father*?"

He starts clapping his hands, applauding me. "You're a regular Einstein. He says hi, by the way. Or he would. If he could talk."

Wait a second. "My father is in that tree?"

"Your father is *part* of the Tree now. That's what happens if you don't get out after the next alignment." James shakes his head. "Didn't you read the pages I scanned? Jesus."

"I didn't get a chance." I reply weakly, remembering the vision I had. My mind races. I can still feel those roots going into my ears and mouth, being stuck in that confined space, my toes becoming roots and --- oh my God. This entire time I thought it was James communicating with me from the Tree! What if it was my father? What if *that* was why my mom wanted to take me home so bad?

James is nearly out of the forest. There's no way I'm letting him get away now. I run after him.

"Wait! How do I get my father out of the Tree of Souls?"

"Quiet!" he barks at me.

I go still. I hear a faint noise in the distance. It could be the wind. But James looks really worried, which makes me nervous, too.

"Stay here," he says. "I'll check out what's up ahead."

James heads for the tree line. Just a few more steps and he'll be out of the forest.

I break into a jog and catch up to him. "Answer the question!"

James turns to me, pissed. "I said, *stay here.*"

"I don't take orders from you," I tell him. This is fucking ridiculous. "How do I get my father out of that tree?"

James clenches his jaw for a second and then relaxes.

"You want to go over this now, huh? Alright, I can't say that I blame you. But could I get something to drink first?" he asks. "I've been trapped in a fucking tree for months, dude."

I slip my backpack off my shoulder and dig through it for my bottle of water.

I look up just in time to see James's fist coming right for my face.

CHLOE

The problem with paralyzing someone is that they become lousy conversationalists. Not that I was interested in listening to Mr. Cole blather on about nature's bounty or soil quality and the like, but eventually silence can be a bit overwhelming. I hear the party music thumping on the other side of campus. Here I am, stuck in this side garden, baby-sitting a very quiet Mr. Cole.

And now my drink is empty. I sigh. This better work.

Mr. Cole sits stiffly on the bench, and I imagine he's a bit bored, too. He tries to get up but can't. He flops back down and moans in frustration. This has been going on for at least ten minutes.

At first, his struggle amused me. Like a spider fighting being washed down a drain. But now I'm bored. I decide to educate him about why he's where he is. I pull the blossom of a trumpet plant from my blouse, where I'd hidden it earlier today. I wave it at him.

"These are such pretty flowers," I say. "James told me how you care for them. *And what they really do.*"

He lifts his eyes to me, slowly. It dawns on him. Finally.

"Paralysis," I say. "Probably sucks. I mean, you're usually so busy around here. Busy with your plants, busy with your beetles and busy in everyone's business." I click my tongue. "But not tonight. Tonight you relax. Courtesy of Professor Linden."

"Please..." Mr. Cole says. I can barely understand him. I know he's saying, "There is work I must do," but it sounds like "Dehzwok-kiemusstoo."

"James was a very good friend to you, wasn't he?" I ask. "Probably your only friend. For, like, *decades*, I bet."

Cole goes limp.

"You probably heard him mention me."

He doesn't answer, the bastard. I tear the blossom and Mr. Cole's eyes go wide. He gasps. *Now* I have his attention.

"And you probably know tonight's a special night, right? *Because he's coming back to me*," I say with a smile.

I tear the blossom again and then crush it in my palm. Cole's eyes close in resignation. Awwww. He worked so hard to keep James from me, confining him in that stupid tree as if that would stand in the way of the bond James and I share.

"That's right," I say, smiling at the beads of sweat forming on Mr. Cole's forehead. "James is coming back. And you can't stop him."

PETER

My jaw explodes in pain. I fly backward and land in a heap. *What the hell?! That son of a bitch just sucker punched me!*

I'm trying to make sense of that, when I see him coming at me with a tree branch the size of my arm.

The adrenaline hits me like a bolt of lightning. I roll to my left and the branch just misses my head. I leap to my feet but I'm dizzy. James swings the branch again. I duck under it and come up swinging.

I land an uppercut as I come up. "What the -"

James comes at me with the branch again. I dodge and throw another punch. This one gets him square in the nose.

"-is wrong with you?"

James takes a step back. Blood drips from his nose and he wipes it away.

"You think I'm going back inside that thing?" he says, his voice ragged. "Hell no." And then he smiles. "But someone has to."

He kicks down at my legs and I try to block.

I never see the branch, which catches me in side of my head. I go down hard and see stars. James is on top of me now, pinning my shoulders down as he punches me in the face, again and again.

LINDEN

Dr. Browning stands at the altar with her head bowed. She is, undoubtedly, putting on this overly pious display just to annoy me.

"I can guarantee you he's not listening," I say, and my voice echoes in this empty chamber. "Not this time, not ever. He isn't interested in your pathetic pleas." I tap my fingers on the back of a pew. "He's probably off water-skiing in Tahiti."

Dr. Browning doesn't even turn around. She raises her head to the stained glass window in front of the chapel.

"A little early to be gloating, don't you think?" she asks.

"Not at all." I gesture above my head. "You're so accustomed to waiting, waiting, waiting, even in times of desperate need, that you can't appreciate my perfect punctuality."

She doesn't move.

"And I'm not gloating," I say. "That would imply I harbored some measure of doubt about the outcome, and *I don't*. Don't you understand? It was all about the stones, Charlotte. They were my real objective. And they're *mine* now."

Everything is going exactly as I had planned. She must be dying inside.

"Don't get me wrong," I continue. "I'd like the manuscript back. But it was always about *the stones*. All this time, Charlotte! While you were your usual naive self, believing in the saintly potential of every soul, that somehow James could be moved to do what's right! What did *that* get you?"

I grasp the opportunity and take a little bow. She doesn't even notice. She's still gazing at that gaudy stained glass.

I don't know what I expected. Some type of acknowledgement of my victory, maybe. Finally she turns around but her eyes are steady, her demeanor calm. She doesn't appear agitated in the least. I expect her to come up with one of her meaningless tropes, telling me "his grace is sufficient," or some other verbal band-aid, like she usually does.

But she doesn't.

"Did you really think I didn't know, Professor?" she asks in an unnervingly strong voice. "That I couldn't figure it out? Or did you think that your darkness is so complete ..."

Wait. *She knew?*

"... that not even the brightest light could see into it?"

She steps up much too close to me and whispers.

"It can."

I take a big step back. This whole idea of the Light illuminating the Dark is something I refuse to acknowledge. It's a hoax. A vicious *lie*! And I won't allow her to steal this moment of triumph from me. I *won't*.

"Peter will spend eternity in that tree!" I tell her, keeping my voice just above a growl. "Just like his father."

"Your critical error, Professor Linden," she says confidently, "was putting the manuscript in play. Poor Cole. He'd do anything to retrieve it. He'd even make a deal with me."

I'm speechless. It can't be. I feel ill. I drop into a pew. "But I took care of Cole!"

Dr. Browning lowers herself into the pew next to me. "Temporarily."

"What did you do …?"

"What I *didn't* do … was underestimate Chloe's vanity. Or yours." Dr. Browning allows herself a small smile.

I wish I could tear it off her face.

"Patience and tenacity is what I always say," she says demurely. "And then victory."

PETER

I'm fading. I can't even feel the punches anymore. James's body is so heavy, and getting heavier.

And then suddenly SMASH! The heaviness is gone and feeling rushes back into my face. There's Sophia, holding a rock! James is a few feet away in a crumpled heap, not moving. I gag and cough.

"Oh my God!" Sophia says as blood drips down my face.

"What are you doing here?!" I ask, gasping.

"Anton kissed me under the arch. Total accident! I thought he was you! And I saw ..." She gestures around. "... what Anton set up. *You going into the forest alone.* To the tree! I just started running and then suddenly I'm here and–"

I get to my feet and stare at James. "I can't believe he just –"

Sophia looks at James lying there. I can't read her face. Sadness? Regret? Anger? I remember their picnic, and how much she once cared about him.

"How did you *do* that?! I thought he couldn't ever ...." she asks.

I rush to my backpack and pull out the stones.

"See these? They're what got him out of the Tree! He told me my –"

"We gotta hurry!" One glance at the stones and Sophia's freaking out. She pulls me toward campus.

"What? I'm not *leaving* him here!"

"Yes, you are! The tree can't be empty, Peter! Don't you get it? He would leave you without a second thought!" She pulls at me again.

"After everything I did to get him out of there? There is no way I'm leaving him!"

"We don't have time for this*! We have to leave now!*"

There's no time to explain. I jam the stones deep into my jeans pocket, grab my backpack and lift James in a fireman's carry. *He's gonna tell me how to help my father whether he wants to or not.*

We step out of the forest, and I'm nearly knocked over by the wind. The rain blows sideways. Sophia hurries ahead of me, her hair blowing in every direction.

I struggle to keep up with her. I shout above the wind. "How did you even know where the Tree was?"

She can't hear me. The wind is too loud. Twigs and leaves fly everywhere.

We stagger on. Thorn bushes I don't remember on the way here tear at our legs. With James's weight on my back, I can't bend over to see what's in front of me, so I follow in Sophia's steps. Soon I feel the scratches on my calves and ankles start to bleed.

"Are you sure we're going the right way?" I shout.

She doesn't turn around.

Just then, I get my answer: the wrought-iron fence of The Academy is there in the distance. Maybe fifty yards away. Thank God. *We can do this!*

The gusts of wind are so strong, they nearly knock me over. This weird shrieking sound comes and goes – it must be the rain, which is sharp, and really cold. I turn my face away for a second to avoid the stinging and trip over something, losing my grip on James. I fall. He rolls off me.

I try to pull myself out of the mud. Everything hurts. I make it onto my hands and knees.

Sophia bends over to help me and we stay that way for a second, resting. She looks at my face and gently touches my bruises. She's about to say something when –

"Such a touching scene."

We look up. It's James, towering above us in his torn, muddy clothes. His face is bruised and muddy but there's a fierceness there that scares me. I jump to my feet and pull Sophia up with me.

James moves toward us, his lips curled in hate. I instinctively push Sophia behind me, but as I do, I catch the look on her face: total fear.

CHAPTER TWENTY

CHLOE

Mr. Cole isn't arguing with me anymore.

He just sits there like he's in a coma, but his eyes are wide open. With no one to talk to, I'm bored out of my mind. I didn't exactly agree to be an old man's *babysitter*. I remind myself it's worth it. Soon I'll have James back, and my face, and I'll be the envy of every girl on campus again! He should be here any minute. My heart jumps a little with something that feels like happiness.

Minutes pass. I look at Mr. Cole again and sigh. Maybe I'll just leave him here. The party is over, anyway. The music stopped half an hour ago and I bet the sun's coming up soon, ending the final night of global alignment. I stifle a yawn.

Then I hear someone coming. Richard stumbles into the side yard as I hide behind a hedge. His costume is a wreck and his hair is a mess. He glares at Cole, who now leans to one side. He doesn't see me yet and limps over to Cole.

"What are you *doing*?" he complains like a girl.

Of course Cole can't answer him. For once, Richard is in a situation there's nothing he can do. *I* hold the cards.

"How can you just *sit* there?" he wails.

"He has no choice," I say.

Richard spins around to see me waving what's left of the torn blossom.

"Yes, it's me, the 'unfeeling, vicious' bitch, remember?" I smile at him like an unfeeling, vicious bitch and it feels *good*. I think his jaw actually drops.

"Mr. Cole here is dying to get out there and help, right?" I ask him. "But the question is: help *whom*?"

"Chloe, you can't do this!" Richard finally says. "You're better than this."

I have to snort. "Uh, you might want to rethink that."

"I know you *can* be," he says, and I roll my eyes. That's exactly the kind of moronic compliment men offer when they want something.

"James was going to ruin everything. Expose everyone," Richard continues. "Without Cole's help, Peter doesn't have a chance. For all I know, he's already dead!"

Like I care. I have to be strong for James.

"I know what you're doing," I say. "You can't understand what James and I have. *He loves me.*"

"Chloe, think about it! If James comes back, he'll destroy everyone. Including you."

"Shut up. James would never hurt me!"

Richard knows I won't change my mind. His eyes fill with dread. Serves him right, for all the things he has done to ruin my fun this last year. He's *not* going to destroy my one chance at happiness with James, the one person who truly understands me.

Suddenly I hear a girl's voice. Her accent is familiar.

"Just call me Victoria, okay? And I'll call you David," she says.

"But that's not my – " a man answers.

My throat closes. I recognize those voices. I look around wildly. *Where the fuck is that coming from?*

" – beats Small Town Loser Cab Driver, doesn't it?"

I can't believe it. No. No. NO! Oh please, God. This can't be happening.

The woman's voice softens a little. I hear the sound of a zipper being undone. "You like what you see, Small Town Loser Cab Driver?"

"Whatever," the man says breathlessly. "Call me David."

Suddenly Charley – Charley! – rolls his wheelchair into the tiny patio. He's holding his iPad up, and it's playing a video of the cab driver. And me.

Me! I can't breathe.

"He is going to expose *everyone,* Chloe," Charley says. "The truth about The Academy, us and even you. That's why we can't let him come back!"

"Where did you get that?!"

"The links on James's hard drive. Remember? He had one on *you,* too," says Charley.

I don't hear anything else. There's this roar in my ears. I go to grab the iPad but he pushes me away.

"Don't worry," he says. "It's off the servers! *Hey…* Get off me!"

I stumble back, reeling at the betrayal. I can't believe it. Not James. *Not my James!*

Charley looks at me with something like sympathy and gives me a half smile.

"Relax. I bought the company that owned the servers," Charley says. "Took me two days flying around the country to negotiate the deal."

I look at Richard as hot tears run down my cheeks. He knows exactly why my heart is breaking.

"I *am* sorry," he continues. "But James has something on *all* of us. He was going to release those links, plus a whole lot more, and destroy The Academy. And *us*."

My head is spinning. I wanted James back so badly. I still do. I love him so much. There's no way James would do this. *Or is there? How could he do this to me?* Half of me doesn't believe it. I replay our time together in a flash. *Can it be that he didn't love me the way I loved – ?* No, that's impossible!

But then the sound of my voice in that cab plays again in my head, and I collapse inside. James recorded everything? *Everything?!*

I'm reeling. What do I do now? I was going to get my looks back, *and James.* And now … this? It hurts so much. *So much.*

Richard kneels by Cole and gently shakes his face. Then he looks at me.

"Please, Chloe," he begs. "Let Cole go. Let him help Peter before it's too late."

I can't do that. I crush the petals in my hand. Why should I care about anyone else? *I've just lost James*, the only man I ever really loved. And he loved *me*! I *know* he really loved me! Doesn't anyone understand how big that is, how much that hurts? What makes him think I'll help *Peter*?

"Chloe. *Please*."

I take a breath and steady myself. A spasm of hate grips me. I admit: one upside of releasing Cole now would be watching James get sucked back into the Tree. He deserves that. But if I let that happen,

Linden won't help me. I will be stuck with this terrible invisibility forever – and I'd rather be dead. What do I care if every student on campus has their secrets revealed?! No one will ever look at me again! I'll be nothing. That's *so much* more important!

I only need to hold out a few more minutes. Then the sun will rise and this will all be over. Maybe I won't have James. But I'll have my face back.

"No," I say.

PETER

"No!" Sophia cries.

But she's not looking at James. She's looking past him. James and I whip our heads around, back toward the forest. And then we see it. A thick wave of grey slime surges toward us like a mudslide down a steep mountain.

Run!

I leap to my feet, pulling Sophia up and pushing her ahead of me. James stumbles toward the gate, too, but the slime races past us and then veers into our path. James gasps in terror and stops. Sophia and I stop.

What do we do now?

James and I look at each other. He nods to my right. I take Sophia's arm and slowly move to the right while James moves to the left.

But we've only gone a few steps when the puddle of slime thins, expanding on both sides to form circle around us. We're only thirty feet to the campus gates! The slime circles us, faster and faster, until it's nothing but a grey blur, rising. And it's pushing us closer together.

"What's it doing?" I shout over to James.

"I don't know!" he says, with real fear in his voice. "It has to take one of us! There must be something wrong with Cole!"

"Cole?"

"The keeper of the Tree of Souls!"

"Yeah, your best buddy," Sophia says with a sneer, still backing away from the slime. "Where is he when you need him?"

The blur is only feet away and closing fast. It makes a whooshing sound that's getting louder, and it's emitting this high-pitched screech. James is so close to the whirling slime, the longer hair on his forehead is getting blown around.

"The Tree needs to be fed," he shouts over the screech. "And since Cole isn't around to decide who it gets, *you'll do just fine.*"

He runs at me. I push Sophia to the side so she doesn't get hurt. But at the last second, James veers to the side and before I can stop him, he pushes *Sophia* into the swirling slime!

I can't believe it. Sophia's arms shoot up for balance and she screams. The whooshing sound gets louder, cutting off the scream.

Sophia falls. The grey slime quickly covers her, pinning her arms to the ground and encircling her waist.

"Peter!" she screams.

I grab her as best I can but I'm no match for the force pulling her back toward the forest. She screams and screams. I kick and tear at the slime, which is wet and cold and sticky, but instead of grabbing me, it dissolves as soon as I touch it.

The slime has almost totally enveloped Sophia. She is quiet now, and fading fast. I reach for it again, thrusting my hands into it. It melts on my skin.

Why isn't it grabbing my arms? Why isn't it taking me instead?

"Get up!" I yell, but she can't get to her feet. I try to lift her. She grabs frantically at my shirt and then wraps her arms around me, but the force of the slime pulling at her knocks us both over. I get to my feet and attack it, these long tendrils of grey goop. It doesn't matter. It vanishes under my hands and reappears somewhere else. I can't rip it off, I can't pull it apart and I can't unravel it because pulls back from my touch.

"HELP ME!" I scream at James as Sophia is pulled toward the forest, but he doesn't move. He's back on his feet now, watching me. He looks up at the sky. One corner of it is lightening.

The slime drags Sophia toward the forest. And she's not even fighting anymore. She's like a rag doll, ready to say good-bye, her head bouncing gently as she's pulled further and further away. I see something besides fear cross her face. Sadness. Like she knows it has won. Like she knows she'll have to give up.

Then I remember the stones. Is it possible that the *stones* are protecting me from the slime?

I pull the stones from my pocket and run to Sophia. I don't even think she sees me. I pry her hand open and put the stones in it, holding her palm closed for her. She stops moving. The slime around her starts to disappear. Moments later, feeling stronger, she pulls the stones, hidden inside her clenched fist, to her chest and holds them there.

In a few seconds, the mist is totally gone.

She slowly turns her head to look at me. Her lip is bleeding.

"What have you done?" she asks in a tiny voice. "Take them back ..."

But before she can reach her hand out to me, the whooshing sound starts up again. The grey slime rears up, expands and forms thick ropes that grab on to my arms and legs, as cold as ice! I fall to the ground stiffly, as if wrapped in a shroud, unable to break my fall. I look up. One last look at The Academy.

Sophia watches in horror, finally free. She can't even stand up. She reaches out weakly to give me the stones.

"No!" I say, and shout at James. "Grab her! And *run!*"

James grabs the backpack off the ground and pulls at Sophia's arm.

"No!" she wails. "I won't ... I won't leave him!"

I'm pulled with incredible force toward the forest, rocks and thorn bushes scraping at my clothes.

James picks Sophia up and half drags her toward campus, my backpack bouncing on one shoulder. Sophia screams "Noooo!" with whatever strength she has left. Their voices fade.

I can feel the life being squeezed out of me.

I'm too exhausted to do anything. The slime is up to my chest and squeezes me so hard I can't breathe, crushing my ribs. I grab onto a thorn bush but it bloodies my hands. I can't hold on. The slime pulls me loose and drags me toward the trees.

The sense of being moved, and the giving up to it, reminds me of my motorcycle accident last year, when they were wheeling me into surgery, just before I flat-lined.

My eyes close. Far, far away, Sophia calls my name.

LINDEN

I can't believe it.

That stupid boy, kicking like a baby and grabbing at thorn bushes and committing himself to a certain death when he could have just walked away and let Sophia take James's place in the Tree. Then he tells James to get Sophia to safety! *Sophia!* I thought he was special! I thought he had potential!

I was counting on him.

"You know what this means," Dr. Browning says, because she keeps talking long after anyone is interested in listening. She always has. "Or shall I spell it out for you?

"It's *surrender!*" I say, not even caring about the spittle flying from my mouth. I hope every drop burns holes in her skin. "It is relinquishing to the inevitable and trying to *spin it!* Nothing more! You *will not* warp it into something else!"

She doesn't look at me.

"It is *weakness*," I hiss.

CHLOE

I don't know exactly why I did it.

We stood in silence, the four of us. There wasn't anything left to say.

Then Anton stumbled into the courtyard. He took one look around, saw Richard, Charley, the listing Cole (and me), and figured out immediately what was going on. He checked his watch. Sunrise was less than ten minutes away.

"Everyone just needs to relax," Anton said. And I knew why. He wanted Peter gone. I laughed. Oh, he would owe me now!

But then Cole grunted. Was that a word? Did he say something? We didn't understand it at first. Richard bent close to Cole and shook his shoulder, and Cole grunted again.

Richard straightened. The color drained out of his face. "He said, 'Sophia,'" Richard said, staring at me in horror. "Does that mean it's got *her?*"

He looked ready to race for the forest and save Sophia. My dear, heroic, idiot brother.

What the hell was Sophia doing in the forest, I wondered? Did she go to meet James before he got to me?

And then it all made sense. No. She went to save Peter. She knew about James's betrayal of us all, and she didn't want him back, either.

She was protecting all our secrets, and she was going to die for it.

I looked at Anton first. The news that Sophia was being killed at that moment didn't seem to move him at all. He looked back at me calmly, counting down the clock. I realized he was perfectly happy to lose her. Why not? He didn't think he could ever have her. Better, then, that she be gone forever. That would teach her a lesson, wouldn't it?

For a second, I imagined Sophia gone. I'd never have to watch anyone fall in love with her instead of me again. I'd get a lot of sympathy and attention after the loss of my best friend, which could be fun. I'd really get into that.

Then I remembered how she sat by my bed all night, the night I realized I would never be beautiful again. The night I wanted to die. Sophia didn't even ask why, she just held my hand. No one was watching. No one ever knew.

I remembered all that in half a second and looked at Anton's smug face.

I ran to Cole's side with the blossom and held it under his nose. He took a deep breath. Anton tried to stop me because Anton is an ass, but Richard took care of him in two moves. Within a minute, Cole's strength was back. He rose from the bench, straightened his shirt and slapped his cap back on his head.

"Thank you," he said to me, stepped over Anton and walked away.

Richard watched him go, shocked but hopeful, and turned to me. I shrugged.

I still don't know why I did it.

But as I headed back to my room, I caught my reflection in a window. And there it was. My face. *I could see my face!* Tears of relief and joy spilled onto my cheeks.

Something moved in the reflection and I turned to see Dr. Browning coming out of the Chapel. She saw me there, still touching my face. And I think she nodded at me.

PETER

The slime has nearly got me to the tree line by now. It's covering me completely. I've pretty much given up.

I think of my mom. I want to tell her that I get it now. I totally understand. I hope someday she finds out that I did the right thing. I just wish I had a little more time.

I'm thinking of everything we left unsaid when I realize ... I've stopped moving. I look down and watch the slime unwind from around my waist, down my legs and arms. It unwraps my ankle and turns to mist.

And then it's gone.

My clothes are stiff with mud, and wet, but I'm not being pulled anywhere. The quiet is almost suffocating. I roll over, exhausted, and squint up at the sky.

The sky. It's nearly light with morning now.

I stand up. My legs shake with the effort, I can't help it. Everything hurts.

In the distance, I see James at the gate, carrying Sophia. I hurry as best I can, but I've got a lot of ground to cover, and I can't move very fast.

I watch James put Sophia down. She tries to push the gate open, but it's locked. Desperate, she tries to climb the fence. I can tell from here that she's too weak, and every time she tries, she falls back.

James doesn't notice, he is ripping through my backpack. *Looking for the stones.*

He asks Sophia something, but she's not paying attention. She's watching me take slow, careful steps toward them.

James turns to see what she's looking at. The smile drops off his face.

I turn. Behind me, a thick mist rises. It spills all around me and I close my eyes, ready to be taken. I can't run. I can barely walk. I'm still in the middle of the field.

But the mist moves past me in a rush of cold. It congeals into that horrifying grey slime that rushes toward *James!*

James starts to climb the fence. But the slime is too fast. It wraps around his legs and then his torso. In seconds, James is completely wrapped up to his neck in grey slime.

Sophia stumbles back, panicked.

Then James is pulled, with terrifying force, toward the forest.

As he flies backward, he screams the most gut-wrenching scream I've ever heard. The slime drags him past me, really fast, past the tree line and then deep into the forest.

And then he's gone. The quiet settles for a long beat. Nothing moves but a gentle breeze.

I walk the final steps to Sophia. Her lip is bruised, her hair is wild and her satin dress is torn and muddy. And I've never been so happy to see another person in my whole life.

She drops the stones into my hands without a word.

We stare at them. They look like regular rocks. But now I know they are so much more. I know what this Academy is really about. I know more than I ever wanted to.

The gate makes a clanging sound and swings open. Too exhausted to wonder how that happens, I let Sophia take my hand as we stagger through it.

EPILOGUE

Morning broke brightly over a campus as still as a photograph.

It wasn't the stillness of expectation. The school wasn't about to awaken refreshed after a long rest. This was different. This was the kind of unnatural quiet that follows an event of great importance. And great trauma.

A leftover red ribbon, the only evidence of a recent party, was snagged on a tree branch.

———

In Dr. Browning's empty office, the center of the abstract painting glowed. There was the white stone.

In Professor Linden's office, something pulsated under the giant oak in his favorite forest diorama. The dark stone.

In the Chapel, hunched in a pew, sat Cole. In his open palm was the grey stone.

Cole studied it for hours, turning it over, examining it, mulling over everything that had happened. Some of it, he acknowledged, was his fault. He had liked James and appreciated his friendship, but he had been too trusting. He never imagined that their friendship would lead to the loss of his Manuscript.

It was the only document that chronicled the moment Dr. Browning and Professor Linden, physical manifestations of the best and worst of human nature, were created! It recorded every attempt, big and small, they made to exert undue influence as they fought for the souls of their students.

Most importantly, the Manuscript recorded the same information the student engraved on their closet doors: the choice, announced on Graduation Day, to spend his or her life serving Dr. Browning and the Light, or to follow Linden and descend into Darkness.

He *had* to get it back. He had to figure out how.

And he had to do that while fulfilling his primary purpose, maintaining the balance in this sanctuary, the only one of its kind. That was no easy job, given both Linden and Browning's fierce determination to win at all costs. But free will *must* prevail; without it, goodness is no virtue and evil doing deserves no blame.

Cole knew Peter's arrival changed everything. Like his father (and his father and *his* father ...), Peter represented a chance to end this conflict forever, making him the ultimate prize for both sides. Here at The Academy, whose students and alumni controlled over half the world's wealth, Peter held the potential to lead the world in one direction or the other.

Which would he choose?

The battle for Peter's soul was about to explode. In the dark of the

Chapel, knowing he would have to justify his actions one day, Cole recommitted himself to this purpose.

———⁓———

In the infirmary, Peter had already been weighed, bandaged and admitted. He'd been given antihistamines for his bug bites. An IV was inserted into his right arm.

And all he could do was wait for the right moment, when he wasn't being watched, to pull the IV and get the hell out of there.

Meanwhile, Linden watched the ribbon snagged in the tree wave in the breeze until it was finally lifted high into the air. Then he headed to the infirmary with a great deal on his mind. This setback was a blow to the cause, he wasn't about to argue otherwise, but he was confident he would soon regain the upper hand.

It was time, he thought, to go back to work.

He hated to rush but he hadn't had sufficient time with the young man this semester, and now an irresistible opportunity presented itself if he hurried.

He didn't have much time. Moments ago, he saw Dr. Browning walking to the parking lot, no doubt meeting Peter's mother there and filling her in on what happened the night before. He picked up his pace.

He expected the suspicion and coldness with which Peter regarded him. He wasn't at all bothered by it, and didn't feel the need to soften it with false pretenses.

"How are you feeling, Peter?" he asked, standing a respectful distance from Peter's bedside.

"I'll live. Sorry to disappoint you."

"Ah," Professor Linden said with a smile meant to convey that he felt mildly wounded. "I see you've been talking to Dr. Browning. She's quite gifted, you know, at telling half truths."

"She told me *nothing*."

"Nothing important, anyway," Linden sniffed. "I'm sure she didn't tell you that *she* is the reason your father is trapped forever in the Tree of Souls."

Peter's eyes flickered with curiosity and then hardened again. "That's not -- Why should I believe anything you say?"

"Because I don't lie. Never have."

Peter looked away.

"The reality is sad but true," the Professor sighed, planting the final seeds. "Your father's blind trust in Dr. Browning cost him dearly. I made numerous attempts to get him out of the Tree, you know, including sending James to free him. But it was too late."

He patted Peter's shoulder. "I knew you'd want the *whole* truth," he said and left, closing the door behind him without a sound.

Alone, Peter tried to make sense of it. He had trusted everything Dr. Browning told him. He believed it in his heart to be true and never questioned it. Is that the same as "blind trust?" Was he making the same mistakes his father made?

And then he remembered what Sophia once told him: "Everything here is a trap, and every choice you make is one you can never undo."

Peter removed his IV, setting it carefully under the blanket so he could reinsert it later, and climbed out of bed.

The infirmary was a squat stone building on the side of campus, out of the way, and he had a short window to make it to the front of school without being seen.

Four minutes later, he stood in front of The Academy's main

gates. The MAGNUS NOVUS ORBIS crest glowed in the light of the rising sun. With one arm bandaged and his breath visible in the cold, Peter reached up with his other arm and, with great difficulty, pried open one section of the crest.

After several exasperating tries, he finally pulled out an envelope, one that matched the ones James Harken was filling in the video so many weeks before.

The Manuscript.

He hurried back to the infirmary and climbed into bed moments before his mother and Dr. Browning entered the infirmary.

———— ∿ ————

Dr. Browning smiled down at Peter. Diana sat at the foot of his bed.

"I don't have to tell you how happy I am to see you," Dr. Browning said as Peter's mother stroked his arm and straightened his blankets.

"You look great, baby," Diana said, tugging affectionately at his hair. That kind of thing used to annoy him. It didn't, this time.

He couldn't lift his arm, or else she'd see he hadn't had time to reinsert the IV. He held it in his fingers beneath the blanket.

Diana smiled and set another Angel Figurine on the shelf by his bed. This one looked down at the open book in her hands, a tear (a small pearl) trapped under her lashes. Peter looked at it. The second his mom left, and he could move his arm, he would toss it.

Dr. Browning put a gentle hand on his.

"But I have to ask," she said. "The manuscript?"

Peter looked at the two women, their eyes so full of love. Then he shook his head regretfully.

"He never told me where he hid it," he said.

Diana smiled lovingly. Dr. Browning searched his face. Then she smiled.

"No matter," she said. "What's important is that you're safe. There's a lot of work ahead. And every day is a new beginning."

———————

Professor Linden, in his office, considered the diorama before him and smiled.

All was proceeding as he expected.

Dr. Browning was right. It *was* a time of new beginnings.

The future stretched before them like a freshly leveled playing field, ready for the start of a whole new contest. This contest, however, had higher stakes, and not just for the Professor. For everyone. *For all humanity.*

He was wondering briefly whether those involved had any idea how critical Peter was in this game when he was interrupted by the soft clearing of a throat.

He turned to someone standing patiently by his side.

"It starts now," Professor Linden said. "You ready?"

Zach met the Professor's eyes with confidence. He smiled.

"I am, Professor," Zach said.

And he was.

31901059549198